X

Death & Strudel

Death & Strudel

A BELLE APPLEMAN MYSTERY

Dorothy & Sidney Rosen

ACADEMY CHICAGO PUBLISHERS

Published in 2000 by
Academy Chicago Publishers
363 West Erie Street
Chicago, Illinois 60610

Printed and bound in the U.S.A.

Library of Congress Cataloging-in-Publication Data

Rosen, Dorothy.
    Death & strudel / Dorothy & Sidney Rosen.
        p.   cm.
    ISBN 0-89733-478-7
        1. Women detectives—Massachusetts—Boston—Fiction.
    2. Depressions—Massachusetts—Boston—Fiction.
    3. Boston (Mass.)—Fiction. I. Title: Death and strudel.
    II. Rosen, Sidney. III. Title.

PS3568.O7648 D39   2000
813'.54—dc21   99-051854

one

Believe me, if the gypsy in the storefront on Cambridge Street would've looked at the lines in my palm and told me what was going to happen, I never would've changed jobs.

Better I should've stayed on tacking belt loops on men's pants for the Classic Clothing Company. On the level, only a crazy woman gives up a steady job with this Depression shlepping along.

But when Harry White asked would I like to come and work in his Charles Street Pharmacy, who could say no? Maybe it was an old memory pulling me back. My husband, Daniel, may he rest in peace, used to be Harry's registered pharmacist. Seems like a million years ago.

So when I came to work for Harry a few days ago and walked into the back room, my heart almost stopped. For a second I thought I saw Daniel standing there, mixing powders in a mortar and smiling at me. But it turned out to be a young man named Eddie Plaut, had the same slender build like Daniel.

Still, a neighborhood drugstore's a homey place, know what I mean? Everybody drops in for a nickel ice-cream cone and some free advice. Way cheaper than a visit to a doctor's office, hoo-ha. Even if you were a brand new baby, could you get along without the stuff we sell?

My best friend Sarah Siegel almost had a fit when she heard. "Belle Appleman, are you *meshugeh*? For a teeny cosmetic counter you're quitting the factory? How come?"

Sarah sells in a fancy dress shop on Boylston Street. A little on the plump side, but a nifty dresser right down to her alligator pumps. A widow like me, only a bit older. I'm thirty-six.

"Listen, Sarah," I told her, "in a drugstore you're dealing with the public, you're alive, know what I mean?"

She stared at me. "But you're giving up union wages and a forty-hour week! Is it because that good-looking union big shot left?"

"Left-shmeft," I said. "Now I'm doing work that helps people, like a nurse."

"Big deal! Drugstores go out of business every day, that's what you should worry about. No kidding, Belle, I just don't get it!" She threw up her hands with their Siren Ruby manicure. "And I kept telling you, that union smoothie wasn't for you—"

That Sarah. Advice on my love life, who needed it? "For instance," I said, "in the drugstore you find out the whole world is scared maybe they'll start a baby by accident. Boy, do they need advice! Because once a baby's on the way, *a nechtiker tog*, forget it! So my work is important, makes me feel good, hear what I'm saying?"

"So what?" She gave me a foxy look. "Besides, Nate wouldn't like it. He's the right type for you, not those glamour guys."

"Nate?" My eyebrows did a Joan Crawford swoop. "Hoo-ha! It's maybe written in the Talmud I got to do what Nate Becker wants?"

"Look, Belle, all I'm saying is good men don't grow on trees. Nate goes for you in a big way, he even got you that job. For crying out loud, in the factory you could see him all the time. And you're throwing all that away!"

Go argue with Sarah, she's a regular matchmaker. So how come she can't see Nate's a born bachelor type? A guy his age, he'll never see forty again. Never took a chance under the wedding canopy, the *chupah*. The only thing he's crazy about is that clothing-workers union. Who needed him, anyway?

The one thing I didn't tell Sarah about was a little fly in the ointment that bothered me. Harry White wasn't the same easygoing guy like in the old days. Daniel and me and Harry and his wife Rosalie used to get together a lot for movies and card games.

Of course, Harry's older now, late forties, pouches under those deep-set eyes. A little heavy for his big frame. But still kind of handsome, with that round Jack Oakie face. So what happened to make him so crabby these days? One day he yelled so loud at Marcia Hicks, the fountain girl, she bawled like a baby right into the simple syrup she was mixing with the crushed fruit. And Marcia's no kid, told me she was twenty-eight.

Today was my day to work late and I came in at one o'clock, Marcia too, and we put on our green smocks. Harry was supposed to be on from one to eleven, but he only rushed in, fiddled with the back cash register, and rushed right out again. Jerry Blocker, a curly-headed high-schooler who helped out part-time, came in also. He was working to save up money for college.

I was dusting the cosmetic counter when a worried-looking woman hurried up to me and handed me a prescription. I went in the back to hand it to Eddie Plaut, our registered man not long out of pharmacy school. He's a regular Fredric March, with brown satin eyes and thick brown hair brushed back from a high forehead. He whistled a lot. Acted like the world was his pie and he was enjoying every bite.

I remember one night when we were working together, he told me what he really wanted to be—a doctor. It all started at Revere Beach when he was in high school. A mother carrying her little girl out of the water was screaming that her baby was drowned. No one in the crowd seemed to know what to do, no lifeguard was around.

"So I took over," Eddie said, "turned the kid on her stomach and started artificial respiration. Got the water out of her, turned her again and breathed into her mouth. And d'ya know what? The kid started breathing again!" His face shone. "That's when I knew I wanted to be a doctor more than anything in the world." He sighed. "But med school costs too much."

Now Eddie was grinning and saying into the phone, "Clara? How did you guess I was just thinking about you?"

Young and all wrapped up in a girl, naturally. I put the prescription on the desk near the phone and went out smiling. The woman asked me how long it would take to make up the medicine, her little boy had a bad cough. Usually we told them an hour, no matter what. But she looked so upset, I went back to ask Eddie if I could tell her sooner.

He was still holding the receiver, but the grin was gone from his face and his eyebrows were making a straight line. "Just like that?" he was asking, his voice husky like he could barely hold himself in. "Just like that—in one second—you're breaking up with me? How can you even think of such a thing, after—no, *you* listen! Tell me what's wrong! Is it your folks? For God's sake, Clara—"

Should I stay and wait? It felt funny to be in on such a conversation.

"I won't even listen to that!" he rasped. "What are you talking about? Something's wrong, isn't it? Are you feeling okay? Tell me, what is it?" He bit his lip. "Stop saying that over and over! It's baloney and you know it! Clara, for God's sake—"

I shifted from one foot to the other.

"No! You listen to *me*!" Now he was yelling. "I don't care! I'm going to see you tonight no matter what, who cares what they say! What? What do you mean, you won't be there—?"

I went back out and told the woman half an hour. Then I took my time going around the counters and straightening up displays before walking into the back room, Eddie was sitting at the desk, receiver in hand, listening to the dial tone.

"Eddie?" I said.

He moved his head a little like he was just waking up. Then he hung up and looked at me as though it was foggy and he could barely see me.

"Eddie, I hope it's okay, but there's a sick baby with a bad cough, so I promised this in half an hour." I pointed to the slip on the desk. What did that girl say to Eddie, I wondered, to make his cheeks go chalky white, like Bela Lugosi in *Dracula* just paid him a visit?

He nodded as if it was hard for him to talk. But his words stuck in my head all the time I was helping two ladies decide on Rachel No. 1 face powder. "Just like that—in one second— you're breaking up with me?" What story did the girl tell Eddie to make him look like he just got sentenced to the electric chair?

The usual parade of customers kept me on the run. I was just ringing up a sale, after explaining to a new father how to use a vaporizer, when I spotted someone near the cosmetic counter and whizzed around to wait on her. But Harry's new floor was polished real slick.

Oops, Appleman skidded and landed on her you-know-what. There I sat, plunked behind the counter, with my flared skirt above my knees. My face felt as red as my hair and my wrist hurt like anything.

Before I could decide was I still in one piece, a man in a tan summer suit was kneeling beside me on the floor. One look and I gave a little gasp. A regular Gary Cooper, looking at me as if I was Madeleine Carroll. He picked up my hand. Right away it felt better.

"Don't move," he ordered. "Just sit there a moment and catch your breath."

Move? Appleman was frozen in space. His eyes were blue

like the July sky over Boston before the clouds swim in from the harbor. Was it those eyes or the tumble made me feel I was floating around like those clouds? It was okay by me, Gary Cooper could run the whole show. Let the customers all wait. From outside some auto horns blared, but to me it was a fanfare of trumpets.

A shock of sandy hair fell over his forehead and a whiff of medicine hung on his jacket, but who cared? The blue eyes squinted at me. "Does anything hurt? Try moving around a little."

I would've danced the hora if he'd asked. "Banged my wrist— it's nothing—" He kept my hand in his long, slim fingers, moved it up and down and pressed the bones in my wrist. Skin against skin, smooth and warm. Suddenly I realized he was talking. "Uh—what?"

"Does this hurt?"

"Only a little, where you touched." I pointed. Gary Cooper's fingers could hold mine forever.

"Hey—" Marcia's anxious face stared down at us. "What happened? You okay, Belle?" Her high-pitched voice woke me up and ended my dying-duck act.

"Fine." I started to get up and he reached out with both hands to help me. We stood for a minute holding hands. Who wanted to go back to work? Not Appleman. Really tall, and smiling but serious, all at the same time.

"I've never seen you before," he said.

For a second I could hardly remember my name. "I'm new here—Belle Appleman."

"Belle Appleman," he repeated, like I just gave him a magic password. "Got a healthy ring to it—just the way you look."

My cheeks got hotter.

"I'm George Parkland. Dr. George Parkland, that is. Just another G.P. Are you sure you're all right?"

Come on, Appleman, where's that snappy comeback you always had at your fingertips? Nothing doing. I just nodded and held on to his hands like they were life preservers.

"Say, lady, could you take the time to sell me some razor blades?" The snarl of a customer waiting at the counter broke the spell. I dropped George Parkland's hands. He turned on that 100-watt smile and went into the back room. All the while I was ringing up the sale, my mind kept replaying a record of my scene with Dr. Gorgeous.

Then I edged my way toward the back register, trying to think of a good excuse to go in the back while he was talking to Eddie. But it seemed too nervy, so I hesitated.

"Thanks, Eddie," Dr. Parkland was saying, "here's a script for the Ergotamine."

Eddie mumbled something.

By the time I decided I didn't need no excuse, Gary Cooper came out and gave me that smile you could drown in and left, nodding to Marcia on the way out. Take it easy, Appleman, I told myself, you're getting a bad habit tripping over glamour guys. Anyway, the after-school fountain rush was on, and I went over to the fountain to help Marcia and Jerry.

While I was waiting for a chocolate frappe to churn, I nudged Marcia. "What do you think of that Dr. Parkland? The cat's pajamas, no?"

She shrugged and squirted whipped cream over a three-scoop banana split. "Yeah, if you like that type. I wouldn't get too chummy with him, though."

"Oh? Why not?"

"Still lives with his mama on the Hill, c'n ya beat it?" She topped the split with chopped nuts and cherries and handed it over to Jerry to serve. "Real blue-bloods, got one of them townhouses on Mount Vernon Street. His mother's high-toned, with that Southern 'you-all'. But I'll bet you dollars to doughnuts mama won't let any girl get too close to her sonny boy. Holy Virgin, save me from those fancy doctors!" She stopped for a minute to cross herself. "Every one of them's got a screw loose, for cryin' out loud!"

At suppertime, with Jerry gone, Marcia and I sat on the fountain stools and ate. She didn't seem gabby like usual so I nibbled on a crabmeat salad roll and flipped through the pages of my favorite magazine, *True Detective*. One interesting case this month, a woman with a two-timing husband. So she put cyanide in his toothpaste. Only she made a mistake, she forgot and used the same toothpaste herself. The cops said it was a double suicide pact, but I knew better.

Eddie stormed out of the back room. "Where in hell is Harry? He's never on time any more!"

"Keep your shirt on, Eddie," said Marcia. "What've you got, a heavy date?"

Eddie gave her a dirty look. But before he could say anything, the door opened and Harry breezed in. Eddie dashed for the back room to hang up his white jacket and flew out the door without a word.

Harry watched him go. "What's eating him?" Nobody answered.

Around nine o'clock it got quiet so I went in back to start marking down some cosmetic sets. Harry was mixing up some ointment mishmash on the glass slab. I heard the front door open and Marcia say "Hi!" One minute later the entryway to the back room was filled with the husky frame of a man topped by a brown fedora hat. Never mind the July heat, that hat sat on his head all year long.

"Glory be to God," exclaimed a voice in a thick Irish brogue, "if I'm not beholdin' the beautiful Belle herself, in the flesh!" My detective pal from the Joy Street Station.

"Stop with the blarney already, Detective Connors," I told him.

"Grab a stool," said Harry. "Gimme a minute to finish this ointment and we can start."

Jim Connors shaded his eyes with one hand and peered around. "Mighty peculiar," he drawled, "Belle's here, but there's nary a dead body on the horizon!"

"Dead body?" Harry put down the spatula. "Have a heart, Jim, business is bad enough already—"

Jim grinned. "Belle and corpses, better watch out—"

I gave him a poke in the ribs. "You're here to investigate a murder?"

"Not exactly." He took off his fedora. "Just checking up on Marcia's crabmeat salad. I'm starving."

Harry was already typing out the prescription label, so I told Jim I'd get the food. It was good Jim was there, his Irish lilt would maybe cheer Harry up a little. When I came back with the sandwich and coffee, Harry was putting the little wooden pegs into the bottom holes of the cribbage board. I went back to my marking, watching them play out of the corner of my eye.

Jim was so different from what you'd expect a big Irish cop to be. You're afraid of them when you're young and a greenhorn in this country. But he used to drive me home at night when I worked at the Myrtle Drug before it went bust, and we'd argue over cases in *True Detective*. When some honest-to-God murders started popping up, we had some real stuff to fight about for a while.

Funny, Jim never talked about his home life. Married with kids, he always seemed to be on night duty. Wouldn't a man so long on the force get to work days sometimes, to have evenings with his wife? And he was a Catholic, so no divorce.

Naturally, such matters I never asked about. Belle Appleman always minds her own business. Jim liked to turn on that Irish brogue to pay me compliments that were half jokes. But he never made cracks or got fresh. So what was it with his home life? Maybe Harry knew, sometime I'd ask him.

A yell came from Marcia, "Front, Belle!" Couldn't she handle one customer by herself? I came out frowning. A surprise. Nate Becker stood there, shaking a dripping umbrella.

"Starting to rain," he said, as if I couldn't tell by the puddle he already made on the floor. "So, how're you making out, Belle?"

Who ever expected to see Nate Becker here? When he found out I was quitting the factory, he made such a *tsimmes*, you'd think I was like that guy in the American Revolution they wanted to hang, that Benedict Arnold. Over the phone he had hollered, "What do you mean you're leaving? After all the trouble I went to, getting you a steady job? Don't you even give a hoot about the union?"

Did Appleman yell back at him? Absolutely not. Instead, I explained everything like a lady, not even mentioning who once saved Nate from the electric chair. But all I got was he hung up on me.

"Out so late?" I gave him a Bette Davis stare. "In this rain yet?"

He shrugged and peered down at me through his thick glasses, he's a regular stringbean. "Just felt like taking a walk." He took off his glasses and wiped them with a big handkerchief.

"Some night you picked!"

He put the glasses back on. "I wouldn't melt." He cleared his throat. "Besides, I need some after-shave stuff—"

"Oh? What kind?"

"Hmmm. You pick, Belle, it's your department."

"How about something with a little class?" I went over to the shelf and came back with a bottle.

"That's what's missing in me? Class?"

Who could stay mad at Nate? I gave him my husky Mae West laugh. "Come on, you know what I mean. Yardley's has IT, hear what I'm saying?"

"What am I, a greenhorn? About Clara Bow and IT, who doesn't know? So tell me how much it'll cost me."

"Ninety-five cents."

His eyebrows did a Jimmy Stewart jump. "For that I could take us both out to lunch! But on your say-so, I'll take it." His eyes glinted at me. "Listen, Belle," he said, leaning over the counter, "how's about taking in a movie with me Saturday night?"

An evening out with Nate and no Sarah along, this was a new one. "Sounds okay to me." Was Nate Becker finally noticing Appleman was a woman?

The front door opened and I looked over. A girl was leaning against it, half in, half out. She had on a little brimmed hat that didn't keep the rain off her dripping navy blue raincoat.

For a minute she didn't move. Then she came in with a kind of stagger, letting the door fall shut. A girl younger than Marcia. Dark hair curling around a beautiful face that was awfully pale.

Her big dark eyes were fixed on mine. She moved past the tables toward my counter and held out her hand. When she spoke, Nate turned around.

"Please," she said in a little voice, "please, can you help me—?"

Then she fell down.

two

Marcia let out a screech. The milk pump she was washing slipped out of her hands and toppled over on the fountain with a crash. I ran around the counter and bent down to look at the girl.

Her eyes were closed and her cheeks looked like they were made from wax. She was breathing kind of funny, also. "Harry! Jim!" I yelled. "Out front, quick!"

"What in hell's going on?" Harry sounded mad, his cribbage game interrupted.

I was untying the belt of her raincoat. "Hurry up, already!"

Jim got there first. He squatted next to me and took her wrist. "Pulse is pretty irregular. I'd better call for an ambulance." He moved his six-foot bulk fast, everything's an old story to a cop.

"My God," said Harry, "I think she's in shock."

I got her coat unbuttoned. "What should we do, Harry?" We all figure pharmacists know what to do better than doctors even.

Talk to the wall. Harry didn't answer. Just stuck next to Nate, frozen like a statue.

I touched her forehead, it felt ice cold. "Marcia? Go get that old blanket off the shelf in back, she's freezing—" Marcia was just standing there with her mouth open. "What're you waiting for? Hurry up! On the top shelf!"

Marcia ran for the blanket and helped me spread it around the girl.

A pair of feet stopped next to me. Jim's. "Ambulance is out on a call right now—"

"Out? Listen, Jim, I'm no doctor, but this girl can't wait. You could take her in the police car, no?" I looked up at him.

He nodded. "Yup, faster we get there, the better. Harry, call Mass. General Emergency and tell 'em we're on our way."

The next couple minutes everything looked like a scene from the Keystone Kops, everybody moving in double-quick time. Nate and I wound up in the back seat of the police car, both of us holding the girl, Jim at the wheel. The siren was blasting away.

In the rain-blurry light of the street lamps we passed, her eyelashes were black against her pale skin. She hardly seemed to be breathing at all. *Gottenyu*, was she dying in our arms right that minute? This girl was so young, the skin of her face so perfect, not a line yet. I gave a shiver. Not just from the dampness of the rainy night but from the feeling that the *Malech-Hamoves*, the Angel of Death, was a silent passenger in the car with us.

Harry must've done a good job on the phone because when Jim roared up to the emergency entrance we saw a doctor, a nurse, and two attendants waiting for us. They had one of those carts made up like a bed. They call them gurneys.

They took the girl from Nate and me and laid her on the gurney. The doctor took one look and told the nurse to start intravenous glucose and get a blood sample. The attendants, with the nurse following, wheeled her down the corridor a mile a minute and into one of the emergency rooms. The doctor stopped, a balding young man in a rumpled white coat with a stethoscope hanging from his neck. "What happened?" he asked.

Jim pointed to me. "She was there . . ."

"Me?" I told the doctor how the girl staggered in and fell

down. "Cold like ice, so we put a blanket over her. Is she—will she—?"

"She's in shock, all right," he answered, and hurried off. A minute later, right after he disappeared into the room where they took the girl, a high-pitched voice began calling, "Doctor Johnson, Doctor Johnson, Emergency Room, Code Blue!" The voice kept repeating the words shrilly.

Hospitals at night make everything seem so spooky, with all those shapes in white floating around like ghosts. Peering down the corridor, I could see how fast those shapes were dashing into the room where the girl was taken.

"Wonder who she is," I said to Nate. The high-ceilinged lobby was gloomy in spite of the bright lights. My voice sounded too loud.

"So why don't we look in her pocketbook?" He held out a brown bag by its strap. "It was on the floor in the drugstore."

"Hoo-ha, Nate, already you're operating like a detective!"

"Tective-shmective," he said, "so open it already."

"May I?" A big hand reached out from behind me and took over the handbag. Jim fished around inside, found a wallet, and pulled out a card. "Clara Borofsky. 124 Leverett Street." He glanced at me. "Borofsky? Ring a bell?"

Nate and I both shook our heads. That smell of ether was beginning to fill my nostrils. Wait a minute. Eddie's girlfriend, when he was talking on the phone. Didn't he call her Clara?

"Jim, I just remembered! When our pharmacist Eddie was talking on the phone, he was having an argument with his girl-friend. And her name was Clara! Could this be the girl?"

"When was this?" Jim asked. "Do you know what they were arguing about?"

I thought a minute. "It was just today, before Eddie left. Sounded as if she was giving him the air all of a sudden. Only I don't know her last name, except Leverett Street is in the West End, so this must be the one."

"You never saw this Clara with Eddie?"

"No, when she came in and fell down, nobody in the store knew her. Maybe she never came to visit him there—"

He nodded, took out his little black notebook, scribbled in it, and put it back. I wondered what he was writing, this wasn't a murder case. "Two young people in love," I said, "look what happened—"

Jim sighed and nodded. In a soft voice, he said:

> "She bid me take life easy,
> As the grass grows on the weirs;
> But I was young and foolish,
> And now am full of tears . . ."

"That's beautiful! And you know it by heart!" Imagine, Jim could spout poetry just like that. My mother, may she rest in peace, always said that people are like onions, you peel away the top layer and you never know what you'll find underneath.

"Now, why is that such a surprise, friend? Because I'm a dumb Irish detective? Maybe you don't know me as well as you think. What about your Eddie? And how well do you know yourself, now?"

I didn't want to tangle myself in that one, so instead I asked, "Who wrote those lines you recited? They're beautiful!"

"Ah, that's William Butler Yeats, the grandest poet of them all. In the Emerald Isle, seventy, still alive and kicking . . ."

"Let's hope the Borofsky girl makes it, she's just a kid," Nate said.

"Right. Guess I'd better call her folks now." Jim's face was set as he went over to the desk and asked the nurse for the phone.

Maybe you never got used to bringing people news they didn't want to hear.

"Let's go, Belle." Nate fidgeted. "We already did all we could."

"Go? Without finding out the story on her?"

He groaned. "Hospitals give me the heebie-jeebies!"

"Who doesn't get them!" It was good to have him for company.

Jim came back. "Her folks'll be along soon, got their own car. No need for you two to hang around." His face looked sweaty, maybe from making that call.

"Talk to Belle, talk to the wall," said Nate.

"You'd have better luck moving the Statue of Liberty, once Belle makes up her mind," Jim said, drily. "I'd better go catch the doctor."

Nate eyed his watch.

Would Harry be mad at me for running out of the store that way? Harry got mad so easy nowadays.

Jim came back shaking his head. "Bleeding inside, she lost a lot of blood. We got her here just in time. The doc is pretty sure she had an abortion. Illegal, of course."

"Abortion!" I couldn't believe it. Abortion was something you heard whispers about but never really met up with.

Jim nodded. "Yup, it's a police affair now."

"Police? You mean you're going to arrest her?" Nate asked.

"Well, not now. But she is an accessory to an illegal act. I'll have to send Rafferty or someone over from the station to stand by and get a statement from her. When she comes to after the operation."

Another shock. "Operation?" I asked.

"Yup, a hysterectomy. Her only chance, they say."

Suddenly two middle-aged people burst through the front door and stopped. They stood there and looked around as if they didn't know where to go. The man was short and stocky, ruddy-faced, breathing hard. The woman was small and pale, her face pinched and frightened.

"Mr. and Mrs. Borofsky, is it?" Jim hurried over to meet them.

"Yes—our daughter's—they called us—" The man couldn't get the words out fast enough.

"Clara—where's our Clara?" the woman burst out. "Tell us—"

"Right this way." Jim led the two of them down the corridor.

"Phew—let's get out of here—" Nate took my arm and this time I didn't argue.

Outside he put up his umbrella. It was only misting now, you could smell the ocean, the salty smell of Boston. We walked in silence, it was enough just to sniff the freshness. When we got to my apartment house on Allen Street I leaned against the brick wall of the building and took a couple deep breaths of the moist night air. The street lamps looked blurry.

All of a sudden I remembered. "Your Yardley's? You took it with you?"

He patted each pocket. "Nope, must've left it on the counter. Never mind, I'll stop by and pick it up."

I started to giggle.

"What's so funny?"

"You, carrying a lady's pocketbook! And I never noticed till you showed it to me!"

"You know what, you're dead tired." He patted my arm. "So go upstairs and have a nice glass warm milk."

"Hmmm. Okay if I take a little Mogen David instead?" Somewhere upstairs a window was being pushed open, a familiar sound. I didn't have to look up to know who was doing it. My nosy neighbor, Mrs. Wallenstein, checking up. *Nu*, let her rubberneck.

Nate grinned. "A little wine never hurts."

The puddles in the street were shiny with the glow from the street lamps. Somehow I didn't want Nate to leave, I was wound up like a Victrola. "That poor kid. Not even an engagement ring on her finger and already in such trouble."

"*Nu*, it's a messy world."

"Hoo-ha, you said a mouthful! Listen, it's tough on kids today, no jobs . . ."

"So who had it easy? I came here a greenhorn without a dime in my pocket, couldn't speak a word of English . . ."

"Me, too, it was no picnic. Still, today's kids can't even afford to get married—" Daniel and me, we had that at least.

Nate's glasses were spotted with mist. "Look, Belle, if it's that girl you're worrying over—girls like that, they go looking for trouble, what can they expect—"

"Expect!" I saw red. "Expect? Hold your horses! It takes two to tango, remember! Girls like that? Says who? A girl doesn't get pregnant all by herself, you know. What about the guy? He's maybe in a nightclub right now doing the cucaracha! And the poor girl's dying in the hospital!"

Nate's mouth was hung open like he couldn't believe his ears. I went right on. "And I thought you were such an up-to-date brain! So thanks for everything and goodnight!" I dashed in and let the door slam behind me. Mrs. Wallenstein got an earful tonight.

By the time I got into my apartment and hopped in and out of a foamy bath, I cooled down. Why did I let Nate get me so mad? Again we ended up fighting. Look what a good sport he was, helping out tonight, hanging around in the hospital just to please me.

Sarah was always arguing that Nate was my type. What she would have to say about that gorgeous Dr. Parkland I didn't want to think about. I sat down and peered into my dressing-table mirror. *Nu*, Appleman, a good moment to start yanking your hairbrush through your curly red mop one hundred times, like it says in the *Woman's Home Companion*.

What was it Sarah kept accusing me of, falling for glamour guys? Good thing she didn't see me mooning over Dr. Gary Cooper. But wouldn't any woman be glad to have someone like that looking after her? Not just his looks, neither. A perfect gentleman.

Come on, Appleman, who are you kidding? Aren't you all set to go floating off in those blue eyes of his? Maybe Sarah's right this time. Maybe you're too quick with the gypsy violins playing in your head.

I put down the hairbrush. Of course, he could just be another of those smoothies. He was a stranger, what did I know about him? Only that he lived with his mother. And had a magic touch. The woman in the mirror gave me back a dreamy smile. Who could believe anything crummy about Gary Cooper?

What would Daniel have said? Funny, when you're young and so head-over-heels in love, you think all your problems are solved. You're positive your marriage means that you'll both live happily ever after just like in those fairy tales. And that you'll grow old together. Who could have imagined I'd lose Daniel so young! Who even knew what loneliness was!

As I slid into bed, the lines Jim recited came back in my head.

> . . . But I was young and foolish,
> And now am full of tears . . .

three

The Charles Street Pharmacy wasn't far from my apartment, but it was in a much classier neighborhood—what we called the "right" side of Beacon Hill. Our customers came mostly from fancy-shmancy places like those townhouses on Mount Vernon Street. If you ever lived in Boston you know the kind of people I'm talking about—bankers, lawyers, doctors, with great-grandfathers who came here when Indians were still pow-wowing along the banks of the Charles River.

Not like me and my mother. We came a little later when President Number Twenty-Eight, Woodrow Wilson, was already on the job. His number I remember because a prune-faced judge popped that question at me when I got my citizenship papers.

And I'll say this for Harry White, he sure kept the place up-to-date. The store sported a shiny tile floor, a giant black-and-white checkerboard, so slick it made me fall down and meet Gary Cooper. On the new fountain, a snazzy marble top from Italy, cream color streaked with pink, it almost knocked your eyes out.

But even if your eyes were closed you could still tell you were in a drugstore. Over the glass top of my cosmetic counter came floating the teasing accent of Elizabeth Arden's Blue Grass, made me feel like dancing. And a man-type perfume from the open boxes of El Productos inside the tobacco counter.

Maybe the tastiest whiff of all, God forbid I should give in to it, came from the trays inside the candy case piled with pastel-colored Jordan almonds, fruity sourballs, sugary marmalade slices, twisted black licorice sticks, and crunchy mixed nuts.

It was such a pleasure coming to work because from the minute I opened the door I sniffed air also spiced from the fountain smells of hot fudge syrup and fresh coffee brewing. Some difference from the Classic Clothing factory, smelling from the oil that my foreman used to squirt in my tacking machine!

The morning after that terrible night with Clara Borofsky, I got almost to the front door of the store at the same time as Marcia. Her eyes had dark circles underneath.

"Gee whiz," she said, "I couldn't hardly get to sleep last night. What happened at the hospital?"

I pulled open the front door and held it for her. "Right away she needed an operation. Maybe I'll give a ring, find out how she is."

We walked into the back room and said hello to Eddie while we hung up our jackets. "An operation, gosh," said Marcia. "How on earth did you do everything so quick—"

Eddie was standing at the prescription counter counting out the cash register change. "Why, what did Belle do?"

"Oh boy, you missed it. It was pouring out, and some girl comes in around nine o'clock, soaking wet. And passes out on the floor! You shoulda seen Belle giving orders like a general—"

"Who was it, one of our customers?" Eddie gave Marcia the money for the fountain register.

"Nope, never saw her before," Marcia said. "Belle, did you get the lowdown on her, what kind of operation?"

Now I wondered if this was Eddie's girl we were talking about, but it wasn't easy to ask. Of course, Clara was a common name,

I knew a couple Claras myself. How much should I describe about Clara's condition? "Surgery, she was bleeding inside."

By this time we were all out front. Marcia was checking the syrup pumps on the fountain, I was getting the coffee started, and Eddie was taking care of the third register on the back counter.

He walked over to me. "You mean she was hemorrhaging internally?"

"That's what the doctor said. Her poor parents, they were nervous wrecks." I hesitated. "Some job Jim has, he had to call them, they came right over." Better get it over with. "A Mr. and Mrs. Borofsky."

It was like I hit him with a baseball bat. Eddie sank onto the end stool. "Clara? Clara Borofsky? Surgery?" He stared at me wild-eyed. "There must be some mistake, I only talked to her yesterday. Are you sure you got the name right?" I nodded. "Oh, my God!" He gripped the fountain with both hands. "Something's wrong, it can't be—"

"Listen, Eddie." I talked fast. "She's gonna be okay, we got her to the hospital in time, the doctor said—"

He jumped up. "What hospital?"

"The Mass. General—"

He dashed into the back room and came back pulling on his seersucker jacket. "I've got to see her!"

"Wait!" I yelled. "You can't leave us alone without a pharmacist! What'll we—" No use, he was gone.

Marcia's jaw dropped. "His girlfriend, how d'ya like that!"

"Listen, Marcia, don't say a word to Harry about Eddie going out, okay? Let's hope he gets back here fast . . ."

Marcia's forehead wrinkled. "Why did she need surgery? What was wrong with her?"

"Don't tell anyone. It was a botched abortion, so they had to do a hysterectomy—"

"An abortion! That's against the law!" Her mouth stayed open in disbelief.

Our first customers began edging down at the fountain, so she had to get busy. Meanwhile I sold a bottle Bromo-Seltzer and prayed for Eddie to get good news and hurry back before Harry fired him. A few people came in with prescriptions, wouldn't you know. I took them in back, made believe I was checking with the pharmacist, and told them each to come back in an hour.

It seemed a long time till Eddie got back. His face was set. He never looked like that before, no smile, not a word. I followed him into the back room while he changed slowly into his white coat. His eyes were red, he rubbed them. Then he sat down at Harry's desk and put his face in his hands. Didn't even seem to notice me standing there.

I put my hand on his shoulder. "Look, Eddie, I know it's a terrible shock. But you got to pull yourself together. There's three prescriptions waiting." He heaved a sigh, got up, and dragged himself over to the prescription counter. What worried me was could he fill prescriptions right in his state of mind without making mistakes.

"They wouldn't even let me see her." He was talking to the cans of powers on the shelves in front of him. "Her parents were there. Her father cursed me."

"Did you find out how she is?"

"Still in recovery. They wouldn't even let me in." He turned to me. "Why was there a cop hanging around there, what was he doing?"

He had to know. I explained what Jim told the doctor.

"An abortion? My God!" He sank down on the chair as if he was ready to collapse. "But she never told me she was pregnant! Why would she do such a thing? Why?" Misery darkened his face.

"You mean—you mean you didn't even know? That she was—?"

"No!" he shouted. "Absolutely not! She never mentioned such a thing! Yesterday she calls me right out of the blue and tells me she's breaking up with me! No real reason, nothing new at all. Just goodbye, our folks will never accept it, it's better this way!"

"But you two—were you—"

"We were getting married, for God's sake! Sure we were sleeping together! We met secretly—and I was always careful—"

"So last night you didn't even know where she was—"

"No! I called all her girlfriends, her house, her father hung up on me! Do you think I'd let her go alone for such a thing—that I'd even let her *do* such a thing? Clara and I, we've been in love since the day we met—planned our whole lives, even how many children—!"

"Eddie," I reminded him, "you got to pull yourself together. Prescriptions are waiting—"

He stood up and moved to the prescription counter. "I know." He yanked out the ointment slab so fast it made a little screech on the counter.

I watched for a minute, praying he could keep his mind on what he was doing.

"Belle, front!" Marcia called. I peeked out the slot in the wall of the prescription counter to see what was what. From out front you can't see in the back room, of course. God forbid, a customer should get a look at how a pharmacist makes prescriptions, they never let you. I learned that from Daniel, may he rest in peace.

The whole business of keeping a mystery what doctors and pharmacists do, he told me, started hundreds of years ago. They had separate unions called guilds, and they didn't want no outsiders should find out their secrets. That's why doctors write prescriptions in Latin. So naturally the Charles Street Pharmacy had the prescription counter hidden in the back room along the dividing wall.

The whole business with Eddie had me in a tizzy, too, but a customer was standing at the cosmetic counter. So I went out and sold her some Sable Blue eye shadow and rang up the sale.

The front door opened and blew in a breezy doctor I learned already to keep away from. I didn't even know his name yet, but he was the kind looked at women like they were chickens ready to be plucked. This time he caught me just as I was coming around from behind the cosmetic case.

"Hey, you're the new one, right?" A tall Basil Rathbone type. Grey-streaked black hair. A hawk nose that made him sort of handsome, if you liked that type. I gave him my Claudette Colbert stare.

His face spread in a wide grin. "Say, where did Harry find *you?*"

I edged away. "Outside the door in a basket, naturally."

He roared, his teeth were like a movie star's, all capped. "Hey, not bad, sweetheart!" He held out his hand. "I'm Dr. Sam Revak. And you're—"

"Belle Appleman." I had to take his hand, he was a customer, after all, but I dropped it quick before he could give a squeeze.

His black eyes gave a flash like what I said should be a headline on the front page of the morning *Globe*. Before I knew it, he reached out and grabbed my hand back. "How's about dinner tonight, honey? Around seven?"

Some crust, could you beat it? "Listen," I said, trying to get my hand back, "This is my class night—" My hand stayed trapped in his.

"Class? Play hookey! Where shall I pick you up?"

There was the crash of a dish breaking at the fountain and

Revak dropped my hand. I turned to see Marcia streaking toward the back room and hear her heels clattering down the basement stairs.

Was this man so in love with himself he couldn't even tell when someone was trying to give him the cold shoulder? "Sorry, Doctor, I don't go out with men I don't know."

He grinned and showed those perfect white teeth. "Sweetheart, I'll get Harry to introduce us." He gave my cheek a tap. "Spunky, that's appealing in a woman. Kiddo, I'm giving you a rain check." He threw me a kiss and went in back, leaving me boiling and wondering what got into Marcia.

Later on she told me, all right. "That louse! Making a pass at you right in front of me! Talk about moxie!"

"You mean you and Revak have been going out together? Don't worry, he's not my cup of tea—"

"Going out together? You don't know the half of it! Took me out on the town, all the ritzy places—" She swallowed. "But it was more than that, honest. He told me I was the only girl in the world for him, he'd been just waiting for someone like me in his life. And I swallowed every word—fell hook, line, and sinker!"

She gave a push at her streaky-blond hair, it dragged right back over her forehead. A funny kind of girl, Marcia, sort of pretty, and yet something always spoiled the effect. Green eyes too heavy with mascara, a nice figure but usually a button missing or a slip-strap popping out.

"Look, if he's such a no-goodnick, you're way better off without him. You're young—"

"Young, swell." She ripped a napkin from a holder on the fountain and dabbed at her eyes. "Watching him trying to make you today made me want to pick up one of those syrup pumps and smash his head in! If my brother ever knew the whole story about him—"

Before Marcia could say any more, the lunchtime customers were piling in around the fountain stools. She never sounded so bloodthirsty before. What was she scared her brother might find out?

When things quieted down I hurried in back to see how Eddie was doing. I asked if he wanted a sandwich, but he just shook his head no. "For crying out loud, where's Harry?" he rasped, looking at his watch. "It's his one-to-eleven day!"

"Take it easy," I said, "you know Harry, he's late a lot."

"Sure, he's the boss, takes his own sweet time," he muttered.

By two-thirty Eddie couldn't stand it no more. "I'm going back to the hospital, Belle, I've got to. Cover for me—"

"But Eddie, what if a doctor calls in a prescrip—" No use, he was already out the door. I looked at Marcia.

She shrugged. "Kid's upset, c'n ya blame 'im?"

"Let's hope he makes it back before Harry shows up," I answered.

Naturally, the first customer came in after Eddie left was a young man who wanted to see the pharmacist.

"Is it about a prescription?" I asked.

He shook his head no and looked embarrassed. What he wanted was for a man to wait on him.

"Listen," I said, "the pharmacist's downstairs, might be a long wait. Maybe I could help you?"

His face reddened.

"Don't worry, drugstore stuff comes natural to me, my husband was a pharmacist. Wait a minute." I went into the back room and took a small packet out of a drawer marked Trojans, came back and showed it to him. "It's this?"

He nodded, not looking at me. I slipped the packet of three into his hand. "Fifty cents, please." He shoved it in his pocket, threw a half dollar on the counter, and ran out.

I was ringing up the sale when Harry's wife Rosalie rushed

by me into the back room and out again. Her round face was extra ruddy, she was panting like anything. "Belle, where's Harry? Should've met me an hour ago! And me walking up and down in Paine's, we're supposed to pick out carpeting. He didn't say anything when he left?"

"Don't worry, Rosalie—" I gave her a hug. "He must've just forgot. You know how it is with business, something maybe came up—"

"He didn't telephone, or anything?" she asked.

I shook my head.

She sighed and looked around. Her forehead wrinkled. "Where's the registered man? There wasn't anybody in the back room . . ."

"Must've gone downstairs. Take it easy." I led her over to one of the glass-topped tables. "Here, sit a minute. A cup coffee? A cold tonic?"

She shook her head. A sweet face with chubby cheeks. Blue eyes that believed you. And a fancy beauty-shop hairdo with a pile of blonde Shirley Temple curls. Rosalie loved being a wife and mother but she never got used to that big house in Newton. She worried all the time she should make a good impression, was so anxious to please that the club ladies were always calling on her to do things. The jobs they didn't want, mostly. Rosalie never said no, she was glad to help.

"Listen, Rosalie, Harry's got so much on his mind these days. Maybe he had a last-minute appointment. He's got a lot of headaches with the store—"

"*He's* got headaches!" The words burst out of her. "Belle, we know each other a long time already, you and I. But this is a new Harry altogether, you wouldn't believe it! I kept reminding him at breakfast, we got to go pick out that carpeting. And where is he, for heaven's sake, that he doesn't even let *you* know, in the store? He's driving me *meshugah*, I tell you! And who's taking care of the business?"

"You're sure you got the time right, to meet him?"

She lowered her voice. "Just between you and me, Belle, it's not the first time, neither. You can't imagine how he is nowadays, a different personality altogether!" Her plump hands wrestled with each other.

"It's true, he's kind of grouchy lately around here. Maybe men have a change of life, like women?"

Rosalie didn't crack a smile. "Belle," she said, sounding choked, "It's another woman, isn't it?" She bit her lip. "What should I do?"

"Do? Look, Rosalie, don't do anything. Just stop imagining." I put my hand on hers. "Harry's not that type, you hear what I'm saying? Listen, leave it to me, I'll find out what's eating him. Tomorrow, you'll see. And I'll let you know, okay?"

The back room phone began ringing and Rosalie glanced toward the back. "Eddie's not answering, how come?"

"Must still be downstairs," I muttered, hopping up. "I'll get it." Praying that Eddie should only beat Harry back to the store, I grabbed the phone. Naturally, it was the fussiest doctor of all. But I put on my soothing Loretta Young voice to convince him that the pharmacist would call back in no time, he was busy with an emergency. It was no lie, neither.

Rosalie was sitting tapping her Pink Satin nails on the table top, looking like the world was going to end in ten minutes. Hurrying over to Marcia, who was back at the fountain now, I gave her a poke and said real loud, "Marcia, is Eddie still busy downstairs?"

She winked at me. "Yeah, he said he'll come up any minute now."

Right away I made a cherry coke and brought it over to

Rosalie, she drank it fast, licking her lips as she put the glass down. "What should I do, Belle, tell me, you've got a good head on you. What do you think?"

"Oh, Rosalie" I put my arm around her shoulders. "Tell you what. I'm going to have a long talk with Harry. I'll straighten this whole thing out, see if I don't."

Rosalie nodded and got up from the table. "Thanks, Belle, you know as much as that Dorothy Dix in the *Globe*, maybe more. You'll call me?"

"Absolutely. You'll see, you're worrying for nothing."

Thank God, Rosalie left, though not without a worried look toward the back room. She was no fool. Eddie was sure gone a long time.

Maybe ten minutes later the door opened and Harry showed up.

"Listen, Harry." I talked fast. "You know that girl we took to the hospital last night? Well, it turns out she's Eddie's girlfriend! Imagine, she had an abortion—"

"Abortion? Holy Toledo!" Harry whistled. "Eddie's girlfriend, no kidding—"

"Harry—" Eddie was shlepping into the store, slow like a sleepwalker. His eyes were even more bloodshot than before.

Harry didn't give him a chance to say another word. "What in hell's the idea? How long've you been gone? All I need is for a checker from the Pharmacy Board to drop in and find no pharmacist here! They'd close us down for a month! It would be the ruination of the store—I'd go bankrupt, lose everything! What're you trying to do—give me a heart attack?"

"Harry, you don't understand—" Eddie swallowed.

"Listen, Harry, have a heart," I said. "He had a good reason to go. You never heard of family responsibilities? Tell us, Eddie, how is she—Clara—?"

"They still wouldn't let me see her." He half-choked. "I'm not considered a close relative. But her mother and father who ruined everything—refused to let us get married—they can be with her all day and all night!" His voice broke.

"Just the same, Eddie, you should've let me know," Harry said. "I would've made arrangements, done something. When people are depending on you, you can't just waltz off—"

"Harry, can't you see the boy's half out of his mind?" I said. "How would you feel if it was Rosalie in the hospital, God forbid?" I put my hand on Eddie's arm. "Look, Eddie, she's young and strong. She'll make it, you'll see—"

He shook his head no. "She's in a coma, the nurse said." His eyes filled. "We're never going to be married."

With the back of his hand he wiped away the tears. "I'm never going to see Clara again!"

four

Maybe Harry had turned into an old grouch, but this time he did just what I would've done if I was boss. Told Eddie to go home and get some sleep. So some of the old-time Harry, the one with a heart of gold, was still around. Meanwhile I told him to call that fussy doctor right away.

As soon as the chance came up, while he was in the back filling prescriptions, I decided it was a good time to have that talk with him I'd promised Rosalie. At the fountain I poured two cups coffee and brought them in back. Harry was folding powder papers and laying them out on the counter.

"Here's what the doctor ordered—a little time out." I put the mug on his desk.

"Well, just for a second. Got a lot of stuff piled up here waiting for me." He sat down and picked up the cup.

I took a sip. Nice and fresh. "Harry, I've got to tell you. Rosalie was here looking for you, all upset—you were supposed to meet her in Paine's. What happened?"

"Oh, Rosalie gets so excited over nothing, you know her." He drank some coffee. "Something came up, that's all, couldn't be put off. What's the big deal, picking out carpeting? She ought to hire a decorator, she can't make up her mind—"

"But Harry, it's not nothing, she waited a whole hour in Paine's, then she came here. She said you promised to come—"

"Sure I did, but I just couldn't make it, that's all. Business comes first, has to—" He gulped some of the coffee and stood up. "I've get to get busy with those powders . . ."

I decided to jump right in. "Look, we know each other from way back. Somehow I'm getting the feeling everything isn't hunky-dory with you. Is something wrong around here? I could maybe help?"

He took a spatula and started measuring out a little of the powders he'd mixed in the mortar into each powder paper. "Ah, Belle, running a drugstore these days is no cinch. A million and one headaches. If it isn't the customers, it's the doctors—"

"Doctors? What kind trouble could you have from doctors?"

He put down the spatula and turned to me. "You don't know the half of it! Bad enough, these rich cheapskate customers on the Hill who take six months to pay their bills. But my doctor headaches, they take the cake!" He went back to folding the powder papers and putting them into a small box.

"Like who?"

"Oh, like one you've seen around, tall and skinny, long face, glasses thick like the bottom of a bottle—"

"Sure, he comes in acting kind of jittery. Never says a word to me, just rushes in back to see you?"

"That's the one. Haskell Somerville, a surgeon. A royal pain in the neck!"

Into my mind came a conversation I heard a few days before between Harry and Somerville. By accident, naturally. Appleman always minds her own business.

"Gimme a break, Haskell," Harry was saying. "It's over two months already!"

"I know, I know. But I've got two gallbladders coming up this week. I'll settle the whole account first thing, believe me, Harry." Somerville's voice got kind of high.

"Yeah, but besides, there's too many of these morphine scripts too close together. If the narcotics checkers come through—"

Somerville's voice changed from a whiner to a beggar. "For God's sake, Harry, I need those T.T.s! Can't work without 'em!

They'll never touch you—here's the script—"

Harry gave a grunt. "Well, okay this time. But stretch them out, for cryin' out loud!" A customer came up to me then, so that was that.

So now I asked, "He owes you a lot of money, Somerville?"

"Don't ask!"

"What are T.T.s, anyway? I heard him asking you for them once—"

Harry stopped typing the label and turned around sharply. "What?"

"I was standing at the back register. He was talking loud—"

He shook his head. "Boy, that detective stuff has sharpened your ears! Well, might as well tell you, so you won't have to listen in next time. Guy's a doper, takes morphine. T.T. stands for 'tablets triturate', the kind you dissolve in water for hypodermic injection. You'd be surprised how many doctors get hooked on drugs—their work is tough, and the stuff is handy."

"Hoo-ha, I wouldn't want him to operate on me!"

He pasted the label on the box of powders. "Needs the morphine to steady his hands. Trouble is, he isn't getting enough work these days. So he owes me plenty."

"Everybody thinks you're a doctor, you're rich," I said. "But you learn a lot in a drugstore. Like that other doctor with the droopy mustache, the one who's always asking for a fifth Johnny Walker and telling me to put it on the bill. Looks like he sleeps in his suit."

Harry gave a snort. "Oh, Tom Herlihy. Another pain in the behind. Owes plenty, also. See how it is? Between people like that and the help these days, it's no picnic here—"

I gave him my Joan Crawford snooty look. "What's wrong with the help?"

"Not you, Belle. But that Marcia, what's eating her lately?

Forgets things, doesn't make the chocolate syrup on time, loads of things. A nice kid, but her head's in the clouds—"

"Don't be hard on her, Harry," I said, "she's having some personal problems—"

"Hell, who doesn't?" He handed me the box. "Wrap that up, will you? It's for Bellamy, two-fifty. Yeah, I know about her problem—Sam Revak. But personal troubles can't interfere with business. Same goes for Eddie, too."

"But his girl's so terribly sick—in the hospital—"

"I know, I know. But how can I leave him in charge, if he's gonna be running out the door every minute? Meantime the business goes right down the drain!"

I touched his arm. "Listen, Harry, don't worry so much. I'll take care of Marcia, keep her on her toes. And Eddie'll be fine, once his girl starts getting better. Everything'll be hotsy-totsy before you know it, you'll see."

"From your mouth to God's ear . . ." He grinned and started measuring out some of the brown stuff in a bottle marked *Tincture Nux Vomica*.

That sounded more like the old Harry, maybe Rosalie was all wrong. I picked up the empty coffee cups. "Look, there's a lot of old stuff in cosmetics, high-class and high-priced, wouldn't sell in a million years. Okay if I mark them down? They'll go like hot cakes—"

Harry put the glass stopper back in the Nux Vomica bottle and put it back on the shelf. "Sure, move the stuff out. That's why I picked you for the job, you know your onions."

"Women love bargains." I went out.

A surprise. Who was waiting for me at the cosmetic counter? Gary Cooper, that's who. I handed the cups to Marcia, who gave me a wink.

"Hello, Doctor Parkland." I sang it out a little extra loud to cover up the sudden *klop* my heart gave.

He came nearer and took my hand. "Just dropped in to see how your wrist is."

"My wrist?"

"You know, the hand you fell on the other day?" The fingers of his other hand stroked my wrist with a soft touch, like butterflies landing and taking off. You know the vaudeville act where a hypnotist makes people from the audience do anything he tells them—cluck like a chicken, dance, whistle? I was waiting for George Parkland to tell me to whistle.

"Belle?" He was flirting. "You look like a woman who enjoys good food."

"Who doesn't, Dr. Parkland?" He sure sized me up.

"George."

"George." My brain snapped back to almost normal, but I didn't pull my hand away. "You must have a sixth sense—"

"Doctors get a lot of practice figuring people out. Tell me, what about dinner tonight?"

"Tonight?" Something cut through the fog in my brain. "No, sorry, I have a class." Appleman sure wouldn't mention that it was Evening English.

"Saturday night, then?"

My heart gave another bang. "Saturday's fine, I'm free—"

"Great! Pick you up about seven o'clock. What's your address?"

Somehow I remembered the number on Allen Street. He let go of my hand to write it down in a little leather-covered book. Then he smiled again, crinkling those blue eyes in a way that made my knees go wobbly. "Tomorrow at seven, then." He went in the back room, where I could hear him saying to Harry, "Heard you had a lot of excitement here—"

"Hey!" Marcia came over to me. "Did I hear right, Belle? You goin' out with him?"

"Why not? Shh, Marcia, let's keep it down—"

"F'r cryin' out loud, you can't trust any of them doctors, don't you know that? Buncha bigshots, they're all full of baloney!"

"Baloney-shlamony, it's only for dinner."

"That's what they all say!" She tossed her head and marched back to the fountain. Parkland was coming out of the back room, he smiled and gave a little wave of the hand when he passed me.

"Seven," he said in a low voice. Appleman nodded and got a crayon for marking down prices as if her legs weren't a bit shivery. Only a voice broke into my dream about sitting across from Gary Cooper while music was playing somewhere. It was Harry standing beside me.

"Belle, did I hear right? You made a date with that *goy*?"

My ears couldn't believe what they heard. "What? What did you say?"

"I'm saying you shouldn't go out with him."

"Why, maybe he's a criminal type? A Jack the Ripper?"

"Never mind, he's a big snob. And a woman-chaser. Don't ask me how I know, I just know."

"Look, Harry, it's only a date for dinner. I'm not marrying him . . ."

"Marry? Hah! Believe me, he's not the marrying kind! He's not your kind at all!" He was practically yelling at me.

"First Marcia tells me don't trust any doctor, and now you. What is this? Am I a teenager?"

"She said a mouthful, for once! What do you need him for? He's from that blueblood world, don't you forget it! *He* won't! Believe me, Belle, I'm only telling you this for your own good!"

I gave him my Bette Davis glare. "Harry, I work here, but I'm not one of your children. I know you mean well, but advice for the lovelorn I don't need, I got my own life to live."

Harry grunted and walked toward the back room. "Kiddo, you're looking for trouble," he flung over his shoulder.

If that didn't take the cake! Here was Harry yelling what a big mistake it was for me to have a date with that doctor.

What was going on in Harry's life, that he couldn't even keep a promise to meet Rosalie? What excuse did he have when I asked him about it, a bunch of hooey! And he'd give the same phoney-baloney to his wife. I hoped she'd give him an earful!

Talking to Harry all that time didn't tell me anything new. Business worries, he kept claiming. Who could tell? A drugstore can seem to be mobbed with customers, maybe they're all buying only a nickel White Owl cigar. Or was my detectiving getting rusty? Still, if there was another woman in the picture, wouldn't she call up sometime, or drop in?

Just the same, something smelled fishy to me. What was Harry doing that he was away from the store so much? Some crust he had, to talk to me like he did. How on earth did he know what women George Parkland took out? George sure wouldn't tell Harry about his social life, Harry wasn't exactly his buddy. So why did Harry want to keep me from dating George?

Something nasty wiggled into my mind, like a worm in a nice golden ear of corn. What about that Ergotamine George asked Eddie for? Wasn't that the same stuff, ergot, that Daniel, may he rest in peace, once told me was used to bring on an abortion? So could that mean that George Parkland was maybe—?

No, absolutely impossible. He couldn't be the illegal abortionist who put poor Clara Borofsky at death's door, he just couldn't. It was only one of those funny coincidences with the same word, that was all. If you work in a drugstore, you soon find out—the same medicine can be used for a million different things. *Nu*, Appleman, ask Harry sometime, then you'll know.

The door opened and a handsome older woman came in.

She had on a cream linen outfit I remember seeing in the window of that fancy-shmancy store on Tremont Street, Crawford-Hollidge. With a snappy Breton sailor to match, sitting on the back of her head. Straw-colored hair pulled back and fastened in a swirl at the nape of her neck. Such a severe hairdo would make most women her age look like old crows. But on her, with those high cheekbones and that porcelain skin, it just made you pay attention. Maybe in her fifties, a regular Ann Harding type.

As she stepped lightly over to my section, Marcia made signals behind her. George Parkland's mother, imagine! She stopped at the cosmetic counter and we gave each other the once-over. I asked if I could help her, my voice had its Myrna Loy professional ring.

She gave me a sweet smile. "I'm sure y'all can. A small gift for a man? Something nice—"

"Does he smoke cigars?"

She made a face. "No, thank goodness, doesn't smoke at all." Her whole face lit up. "Just a li'l something for my son. I worry about him, the darlin' boy works such long hours. Weekends, evenin's, always at the hospital—" She gave a sigh. "Maybe you know my son, he comes in here—Dr. Parkland?" Her voice lingered on his name.

"Oh—yes, we see him often." I went over to the shelves of shaving stuff and came back with a bottle. "How about this? The best after-shave lotion on the market—Yardley's. Here . . ." I opened it and held the bottle under her nose.

"Mmm, lavender. Lovely! I'll take it."

"It's ninety-five cents, please—"

"Oh, you're new. We have a charge account here. Beatrice Parkland—just ask Mr. White."

I didn't have to ask. Harry was coming out of the back room, a big smile for a good customer stretching his mouth. "Hello there, Mrs. Parkland. Nice to—"

Before he could get another word out, the front door flew open with a crash against the magazine rack. Eddie Plaut stood there, his hair wild, tears streaming down his face. "She's gone! I knew I'd never see her again!"

We all stared at him. "Eddie, I'm sorry—what happened?" I asked.

"An embolism, they said. Just like that. Clara's gone and I never even got to see her, can you believe it? She's gone. I wish I were dead, too!" He was choking back sobs.

"Oh my God," said Harry. Mrs. Parkland didn't say a thing, just gave a shudder.

I hurried out from behind the counter and put my arm around him. "Oh, Eddie—"

He lifted his face. "She was murdered," he said in a strangled voice. "That abortionist murdered her! I'll kill that son-of-a-bitch if it's the last thing I do!"

five

My heart gave a leap, like always, when I got to the McLean Street School and walked into Room 136. It pepped me up every time I saw those rows of kids' chairs and desks, the blackboards, and the American flag in the corner, and sniffed the nice cozy smell of chalk dust. Coming to Evening English made me feel like an American.

And now I had a special reason for coming here. Harry's words about George Parkland kept clanging around in my head: he's from that blueblood world. So I had to make the big jump to using good English. Enough with the double negatives, Appleman. Remember all those lessons Miss Wallace kept harping on last year? Don't just open your mouth, think first!

Sarah and Nate were already there, squeezed into chairs in the second row. Those desks and chairs were made for kids in the fifth grade, and Sarah's girdle size is I don't know what lately, so you can imagine. With Nate, the problem is what to do with those long legs of his. I stuffed myself into the space next to Sarah while I said hello to them both.

"Belle, I was getting worried maybe you were sick or something," said Sarah, a frown creasing her forehead. She patted her marcelled blonde hair and gave me a once-over. "You're always first one here."

I tucked my shoulderbag under my chair. "I got held up, a terrible thing happened at the store."

Nate finished polishing his glasses and put them on. "What terrible thing?"

"The girl we took to the hospital, remember? Clara Borofsky? She died this afternoon!"

He sat upright. "*Gottenyu!*"

"Clara Borofsky?" echoed Sarah. "You mean Jennie Borofsky's daughter? That gorgeous young girl? My God, what happened?"

"You know the Borofskys?" I asked, surprised.

"Sure, we were neighbors in the old days. They lived in the apartment house two doors down on West Cedar Street. But what happened—?"

"An operation—" Before I could say any more, our teacher came in and went to her desk in front. Miss Wallace was maybe only in her thirties and if she didn't pull her straight brown hair into such a tight bun, she would've looked pretty. Her fingers were already tucking back imaginary wisps of hair. She wasn't exactly a Hollywood type, she wore print dresses with dark backgrounds, but we all loved her.

She was holding a small book in her hand. When the babble of talk died down she told us that it was *Romeo and Juliet*, a play by Shakespeare. "Some of you may be familiar with it, it's been translated into many languages—"

Mrs. Chen in the front row raised her hand. "Miss Wallace, I see the movie last night—at a thee-ayter—"

Miss Wallace smiled, said yes, reminded Mrs. Chen that the past tense of *see* is *saw*, and had her pronounce the word *theater*. She never let a mistake get by her but she didn't make people feel bad.

Romeo and Juliet I already knew about. My Daniel, may he rest in peace, loved to go to plays. We sat mostly in the second balcony, the fifty-cent seats. But that time was the date of our second anniversary. I should've been happy, but I just found out that there'd never be a little Appleman.

So Daniel tried to cheer me up by getting seats in the third row orchestra, two-fifty each, imagine. Some of the words were hard to understand, English from the old times, but with good actors it didn't matter. What happened with the young lovers made you want to cry.

While Miss Wallace was talking, I dreamed a little about that night at the Wilbur Theater, with Daniel sitting next to me holding my hand and whispering in my ear why someone called Mercutio and a guy named Tybalt were mad at each other. He kept my hand in his the whole time.

Miss Wallace was saying that we were going to read parts like we were the actors. It turned out to be fun. Lee Fong, who had the laundry on Spring Street, had the most trouble with the words, but Miss Wallace coached him till he did it okay.

When my turn came, I got some lines that made me shiver at the Wilbur Theater. I was Juliet, standing on the balcony, almost dizzy with love, reciting in a Greta Garbo voice, "O Romeo, Romeo, wherefore art thou, Romeo? Deny thy father, and refuse thy name; Or, if thou wilt not, be but sworn my love, And I'll no longer be a Capulet." Miss Wallace smiled and nodded.

Sarah read the part that goes: "What's in a name? That which we call a rose, By any other name would smell as sweet."

And that got me thinking about Eddie again. Two families, Plaut and Borofsky. What was in those names that made such a difference? Enough to cause a young girl to die in a hospital from an illegal act, an abortion?

At the end of the reading, Miss Wallace talked about why Romeo and Juliet were called star-crossed lovers. It was because they were doomed to die from the day they were born. That idea came from long ago, when people believed that the stars in the sky were in charge of everything that happened to you. If you were born when certain stars were in a bad position, you were star-crossed. Wasn't that what Eddie and Clara were? Star-crossed lovers. But was it really written in the stars that Clara should die?

Nate whispered in my ear that maybe I went into the wrong kind of work, I should better be on the stage. Hoo-ha, a compliment from Nate, imagine. The Yardley's after-shave stuff on his face made him smell great, it was supposed to make women fall into a man's arms. But all it did was make me remember George Parkland would wear the same stuff Saturday night.

After class the three of us stood a minute, deciding where to go. Usually we went out for ice cream, or to Barney's Delicatessen for a corned beef sandwich. But Sarah said not for her this time, she ran around all afternoon on her feet in the store, she just wanted a warm bath. So we walked her home.

Meanwhile I told her what I knew about Eddie and his girl. "How good did you know Clara's folks?" I asked her.

"What? We used to see each other all the time! Sol and my Sam, may he rest in peace, were in the Workmen's Circle together. Neighbors, all from the old country, all trying to make a living and bring up families. Poor Jennie, I'll have to go see her right away. Clara was her youngest, the prettiest."

"Did you ever know a family named Plaut, Eddie's people?" I asked. "They also lived in the West End when he was a kid—"

"Plaut?" Her brow wrinkled. "Plaut. Yes, there was a family. But they weren't so friendly, and they moved away. Hilda Plaut, that's it, I remember her name now. A different type altogether, not like the rest of us—"

Nate spoke up. "Marcus Plaut I know. An accountant, did some work for the union once. A quiet type."

"Some wife he's got, a regular iceberg!" Sarah shook her head. "Who can figure it, how men pick wives!"

"But why would both families be against the marriage?" I asked. "Eddie told me, he and Clara were miserable over it. Two nice young people, who could find fault?"

"You don't know them like I did," said Sarah. "Those Plauts

were *Deutschen*, Germans, you didn't know that? What could you expect? They're all stuck-up!"

"*Deutschen*—from another world!'—that's what my mother used to say," I said slowly. And Eddie Plaut's mother I met when she came in the store one day to bring his umbrella, she worked a few blocks away in the Mass. General Hospital. A tall woman straight like a general, a no-foolishness type. Hair pulled high in a coronet of braids, a dress of good material but no style at all. But she spoke real good English, like the German Jews did.

Nate spoke up. "Same old story, just because the Borofskys probably came from someplace in Eastern Europe, like we did."

"But that's the old country, we're all Americans now," I said. "Who cares, anyway?" But Hilda Plaut must've cared. Enough to put the kibosh on any girl she didn't pick out herself from some high-toned *Deutschen* family. Funny how parents are always so sure they know what's best for their kids.

"Oy," said Nate, "a regular baby in the woods! Look, Belle, the German Jews are still different from us like day and night, even today. Because in Germany, Jews got assimilated. What's more, they started coming over here long before any of us. And they came here already educated. When we were just starting with the pushcarts, some of the German Jews were already businessmen and storekeepers. I remember a friend of mine from New York called them 'the uptown Jews'."

"But why should Eddie's people worry if someone came maybe from a little Russian village, like we did? It was Clara's parents, not her—" I said. "She was born here, an up-to-date girl, educated. Just on account of where her parents came from, she wasn't good enough for their son, can you believe it?"

"Believe it," said Nate. "Because that bunch saw us coming off the boat from steerage, all penniless. We came dragging our bedding, it was all we had, on our backs. Imagine what we looked like to them! Ragpickers!"

Sarah nodded. "They always lived different, even the poor ones. I saw their apartments—bookcases full of books in English—shabby but classy."

"Okay, so Hilda Plaut wouldn't give Clara the Good Housekeeping seal of approval," I said. "But tell me this: why didn't the Borofskys like Eddie, a nice, clean-cut boy with a profession?"

"What's the matter with you, Belle?" said Sarah. "Clara wasn't good enough for Eddie's people. So the Borofskys figured, why should their Clara be mixed up with them or their son? In front of Sarah's house we said goodnight and Nate and I walked toward Allen Street. "To die so young," I said. "Barely had a taste of life. Just because a doctor was greedy."

"*Nu*, we're alive," Nate said. "So Saturday night let's live a little. How about dinner at Meltzer's before the movie? What do you say?"

Saturday night? The movie? Then it dawned on me, he asked me in the drugstore the night Clara came in. "Oh, is my face red! Nate, I'm sorry—I already got a dinner date Saturday. What happened was—"

"What?" He didn't let me finish, just stood still glaring at me. "What do you mean? When I asked you in the store, it was all set—"

"I know, I know. But with the whole Clara business, I just forgot. And this doctor asked me out, so—"

"Terrific!" Nate eyed me. "A doctor's a big shot, way ahead of a cutter in a factory. Has an office, and a lot of dough coming in. All I have is my union card. So you forgot."

Oh, boy. And he was right, too. I started walking and talking fast. "Look, Nate, I'm terribly sorry. But this doctor's a good customer in the drugstore, what can I do now? So let me take a raincheck and we'll go next week, okay?"

Nate growled something. We were at the door of my apartment house on Allen Street. Time to change the subject. "Besides, Nate, I feel I got to help out Eddie. He's so crazy and upset over Clara, God knows what he'll do. So I'll try to find out who's doing abortions on the Hill before he does. He could go kill someone and get the electric chair!"

Nate's eyes glinted behind his glasses. "Sure, Belle, with you it's the same old story. Any excuse to go find trouble!"

"What? I want to stop trouble from happening!"

"Swell. Who are you, the police? If a doctor's doing illegal abortions, let the cops figure it out, it's their job. I'm sick of telling you, Belle Appleman. Why don't you stop putting your nose in where it doesn't belong?" He shook his finger in my face.

"Where I'm not gonna put my nose, Nate Becker, is in a movie theater with you!"

And with that I slammed into my apartment house before Mrs. Wallenstein could open her window to see which man I brought home that night.

six

Sarah called me in the drugstore early in the morning. "The funeral for Clara is today at eleven, you want to go?"

I couldn't get away from work, so we arranged to go to the Borofskys the following night, it would give me a chance to bake something. It's an old custom, to bring food to the mourners.

Right after I went out front, Dr. Thomas Herlihy walked in. Reddish hair thinning on top and a saggy mustache. His mouth was split in a big grin. He waved to Marcia, who was pouring coffee into two cups, and came up to my counter.

"Hi, there!" He leaned over the counter and I could already smell the whiskey on his breath. He was a big man, heavy, with a stomach that was pushing his belt out too far. The reddened nose of a *shiker*, a drunk. "You're Harry's new girl, right?"

"Can I help you?" I backed away from his breath a little.

"I need all the help I can get!" He belched.

"Oh? I'm Belle Appleman."

He gave a hiccup. "Here, lemme show you something, liven up your day—" He pulled a magazine from his pocket that said MEDICAL PRACTICE on the front and opened it. "Look—pretty funny, huh?"

The picture showed a nurse chasing a patient wearing nothing except eyeglasses down a hospital corridor, with a pair of scissors in her hand. A doctor was running after them, yelling.

"See, the doc is saying, 'No, no, nurse! I said to slip off his spectacles!'"

Who needed such jokes from this drunk? I didn't smile, just gave him my prim Loretta Young look and said, "What's funny?" and walked over to the back shelves. He roared and went in back to show it to Harry. Pretty soon he was asking for a fifth Johnny Walker.

"What?" said Harry. "Don't you know how much is on your tab already?"

"Have a heart—I'll put some down on it this week, for sure. Couple of big cases coming in. I need it, honest."

"Raspberries, you need it like I need a heart attack."

"Harry, be a friend!"

Harry gave a groan. Muttering, he stomped out to the liquor shelves, picked out a bottle, and shoved it in a bag. Herlihy grabbed the bag like it was filled with gold, gave us all a drunken grin, and pranced out.

"Harry," I said, "what kind doctor is that? Does anyone go to him? Maybe he does abortions to get money for booze?"

"I got troubles enough with him not paying his bills. Who cares what goes on in his office?" He stalked in back.

Some morning. Who should come in next but that tall, skinny Dr. Somerville, gray-haired and gray-skinned, looked like a ghost with glasses. Right away he began arguing with Harry about filling a prescription for morphine. Why didn't Harry put his foot down? Would the other doctors care if he threw out such characters? But he gave in as usual and Somerville floated out. Another good possibility as the abortionist. How else could he pay for all those pills? *Nu*, Saturday night would be the perfect time to talk to George about those two. Each one a regular lulu!

Around eleven o'clock the day got better—in came my favorite doctor, Arnie Silverstein, the psychiatrist. Since I was bending down arranging stuff inside the cosmetic case, I didn't know he was there until I heard him order a double banana split from Marcia. I popped up smiling.

"Hiya, gorgeous! How's tricks?" He was chubby like a Teddy bear. As soon as Marcia put the finishing cherry on the four scoops of ice cream swimming in strawberries, pineapple and sliced banana and peaked with a mountain of whipped cream and nuts, he brought the gondola dish over to a table. No other customers were around so I took a cup coffee and joined him.

"You're celebrating something, Arnie?" I asked.

"Just trying to drown my sorrows." He spooned a hill of whipped cream with chopped nuts into his mouth. "Muriel's lawyer informed me this morning that she's serious about the divorce, they're starting proceedings."

Muriel was his second wife already. Poor guy, he always managed to get hooked by the wrong woman. "That's a shame, Arnie. But maybe it's for the best."

"Should've married you instead, Belle." He wagged his head, stuffing down ice cream and banana.

My eyebrows did a Mae West uplift. "So ask me when you're single again! Listen, Arnie, I can ask you about something serious? You know what goes on in people's heads, no? So what do you make of this? An engaged girl gets pregnant but instead of asking the man to marry her, she breaks the engagement and has an abortion without telling him. What would make her do such a crazy thing?"

Arnie shrugged. "Women have been known to change their minds. Even after they're married." His voice was dry. "You mean she didn't want to marry him, she met someone else along the way?"

"That I don't know—"

Arnie chomped on the cherry. "Sounds pretty complicated. Too many variables, things we don't know about. The relationship itself, for instance. Maybe if I could talk to her doctor, or to the girl herself. Someone around here?"

"You can't talk to her because she's dead." I told Arnie the story. "You maybe heard some talk about a doctor on the Hill who might be doing abortions?"

Arnie shook his head. "No, and I don't want to hear any." He spooned up the last trickle of strawberry syrup and looked at me. "Say, Belle, how about dinner Saturday night? Tell you what—we'll go out on the town. Dinner at the Copley-Plaza? Dancing at the Coconut Grove? You owe me a raincheck from the last time I asked, remember—?"

"Oh, Arnie, it's too late!" My mouth made a Bette Davis pout. "I already got a date for this Saturday. So take another raincheck, okay? Only next time, please ask earlier—" Too bad, Arnie was a lovable roly-poly.

"Your loss, Belle," Arnie said. "Well, we'll do it real soon. S'long now, got to run." He got up, went over to the candy counter, picked up a handful of Hershey Bars and Milky Ways, and paid Marcia.

Oh, boy, Appleman, three men in a row asking for the same Saturday night, who could believe it! Working in a drugstore, look what happens. Sarah didn't figure on all these men around here—two of them doctors yet!

By one-thirty the lunch rush was over, Jerry came in to relieve Marcia and Eddie to replace Harry. Eddie was pale like anything, in a navy blue suit, must've gone to Clara's funeral. But I wouldn't ask him about it, let him tell me. The cemetery must've been awful in this heat.

As soon as Harry was gone I made myself a foamy big mocha frappe. And a fat tuna salad sandwich, the 35-cent special. Why did I always wait till Harry left? Maybe because he yelled at Marcia for putting too much stuff in the lunch sandwiches.

"What're you doing?" he roared at her. "The way you're piling it on, the fountain profits are down the drain!" Poor Marcia, her face got red and tears smeared her mascara. She cried easy these days.

So it was better that Harry didn't see how the yummy salad was oozing out of my roll. And how much coffee ice cream followed the chocolate and coffee syrups in my frappe. It sure beat brown-bag lunches at the factory!

Of course, at the same time, I was turning the pages of *True Detective* magazine, reading how you can find clues in the smallest details, things most people don't even recognize. The door opened and in came Hilda Plaut, in a long-sleeved dark print dress, on such a steamy day.

"Hello, Mrs. Plaut," I greeted her as she came by my stool.

She stopped and managed to bend her lips in a smile. "Oh, hello, Mrs.—uh—Appleman, isn't it?"

"Belle Appleman—"

She nodded and looked toward the back room. "Eddie's in, isn't he?"

"Yes, he's in back. Terrible about Clara Borofsky—she collapsed in here, you know. Poor Eddie, at the funeral this morning—"

"I warned him all along, but he wouldn't listen to me." The straight back got a little stiffer. "I told him a thousand times," she said in a voice like the winter wind, "that girl wasn't for him. Now it's plain what she was, out to trap my son. But these tricks never work, you see how she ended—"

"But Eddie was so in love with her—"

Hilda leaned toward me and spoke quietly. "He's just out of school, too young to be saddled with the responsibilities of marriage. After all, he's only getting started with his career. He didn't need to be tangled up with that girl." She turned and walked toward the back room.

I gaped after her. What kind of person was she? Imagine, Clara got pregnant to push Eddie into marriage! But anyway, couldn't she spare a tear for a beautiful young girl who was already dead and buried?

Right after his mother left, Eddie came out of the back room. "Belle, can you watch the phone for a minute? I've got to go downstairs for some elixir terpin hydrate and codeine—"

Naturally, the minute he left the phone rang. "Belle? It's me, Rosalie. Can I talk to Harry?"

"He left when Eddie came—"

"So where is he? He was supposed to come right home! Belle, he's driving me crazy! Did you talk to him?"

"Sure I did, I asked plenty questions. Rosalie, his head is filled with worries over business, that's all. A million things—"

"Business!" She gave a snort. "Banana oil! He's a scream, my Harry. Monkey business, more like it!"

"Rosalie, don't make yourself sick over this, you don't really know—"

"Sure, it's just ducky! I'll sit home like a good sport, while he's out getting all hot and bothered over some tramp!" She banged down the receiver.

Rosalie never got mad like this before. So where could Harry be? What was going on with him? Maybe Rosalie was right, he was sure forgetting about the store.

Eddie came up from the basement with the gallon bottle of cough mixture and began filling the quart bottle from the medicine shelves. "Who was that?" His jaw was tight.

"Rosalie, looking for Harry." I hesitated. "You went to Clara's funeral this morning?"

He put the stopper in the bottle and nodded, his face was turned away from me. "How could I stay away, I had to be there—"

"Of course you did."

"I stayed way in the back so her folks wouldn't see me. It's the last thing I'll ever do for Clara . . ." He choked.

"Why should they blame you, Eddie? You wanted to do the right thing. She was the one who broke off—"

"I've been over it in my mind a thousand times—" Eddie turned, his teeth clenched. "One thing's for certain, I'm going to find the bastard who killed her. Whatever it takes. And I'll arrange a slow, painful death for him, I swear it—"

"Eddie, don't talk crazy. If you did something like that, you'd only get the electric chair! Try to keep busy, try to forget—"

"Forget? Fat chance!" Eddie snorted as he screwed the cap back on the gallon bottle.

"Listen, Eddie, I'm the one who helped take Clara to the hospital, so I'm in this, too. And no question, she was murdered. So I'm going to figure this out. Believe me, I'll find out who did the abortion, honest. So give me a chance, okay? Meanwhile, you take it easy—"

He shook his head. "Thanks, Belle, but I'm the one responsible for what happened. You shouldn't get involved. Somehow, I'll find him. And I'll kill him, dammit! He's a butcher, doesn't deserve to live!"

Who could argue with him? Meanwhile Jerry was calling, "Front, Belle!" I went out to see who it was. A heavy-set man in a white short-sleeved shirt stood near the fountain, something familiar about him.

He held out his hand. "I'm Sol Borofsky. I wanted to meet you, Mrs. Appleman." We shook hands.

"I heard how you helped Clara the night she—she—" His voice shook a little and he stopped.

"I was so sorry to hear what happened," I said. "Such a beautiful young girl—"

He nodded. "I just want to say thanks for what you did. I'm

speaking for my wife—Jennie—also. We're sitting *shiva* this week, maybe you'll come visit us?"

"Thanks, I'd love to meet your wife."

He took out a handkerchief and wiped his forehead. "You didn't really know my Clara. A girl in a million, smart as a whip. Worked in the library on Cambridge Street, took college courses nights at B.U. And pretty? She could've had any fellow! Raymond Green, on our street, in dental school—crazy about her since kindergarten, carried her books—" His voice broke and he took a breath. "So we'll see you at our house, then?"

"Belle, do you know where the—" Eddie had come out of the back room, but when he saw Sol Borofsky he stopped.

Sol's eyes flashed. He sucked in his breath and pointed at Eddie. "You!" He spat out the word. "She's gone, my beautiful Clara, my baby! We buried her today—if it wasn't for you, she'd still be alive!"

Eddie put out a hand like he was blocking a punch. "Oh, no." His eyes glistened with tears. "No, Mr. Borofsky. As God is my witness, I loved her." He swallowed. "*She* broke off our engagement all of a sudden. I wanted to marry her, you know that—"

"Liar!" Sol shouted. "It was you! You threw her over after you knew—" He shook his fist at Eddie. "Today we laid her in the ground. In the dirt, in the cemetery! If she never met you, she'd still be here!"

His voice rose. "You killed Clara!"

seven

The July sun sparkling on my apartment windows gave me the message it was summer outside, maybe the best time of all in Boston. It also showed streaks of soot on the glass.

Almost time for Helen Trent on Station WNAC, a story about an actress who has all kinds problems with men, so I turned on the radio. Naturally, I missed a bunch episodes during the week, but it was such a mishmash you could tune in any time and follow her troubles. While I took the Bon Ami from the cupboard, a voice told me that when Nature forgot, I should remember Ex-Lax. Then the strains of an orchestra poured out and a tenor sang that when your heart's on fire, you better realize that smoke'll get into your eyes.

Was that what happened to Eddie, smoke got in his eyes? He was maybe so crazy in love he didn't notice that Clara changed. And that dental student right on their street that Sol talked about, Raymond Green, was that flame still burning? Or did she get sick and tired of fighting her folks over Eddie—his folks also—their two families were just like the Montagues and the Capulets. That kind of constant hammering could sure do a job on young love.

But she wasn't the kind gives up easy. A hard worker, a job in the library and college too, she had a lot of gumption. Would a type like that be so deep in with Eddie and then tumble for another guy overnight? No, this was no butterfly that drifted around, she was a serious type. The kind that would never sleep with a man till she was positive in her bones he was the one, for keeps.

Till death do us part.

And when you're so deep in love, what's more delicious than the idea of a baby that's part of your feelings? When Daniel and I dreamed about that, what I really longed for was a carbon copy of him even to his fingers. It shook me something terrible to learn that was impossible.

But how could a nice girl, sleeping with Eddie because she felt as good as married, want to do away with their child? Not because the families were against them. Impossible! When babies come, grandparents usually forget all their grudges. Who can be mad at a baby, especially when it's your own flesh and blood?

Think, Appleman. What was it Arnie Silverstein said? You'd have to talk to her doctor to learn more, that was it. But which doctor told her she was pregnant? A good bet it wasn't the family doctor. So did that doctor also tell her something terrible that made her want to get rid of the baby?

Anyways, how come she never told Eddie she was pregnant? In my whole married life there was never a thing I couldn't tell Daniel, may he rest in peace. Even if she thought her parents would be shocked or sore about it, she had Eddie. What more did she need? He was dying to marry her, they could've lived happily ever after like in the storybooks.

Instead she went to the telephone, called Eddie to say their whole romance was a mistake, it would never work out with the parents carrying on, so goodbye forever. And went right out to have an illegal abortion. All alone, at night. What would make a girl do such a thing? When did she make up her mind to do it?

An abortionist right on Beacon Hill, imagine. Who was it? I only knew four doctors from the store. George Parkland, he

was getting that Ergotamine stuff from our store. Tom Herlihy
and Haskell Somerville both needed money real bad. About
Revak's practice I didn't know—except he was a gynecologist.
He was in the right department, for sure.

While I was polishing the window, another idea came to me.
Did it have to be a doctor? Didn't I read once in a *True Detective* story that sometimes people who lost their jobs as nurses
or hospital workers did private abortions? In shabby rooms hidden away somewhere, with unwashed tools? How many poor
girls died from what went on! Was that the kind of place Clara
Borofsky went that night?

Just thinking about it shook me up. It was no cinch, neither,
to find out who was running such an outfit to make money.
Because girls in that fix couldn't bargain, they had to pay whatever the asking price.

Meanwhile Eddie was drowning in guilt. And the Borofskys,
who didn't want a wedding, had a funeral. It seemed the Plauts
had no tears for Clara, if the father felt the same as the mother.
But they had plenty to worry over with their son and how
churned up he was now. Maybe Clara thought she was doing
the right thing, but now two men were ready to kill.

This week the Borofskys were sitting *shiva*. That Hebrew
word means the number seven, the number of days an ortho-
dox Jewish family sits at home and mourns the dead. The very
religious don't even wear street shoes, only slippers. Friends and
relatives come to visit the family so they shouldn't be alone with
their trouble. They bring food, since the family is not up to
cooking. It's supposed to be a quiet time to speak of your memories of the departed and to show sympathy for the living.

Sarah called. "Oy, that funeral, I cried oceans. So, pick you
up at seven tonight? I made mandelbread to bring—"

"Okay, seven. I'll bake right now—strudel—"

Strudel-making my mother, may she rest in peace, taught me to do when I was a girl, so later I could make it for my husband. I remember how wonderful our kitchen used to smell when the strudel came out of my mother's big black stove. That stove got heated with coal that you pushed in with a little shovel after you lifted the top lid. White gas ranges like I had here in my Allen Street apartment we didn't know from.

Who had a fancy-shmancy temperature knob and timer in those days? My mother just stuck her head almost inside the oven from time to time to check. Finally she'd pull out the strudel, always done just right, light brown and crisp. Once I was so greedy to bite off a piece to taste, I burned my fingers on the hot pan.

Strudel isn't something you can throw together one-two-three and it's done. Especially if you didn't make it for a long time, like me. But it's a recipe I didn't need no cookbook for. My mother taught me her way, a pinch of this and a handful of that. First I got out my breadboard. Then I threw a couple big handfuls flour on it, added a pinch of salt, and made a hole in the middle. Into the hole I plopped an egg-white, some oil, a good splash lukewarm water from my kettle, and a dash vinegar.

Now came the part I liked best, making the dough. I squeezed everything together with my hands until the squishy dough felt just right. Then I picked up the ball of dough and slapped it down hard a couple times. Next I just kept folding it over and punching it. Along with getting the dough right it gives you plenty exercise. When the dough got nice and stretchy, I brushed it with oil and let it sit in a warm bowl for a while.

So far, so good. While the dough was resting I sliced up a pile of peeled apples. Now I took everything off the kitchen table, opened the drop leaves to make room, and covered it with a clean old tablecloth. My rolling pin I pulled from the drawer, sprinkled plenty flour on my hands, the rolling pin, and the whole cloth. Then I lifted the dough out of the bowl, plopped it on the table, and started rolling it out till it was good and thin. Again a brushing with oil. Now came the tough part.

Nobody should have to make strudel alone. Just like with blintzes, stretching the dough was way easier with someone helping. Daniel, may he rest in peace, used to help me, both of us going round the table, stretching the dough as thin as we could. You have to use the back of your hands under the dough and pull the dough toward you real careful or else you make holes. Over and over, flour your hands and stretch the dough till you can nearly see through it. We always got flour all over our noses and clothes. Daniel would sing "Ring Around the Rosie" till we finished, then he would lean over and kiss the end of my nose clean.

Now I had to do the stretching all by myself. Some job! I yanked too hard and a hole opened up. So I picked that part up and pressed the edges together in a little fold to hide the hole. Oy, Appleman, you're sure out of practice. But at last I won the fight. The dough was stretched all over the table, with a little even hanging over the edge. Only a few small holes. I lopped off the extra hanging part and spread a little more peanut oil over the whole business.

The filling was a cinch, just a mishmash of the apples and a handful of sugar with some chopped walnuts and raisins mixed with cinnamon. Now the whole thing had to be rolled up together, lifting one side of the tablecloth a little at a time. Daniel and I used to giggle like kids while we rolled it together. What were we always laughing at? "Wait—you're going too fast—it's lopsided!".

But strudel by yourself is a different story altogether. I had to roll one side, then run around to the other side to roll it up to match, then back again. Some business! But maybe it's good to lose the weight you'll gain eating it. Finally it was done. The last part was the easiest. I cut the strudel into two parts, to fit in my baking pan, and shoved it into the hot oven. I put the radio on to hear the news while cleaning up the mess.

Not much to make anybody feel good nowadays. German Jews all over Germany were being kicked out of their jobs. Jewish stores had to close, Nazis were throwing rocks through the windows. What was hard to figure out, if the German Jews were so educated like Nate said the other night, why didn't they have sense enough to get out before that crazy Hitler went so far?

The only thing made me feel better was the weather report, fair and warmer for Saturday. A good sign for my date with George. The aroma of the strudel was filling the room, I hopped up to take it out. While I was cutting it in fat slices I gobbled up a couple end pieces. Mmm, peachy.

By now Jim Connors would probably be at work, he was usually there afternoons. How would the police go after an abortionist? Why not call him.

"Jim? It's me, Belle. Terrible about that Borofsky girl, no?"

"You can say that again." His voice was dry. Death was nothing new.

"So—got any ideas, who was the abortionist?"

"Why, you got any leads?" All ears now.

"No such luck. But lots of doctors come into the store—are you checking every doctor on the Hill?"

"Yeah, but if you hear anything, I'd sure appreciate it . . ."

"You know me, Jim, I always mind my own business—"

"Yeah, and Mayor Curley just made me Police Commissioner!"

"*Mazel tov*, congratulations!" But he already hung up.

When the strudel was cool I piled a mountain of it on a

plate, wrapped it up, and tied it with a ribbon. The fragrance made me start supper early. A lamb chop browned in the pan, some of those tiny green peas, with lettuce and tomatoes. Funny, I hardly ever read while eating at home. Food was so expensive—lamb chops fifty cents a pound—so it didn't seem right not to give it your whole attention. For company I had the Goldbergs on WNAC. Who could be lonesome listening to Molly yell, "Yoo-hoo, Mrs. Bloom!"

Right on the dot at seven the bell rang. I grabbed my shoulder bag and the strudel and hurried downstairs. When I came out, a surprise. Nate Becker was standing there next to Sarah.

She was beaming. "Nate's coming with us, isn't that nice?" To Sarah, Nate was Mr. Ideal.

Nate cleared his throat. "Since I was mixed up in the whole thing at the drugstore—" He shifted from one foot to the other, remembering our argument, maybe.

"Why not," I said. "To go there is a *mitzvah*, a good deed." We headed up Allen Street to Chambers and across Ashland to Leverett Street, not talking much. Because talking was what we'd be doing when we got there. Who's smart enough to know the right words for people numb from such a loss? All the usual stuff begins to sound phoney in your ears. When people came to see me that awful time, better than words were the warm hugs.

The Borofskys' place was crowded, a mob of family and friends were there. The windows were open but the apartment was plenty warm. Sarah brought us to meet Mrs. Borofsky, a slender woman in navy blue. She got up to hug Sarah. Then Sarah introduced me and Nate. "They're the ones who were there that night—"

"I've been wanting to meet them," said Jennie Borofsky. Dark eyes and dark hair with teeny wings of silver around her face. Pale and red-eyed, but you could see where Clara got her good looks. She shook my hand and Nate's. "I'll never forget what you two did for my Clara. She was my baby, you know." Her eyes filled.

She thanked me for my covered plate, Sarah brought her package to the older daughters. "It was kind of you to bring this, come, let's put it on the table," Jennie said, and led us into the dining room. The table was covered with a beautiful white tablecloth you could hardly see, so much food was piled on it. The room had a fragrant smell of fresh cakes mixed with delicatessen smells of corned beef.

Jennie unwrapped the dish. "Strudel! My favorite! It looks wonderful, you worked hard on it—" She found a bare spot and put the plate down.

"Jennie," I said, "Sol told me your Clara worked in the West End library branch. I was trying to remember if I ever saw her there—"

"Oh, you wouldn't have seen her, probably—she worked upstairs in the children's room."

"Jennie, dear!" A crowd of people swept around her, so I moved away and found myself face to face with someone I knew. A round-faced girl with glasses.

"Hello, aren't you Miss Mullen—from the library?" I asked. "I'm Belle Appleman—you helped me to find something for Evening English—"

She nodded. "I remember, Evening English. But you're a good reader—"

"Listen, Clara worked with you in the library, too. So you knew her pretty good?"

"Of course, we used to eat lunch together. Poor Clara, what a terrible thing to happen! All from a burst appendix!"

"Terrible," I said. "Tell me, Miss Mullen, the last time you saw Clara, did she seem okay? She came to work last Thursday?"

Miss Mullen took out a handkerchief and blew her nose. "Funny you should ask. She wasn't herself the day before—before it happened. I asked her if she was feeling all right, but she said it was an upset stomach, that was all. Didn't want any lunch, not a bite."

"You knew she was going with Eddie Plaut?"

"Eddie? Oh, sure, we all knew him, he called for her all the time." She shook her head. "The way he used to look at her, I've never seen anything like it—"

"She never went with anyone else?"

"Anyone else? You're kidding!" She frowned. "Of course, I only got transferred there this year. But Eddie was all she talked about. Why, she started knitting a sweater for his birthday not long ago. She was crazy about him!" She peered about the room. "Funny, I thought he'd be here—"

"Maybe he'll come later. Nice to see you again, Miss Mullen, I'll look for you in the library."

Jennie was still standing in the dining room. "It's good you have so many friends," I said.

She nodded. But I saw her look past my shoulder, so I turned around. A man in a gray suit was coming toward us holding a package. White hair topping a youngish face, an uptight expression behind horn-rimmed glasses. He stopped in front of us and said, "Jennie—" and just stood there.

"Marcus," she said. "You came!"

"Jennie, we're so sorry about—everything." A nice speaking voice, American, only a Boston accent. He could've been a schoolteacher. "Hilda couldn't come, but she feels the same." He held out a package—"She sent this."

"Thank you." Jennie took the package and laid it on the table. "And thank Hilda for me—" Then she remembered I was there. "This is Belle Appleman. Marcus Plaut, Eddie's father—"

He shook my hand. "Eddie often speaks of you—"

"He's a nice boy, we all like him—I'm glad to know you." For a minute nobody spoke. It felt like I was maybe horning in, so I quick made an excuse and got away. But I couldn't help hearing him say, "You mustn't blame yourself—" Then something happened to keep me from hearing any more.

It was Sol Borofsky, rushing past me to plant himself between Marcus and Jennie. "What are you doing here?" he shouted at Marcus. Everybody turned around to stare.

Marcus hesitated. "I only wanted to offer our sympathy for your loss—"

"Your sympathy we don't need!" Sol's face was purple. "My Clara, my baby's dead! You're not welcome in this house!" He waved his hands like a wild man and crashed a fist down on the dining room table.

Where did Sol's fist land? Next to Appleman's strudel, naturally. The plate gave a jump in the air and crashed in pieces on the floor, scattering pieces of strudel all over the place. Marcus Plaut's startled face flushed dark, his mouth opened and closed without saying a word. Then he turned, made his way through the knot of watching people, and went out the door.

For a minute the place was filled with silence. Then Sol stomped out of the dining room toward the kitchen. Jennie just stood, tears streaming down her face.

Conversation broke out again. Sarah and Nate came over to us. "Can I get you some water, Jennie?" asked Sarah.

Jennie wiped her cheeks and shook her head no. "Oh, I'm sorry you had to hear all that." She gave a deep sigh. "But you know Sol, he has such a temper. I tried to talk to him, but—" She stopped and turned to me. "Belle, your strudel, after all your work—" She bent down and began to pick up pieces. I got down to help.

"Get up, ma—everyone, please—" A pretty young woman stood there with a brush and dustpan, one of the daughters.

"I'll clean it up in no time—" She started.

"Your plate—" Jennie said, as she stood up.

"An extra one, from dish night at the movies—"

She smiled, then she gave me and Sarah big hugs, and shook Nate's hand.

The night air was still warm as we walked up Leverett Street. A roadster with the top down passed, full of fellows and girls singing off key. The strains of "I can't give you anything but love, baby . . ." floated after them.

"Love, it's a big deal at that age," said Nate, looking after them. "But it doesn't always end so happy, look what we saw tonight—"

"Did you forget the poem Miss Wallace told us? 'Better to have loved and lost, than never to have loved at all'—" I reminded him. Some world if everyone was like Nate, couldn't take a chance on love.

"All that beautiful strudel in the garbage!" Sarah gave a couple of clucks with her tongue.

"D'you know what's funny?" I asked. "Once already I made a special dish for an occasion. And the same thing happened, somebody died."

"Some combination," Sarah said. "Food and funerals."

My eyes did a Bette Davis roll. "And this time it's death and strudel!"

eight

"What a business, tonight," Sarah said. By now we were all standing in front of her apartment house. "The way Sol carried on—did you ever see anything like it? Poor Marcus, I felt so sorry for him—"

"You know what's funny?" I said. "In the drugstore Hilda Plaut claimed it was all Clara's fault, for plotting to trap Eddie into marrying her. But Marcus Plaut came full of sympathy, didn't even answer Sol Borofsky after the way he yelled—"

"So mothers never think a girl is good enough for their son, what's new about that?" asked Nate. "And some things, like what went on between Eddie and his girl, it's better not to know, she's gone now."

"Eddie and Sol are both talking revenge, that could mean real trouble," I said. "Sarah, you knew the Borofskys when they were neighbors of the Plauts. So maybe—"

"Listen." Nate pushed up his glasses. "This is no murder, the poor girl died, that's all. So what's the big deal?"

I gave Nate my Myrna Loy stare. "It's murder, all right, don't worry!" I turned to Sarah. "Maybe you can remember a little about way back when you were neighbors with all of them? For example—"

"Belle, what're you starting?" Nate shifted from one foot to the other. "The Borofskys just buried their child, and the Plauts got plenty with their son now. Already you're hunting for an abortionist, right? So why mix in on these people, they got trouble enough! Go digging up old gossip, what for?"

"Thanks a million, Mr. Becker! So that's how you see me, just digging up gossip to spy on people?"

"Listen," Sarah the peace-maker broke in, "let's go upstairs and have some tea and mandelbread, I never had a bite over there—"

"Thanks, but tomorrow's a work day, some other time. Goodnight, ladies—" Nate loped down the street. Who needed him, anyway.

So Sarah and I went upstairs and she put the kettle on. "I can't get over it, the way Sol carried on tonight. In front of all those people, yet." She clucked her tongue.

Thank goodness she wasn't lecturing me for yelling at Nate. "Telling everyone Clara died from a bad appendix—who could blame them, why blacken the girl's name?"

"Sometimes a little lie is better—" Sarah set down a plate of mandelbread.

I munched. "Mm, delicious, Sarah. Listen, I know you weren't in the same building with the Borofskys when they were neighbors with the Plauts. But can you remember anyone else, someone who lived in their house? Who's still around here?"

She poured the tea. "Oy, it's a long time back, let me think. Oh, I know—Fay Winkler! What was her husband's name— Leo—no, Leon, that's it. They were on the floor underneath the Plauts and the Borofskys, I'm positive."

"Oh, those two were on the same floor?"

"That's right. And the Winklers on the first floor."

"These Winklers—where do they live now?"

"Who knows? I lost touch ages ago. Wait!" Sarah went into the hall, came back with the phone book, and began shuffling through the pages. "Aha! Here they are, in Brookline, 149 Babcock Street."

"Sarah, you're a whiz. So the Borofskys and the Plauts lived right on the same floor, imagine. Hard to believe they could be so strong against their two children wanting to marry, no?" I sipped my tea. "Do you think she maybe told her mother her secret?"

"What mother in her right mind would let a daughter do such a thing instead of getting married right away!"

"Seems impossible," I said. "Look, it's getting late, thanks, Sarah. It was good to have a quiet minute after all that—"

Sarah's eyes gleamed. "So we're starting to figure out a mystery, Belle, right?"

I winked at her.

The next afternoon when I got to work I noticed that Marcia seemed more upset than ever. So later on when Eddie was busy with prescriptions I went over behind the fountain.

"Look, Marcia, maybe it's none of my business. But the way you're looking today—something happened this morning? Harry yelled at you?"

She shook her head. "No, not that, it's—nothing."

"Nothing?" My eyebrows gave a Joan Crawford jump. "It's nothing when you got two sandwich orders and three drinks wrong in a row? A customer asks for a large Coke and you give him a glass Moxie? Come on, Marcia, what's wrong?"

A flood of tears poured down her cheeks. She yanked a napkin from the holder and mopped them. "Oh, Belle, I don't know what to do! I'm late this month!" She gulped. "A whole week already!"

"Oh, boy. You're positive?"

She swallowed hard. I filled a glass with water and made her drink. "I don't know what to think. Trouble is, it's happened to me before. When I got real worried about something, y'know. So now I'm not sure if it's that, or if it's—if I'm—" She couldn't finish.

Pregnant, it wasn't easy to get that word out. Some business! First Clara, and now Marcia. I gave her some more napkins to wipe her face. "So—shouldn't you tell him what happened?"

"Not yet! Not till I'm absolutely sure!"

"It's not good to wait. Go see your doctor, he'll check with a rabbit—"

She shook her head. "No, no, what if it's nothing? God, I'd feel so dumb—I'll wait a while, then, maybe—"

What you don't want to know, you foolish girl, I said to myself, is the truth. "Okay, but don't wait too long. Look, you're probably worrying for nothing." I gave her a pat on the shoulder and went into the back room.

What I saw gave me a little shock. Eddie wasn't making no prescriptions. He was standing holding a flat bottle tipped up to his lips. I didn't have to read the label, the smell was enough. "Eddie, what're you doing?"

He put down the whiskey bottle and screwed on the top. "Helps me keep going—"

"Helps-shmelps, if Harry catches you, you'll be going, all right! How're you going to wait on customers smelling like a saloon?"

He patted his pocket. "So what, I've got some SenSen." He took out a little package, shook one of the tablets out, and popped it in his mouth. "Belle, you don't know what it's like, going over and over it in my mind—I can't sleep nights—"

"You got a worm eating inside you, you're going to kill it with a bottle *schnapps*? Get hold of yourself, Eddie! You're a professional man, you got a reputation. What if you get so mixed up you make a mistake with a script and somebody gets twice as sick? Or dies even! Then what?"

A flash of pain twisted his features. "Somebody *is* dead. Someone that deserved the best in the whole goddam world. And it's my fault, all right, don't you see that? Didn't you hear what her father said, right here in the store?"

"Sol Borofsky has some temper, one day it'll get him into real trouble. And he's a father, crazy from the shock, give him a break. But you can't take him serious, Eddie, you're too smart for that."

"Yeah, smart," he said bitterly, picking up a prescription and staring at it. "A real genius. Thought I knew Clara backward and forward. And look what happened!"

"Go ahead, let guilt eat you up. Become a drunk, lie in the gutter. All on account of what a father half out of his mind said! If that doesn't take the cake!" I wanted to shake him. "Did you ever think, maybe he's screaming because he's so piled with guilt himself? He tried to stop you two from getting married. So he's the guilty one, not you! Have a heart, Eddie!"

He took down a box powder papers. "He's guilty, they're guilty, I'm guilty. She's gone and I don't even know why. I go over and over it—but I keep coming up zero, can you beat it?" He started folding the papers and laying them out on the counter. "Oh, God—" He picked up the whiskey bottle.

"Eddie, stop it! You think nobody else ever had *tsuris*, trouble? Keep it up, drown it with *schnapps*! Some memorial to your Clara! You'll end up like Herlihy—or worse—"

"If you were a man, I'd tell you to go to hell." He took a long swallow.

So the Charles Street Pharmacy wasn't so chummy no more. Between the two of them, Marcia and Eddie, there wasn't much conversation going on. And Harry wasn't exactly his regular self, whatever that was these days. When a prescription came in, I handed it to Eddie with only a polite question of how long it would take. At suppertime, Marcia left without saying a word.

Jerry came in and made me a tuna salad on toast. I sat alone at one of the tables and looked at *Black Mask* magazine, but I couldn't get into it. Those stories with their tough private eyes shooting and getting shot and grabbing beautiful girls didn't give me the same kick as the real-life stuff in *True Detective*.

As if Eddie's problem wasn't bad enough, now Marcia was worried sick, and she had a good reason. Like I told Sarah that time, once a baby is started that's it, the whole world changes. You can't go back, Clara tried, look what happened. No wonder Eddie was drinking.

Around nine o'clock a young man came in, looked around, and came over to where I was filling in some stock on the shelves. Jerry was downstairs making some fresh chocolate syrup and Eddie was in back, doing God knows what. This fellow was kind of stocky, with blotchy skin, and wearing the type clothes told you he wasn't no banker.

"Say," he said, "you Belle Appleman?"

"That's me, can I help you?"

He leaned toward me over the counter. "You bet you can. You know this jerk doctor, name of Revak?" His voice was kind of hoarse, like he had laryngitis.

"What?"

"I ast you, sister, you know this Revak?" His voice got louder.

"Maybe. Who wants to know?"

"Me, I wanna know!" He leaned closer. "Marcia's my sister, see, and that louse has been messin' her up!"

"Oh." I moved back a little. "You're Marcia's brother John? She told me about you. Okay, I know who Revak is. But I don't know a thing about him, honest."

His voice got louder and hoarser. "That punk's been leadin' my sister down the primrose path!"

Eddie came out of the back room. "Anything wrong, Belle?"

"Keep outa this, buddy, it's none a your beeswax!"

"Sir, if you don't keep it quiet I'll have to ask you to leave the store!" A surprise. Eddie was slim, no match for this tough Irisher. Maybe the whiskey made him brave.

John Hicks gave a guffaw. "Who's gonna make me? You and what army?"

"Now, listen—," Eddie began, but I cut him off.

"Never mind, Eddie, you got to fill those prescriptions, you go in back. I can handle this. Please."

Eddie scowled at Marcia's brother but he walked on into the back room. I looked John straight in the eye. "All right, Mr. Marcia's brother, what is it you want from me? You want I should order Revak to marry her?"

"You bet your sweet patootie, that's what I want! You tell him he'd better straighten up and fly right or else—"

"Hold your horses, I'm no Western Union messenger! You want Revak, go find him and tell him yourself!" Could Marcia have asked John to talk to me? No, she'd never do that. So why was he pestering me?

John Hicks glared at me. "You're s'posed to be Marcia's friend—"

"Sure, I am her friend. But I can't make a miracle happen. Use your bean—"

The door opened and three customers came in. Hicks gave a loud snort and turned to go. But first he banged his fist on the counter, making a package cologne fall over.

"You see that hot-shot doctor," he snarled, "you tell 'im he's not gonna get away with it! Or he'll get some action he wasn't expecting!"

nine

Harry wasn't exactly thrilled when I asked if it was okay for me to leave at five o'clock. "Listen, I only took ten minutes for lunch, Marcia had such a headache, and I'm opening in the morning—"

"Don't tell me about headaches, I got my own." He was making up some pungent, gooey ointment on the slab. "So you're going to make whoopee with that Parkland?"

"Whoopee-shmoopee, we're just going out to dinner, Harry. Besides, it's partly business—I'm checking out all the doctors around here, too."

"Yeah, yeah." Harry shrugged. "It's just that I remember Daniel, that's all."

I stood there. "And I don't?"

"For crying out loud, that's not what I meant—listen, go already, it's almost five now. And you're the only one around here that's not a real lulu! Go on, get going, have a good time—" He waved the spatula.

I ran. What he said didn't exactly pep me up but I decided Harry wasn't going to spoil the evening for me. This was one evening Appleman was going to enjoy. What woman wouldn't get a kick out of spending Saturday evening with Gary Cooper?

Maybe getting ready for a date was the best part of it. I took a long time in the shower, washing my hair till it squeaked, and a longer time towelling it dry and brushing it different ways around my face. My mother always worried over my red hair, what color clothes to go with it, but curly hair makes life a cinch. I peered at myself in the mirror, picturing how I would look on Dr. Gorgeous' arm. A whole evening with him, imagine.

While I was stroking on some Coty's Emeraude, Harry's words came back to me. How did Harry know so much about George Parkland, anyway? Maybe Harry was like a kid who hates to see his widowed parent go out on a date with somebody new. Did Harry know how few dates I'd been on? In the factory and the drugstore I mostly met that wise-cracking type that never appealed to me. On one count Harry was right—I never went out with a *goy* in my life.

So what was there to be scared of? Look at Jim Connors, a big Irish cop, but a perfect gentleman. Of course, he's married, so that's different. But who cared what church Gary Cooper went to, or if he went at all? We weren't exactly going to say prayers together!

Only you better remember Miss Wallace's lessons, Appleman—can you get an A tonight in grammar? Because George spoke such perfect English. Easy for him, he was born here. Blue blood in his veins, Harry pointed out. So what was in Appleman's veins—chicken soup?

Or—did Harry know George did illegal abortions? Just thinking that made me shiver.

Now, what should I wear? It better be something cool in this weather. I fluffed Coty's Natural all over my face, supposed to give my skin a pearly glow, and wondered where he would take me. My lips got outlined with Richard Hudnut's new shade, Ripe Berry—advertised as kiss-proof. Of course, a lady never kissed on the first date, Dorothy Dix always warned in her columns it could lead to all kinds trouble. How did she know, did she try it?

The whole man-woman game seemed different nowadays.

Did it change when the Bolsheviks won out in Russia, was that where all this gab about "free love" started? Free for who, I'd like to know. Not for Clara Borofsky, she paid with her life. Not even for Eddie, guzzling that smelly whiskey in the back room. Maybe the old-fashioned ways were better, like my mother brought me up.

And Marcia? Even if her brother held a gun to Revak's head? Jack Benny was full of jokes about shotgun weddings. Some way to start a marriage, chock-full of hate.

But do woman set traps, like Hilda Plaut claimed Clara did? The cosmetic counter is loaded with stuff to make your skin touchable, your cheeks blushing pink, your lips like roses. Perfume to make a man faint from it. Like that tenor was singing on the radio, the night was cool and I was glamorous, so if he got over-amorous, what could he do?

Nu, decide already, Appleman. I pulled out that dress Sarah egged me into buying in Filene's Basement. An odd color, she called it Nile green. From some fancy shop in a place called St. Louis, imagine. I slipped it on and ran to the mirror, fastening the belt. Silk crepe with a big cape collar that fluttered little wings over my bare arms when I moved. Gave me a nifty small waist and swirled around my legs. Ladylike, even Harry would've grunted okay.

By the time the downstairs bell rang I only changed my earrings three times and my shoes twice, but I was ready. When he knocked at my door and I opened it, my heart gave a little jump. He was wearing a light gray suit that didn't come from no bargain rack, even his white shirt and striped silk tie had class. The thick sandy hair was brushed back and the blue eyes, up close, held little flecks dancing around as he smiled.

"Belle Appleman, it's been one long day!" he let me know. No smell of medicine this time, just a mingled whiff of Yardley's aftershave with clean linen and soap and something man-type.

"Waiting for tonight, I mean." He inspected me. "Hey, you look wonderful—so different—" His voice sounded boyish and light-hearted. "May I come in?"

"Of course, please come!" Appleman, you flunked the beginning already! I swung the door wider. He walked in and I closed the door behind him.

"For you—" He handed me a box. "This flower outshone all the others in the florist's—reminded me of you, just the way you shine among all that stuff in the drugstore—"

"Oh, thank you!" I took off the cover. A white gardenia. "It's beautiful!" I took a sniff.

"Here, let me—" He got the pin out of the box along with the flower. "Let's see, right here should do it—" His fingers were long, they had little hairs on the backs. They moved across my shoulder and touched my neck for a second as he fastened the pin. "Didn't stick you, did I?"

Appleman was tongue-tied. "No, no—it's—" Before I could finish, his face bent down and his lips brushed my hair. Then they moved down lightly across my cheek and finished up at the place most men start. On my lips they lingered, soft but firm and warm, and suddenly I was in his arms. It was so delicious, so easy to be wrapped up in his hug, like opening the door to a magical country visited long ago. His arms tightened around me, as if they meant business.

Where were we drifting?

"George, please!" I put my hands against his chest and gave a push. "Let's get things straight right now. Because I live on the wrong side of Beacon Hill, does that mean it's open hunting season around here?"

"Oh, no, Belle, you've got me all wrong!" The blue eyes widened. "It's just that I can't get over you—not just your hair and your skin, but the way you are—so alive, all lit up—I've never met anyone like you. Don't you see—it's as if I've been struck by lightning—so it's really all your fault—" His features crinkled into that boyish grin.

Who could be mad at Gary Cooper? "I'll get my things," I said real fast, and scooped up my bag and my cape from the hall chair.

He put his hands out palms up. "Your wish is my command—"

I breathed a sigh as we went downstairs and out of doors and got into his gleaming black car. Appleman, watch it. Only two minutes after he came, and look at you, melting. How would the evening end?

The sun setting over the Charles River trailed wavy streamers of pink and violet across the sky. "No wonder it's stuffy, your window's closed—here, let me open it—" He leaned over and rolled down my window, his cheek barely brushed mine, and my heart jumped and did a nose-dive. Then he started the engine and we began to move down Allen Street. "Tell me—I want to know all about you—have you lived in Boston most of your life?"

"Always—ever since I came to this country as a young girl. I wouldn't nev—uh—ever want to live no—anyplace else." Appleman, for one night can't you clobber double negatives? "The Esplanade and that smell of salt when the east wind blows on a hot day. Just sniffing it makes you feel good. Boston is home, no matter what."

George smiled. "Hey, we have a lot in common, I knew it, I was born here! Used to coast down the hill on the Common in winter and ride the swanboats in the Public Garden in summer—"

"What about college—you didn't go away?"

"Nope, stayed right here. Even through medical school. Still living in the house I was born in, as a matter of fact." He gave a sigh. "Although that I wouldn't mind changing—"

"Oh? Then why don't you?"

"Well, my mother's a widow, she'd be all alone, miserable. So it's easier this way—"

"I'm a widow and I live alone."

He was silent for a minute. "You must've married young—"

"Too young, my mother thought. Funny, the things mothers worry about—"

"You can say that again." His voice was dry. "But don't get me wrong, my mother's bucked a lot of odds for me. I owe everything to her, absolutely everything."

I leaned back, the evening breeze fanned my cheeks. Don't get carried away yet, Appleman, you got to lead the talk where you want it—illegal abortions. Who would hear more about that than a doctor? And stop talking about mothers, what man wants to remember mama on a moonlit night? That'll sure kill romance fast! So is that what you're after, Appleman, romance?

"Here we are." He was parking the car already on Winter Place right next to a sign that said NO PARKING.

I sat up. "But look at the sign—you'll get a ticket!"

He grinned. "Not with the MD on my license plate, I won't. Might as well make the most of it." He turned the key and took it out. "And it's practically at the front door of Locke-Ober's." He gave a chuckle like a small boy who'd just put one over on the teacher. So bluebloods were no different, they liked to cheat a little, too.

Funny, the restaurant was right in the heart of Boston but I was never there. Expensive, that I knew. Walking in there with George Parkland's warm hand holding my bare arm with a light touch was like he was taking me into his world. Walls paneled in dark, satiny wood, soft, shaded lights, and crisp, snowy table-cloths.

The talking and even the laughing all hummed in a low key. The women's dresses glowed silky and pale, everything looked rich and immaculate. A faint aroma of perfume and cigars and good food drifted to my nostrils. Newspaper headlines said that one-fourth of Boston was unemployed. But not this bunch.

The headwaiter greeted George like an old pal. "Ah, Dr. Parkland, how are you—?" Did I imagine it, or did heads turn as we were led to our table? Even in that crowd, George stood out, I'd forgotten how tall he was. Made me feel like Queen Marie of Romania.

The menus came and we studied them. The prices were something terrible so I closed my menu and said, "You seem right at home here, George. Why don't you order for me?" I learned already that men like being in charge.

His whole face creased in a smile. "My pleasure!" So men in George's world were like men everywhere.

He sure knew how to pick a restaurant. The service here was some difference from Meltzer's, where I ate with Sarah, with waiters who told you what you should eat like they were your mother. Here the waiter spoke with an accent, also, but a different type accent, it sounded fancy like the menu.

"And your usual?" he asked George right off.

George nodded and looked at me. "—and you'll have—a Martini? a Manhattan?"

I made a face. "No, nothing, thanks."

He laughed. "A champagne cocktail," he told the waiter.

The waiter moved like an Indian on the trail, and was back with the drinks in a flash. George ordered Beef Wellington and checked if it was okay with me. Spinach salad, braised endives, broccoli with Hollandaise sauce, and Burgundy wine. The waiter seemed happy with every choice, nodded, and melted away into the dark paneling.

"Try it," George urged, motioning at the drink in front of me. I took a careful sip and sneezed from the bubbles. George grinned. "You'll never be an alcoholic, that's for sure!"

Better start asking the right questions, Appleman, before all the rich food and drink turn your mind to mush. "George, did you hear about the girl who collapsed in our store? And died from an illegal abortion?"

His eyebrows jumped a little. Was that on account of guilt? Or was abortion not a lady-like choice for the dinner table? Then he nodded. "Oh, sure, Harry filled me in on the whole story. How you stayed calm and collected the entire time. Good for you, that's pretty tough to do. Keeping your wits about you— it's one of the hardest parts of medicine." He sighed. "That's what being a doctor is—one emergency after another."

"So did you ever hear of abortions being done on the Hill?"

He pursed his lips, frowning. Then he took a sip of his cocktail. "Nope, can't say that I have. Are you sure it was done on Beacon Hill? She could've gotten out of a cab, you know—"

"But if she took a cab, why not go right home? Or if she felt so sick, right to the hospital? No, it must've happened right on the Hill—"

George gave a shrug. "Remember, doctors are only people. We're not exactly the gods some people think we are. And people are greedy. Besides, some practitioners believe abortion should be legalized. So they might be doing it outside the law, thinking that they're helping women in trouble."

He sipped his drink and went on talking. "But the fact is, any medical setup that's not legal spells trouble. Because even under the best conditions, things can go wrong, unfortunately. Even in hospitals. So doing it in the wrong setting is like playing Russian roulette—"

"The way you explain things—it's a pleasure to listen," I said, and drank a little of my champagne. "Only let me tell you, whoever did it won't get away with it this time! Sending Clara out in that condition, it was a regular murder!" I lowered my voice, nobody spoke loud in that restaurant. "And I'm going to find out who he is, you'll see!"

He looked puzzled. "Why, was the girl a good friend of yours?"

"No, no, I never saw her before. But if somebody doesn't find him soon, there'll be another murder. Did Harry tell you that Eddie, our pharmacist, was Clara's intended? He's a good kid, but he's in terrible shape now, swears he'll kill the abortionist. So does Clara's father. Hear what I'm saying? I've got to make it snappy and beat them to it!"

The waiter appeared with rolls and butter and filled our water glasses. I sampled a tiny blueberry muffin. Mmm, way better than the fizzy drink. "George, did you always want to be a doctor? When you were growing up, I mean?"

The blue eyes opened wider, then he smiled. "You have a way of getting right down to the nitty-gritty, Belle, did you know that?" He buttered a piece of a Parker House roll and swallowed it. "Most women play it cozy, don't go very deep. Know what I really wanted when I was a kid?"

"What?"

A dreamy smile lit up his face. "To play pro baseball. I was on the team all through school, college, too. You can't imagine the excitement of it, out there. Every time, in every game all over again." For a few seconds he was far away, then he shook his head. "But that's kid stuff, you've got to grow up some-time—"

"Bet you were good at it—" Some build he had, a regular athlete, tall and lean.

"Even had a bid from the Red Sox," he said, staring into his drink.

"The Red Sox! That's terrific! Why didn't you snap it up? Just what you loved and a big career too!"

"Well, it wasn't that simple." He frowned. "My mother, for

one thing. She felt pro baseball would be a waste of my education. In with a bunch of tobacco-spitting roughnecks, she said." He fiddled with his fork. "Sure, they're pretty earthy characters in those locker rooms—"

"But what about the famous ones—like Babe Ruth?"

"Oh, lots of them are great guys, no question. But mother pointed out how medicine would give me a profession my whole life long. Serving my fellow man in an important way—" He put down the fork and finished his drink.

"Serving your fellow man—that's wonderful—" My voice trailed away. "So it was your mother's idea—"

"She was absolutely right, she always is."

It was unusual, the way he talked. So many people only got gripes about how their mothers wouldn't let them do this or that. Meanwhile our waiter was sliding our salads in front of us. Regular works of art, shining leaves crowned with huge, white mushroom caps and avocado wedges. Spinach I thought you had to cook, but these tender leaves with a lemony dressing were way better, no bitterness at all. It sure beat Mr. Schipper's head lettuce.

Our main dish appeared, beef hiding inside a huge puff of flaky pastry. The braised endive was a new one for me, also, a little sharp at first but nutty when I got used to it. Broccoli at least was familiar, but now it had it under that rich sauce.

George looked at me. "What do you think?"

"This pastry—out of this world! So's everything—"

He laughed. "Eating with you is a pleasure—you really relish food. The way your eyes gleam! So many women pick at it—"

"When you've been as poor as I was, you learn to appreciate good food, believe me." I gave him my Ginger Rogers smile.

"Try your wine—"

Ruby red, a gorgeous color. I took a sip. "Isn't it sour?"

"No, it's dry—Burgundy—" He shook his head. "Never mind, just enjoy the food. I can see I'm never going to be able to get to first base by plying you with liquor. Have to find some other way . . ." His eyes teased me.

I just smiled and went on eating. "So now you've been a doctor for some time. Some difference from baseball, with so much responsibility. You have long hours, too—so do you like what you're doing?"

His eyes narrowed. "I'd better," he said. "The Red Sox wouldn't look at me now, all out of practice."

I speared a broccoli floret. "It must be terrible to get a case like Eddie's girl. I saw how the nurses and doctors ran down the hall to help her—but she died, anyway. Twenty-two years old, imagine."

Lines crossed his broad forehead. "That's the toughest part, when all the equipment and all the training put together just don't do it. And then? And then you have to go out and tell the family. Oh, brother—" He gulped down some of the red wine. "I've been practicing a good seven years, but some things don't get any easier. How come they weren't married, Eddie and his girl?"

"The families were both against it, like Romeo and Juliet." I explained about the Germans and the Eastern Europeans. "But there's one big puzzle. Why would such an intelligent girl go out and have an abortion and not even tell Eddie? He was crazy about her—"

He shook his head. "No one'll probably ever know the answer to that one."

"Oh, yes, we've got to," I told him, putting down my fork. "I'll find out that, too, see if I don't!"

"Harry told me about your detective accomplishments. Sure glad you're not on my trail—" His blue eyes were laughing. "And you're up on your Shakespeare, too—"

I wasn't about to mention Evening English, I just gave him my Myrna Loy mysterious look.

The waiter came and mentioned some fancy desserts but we both decided no, so he brought coffee. Then George checked his watch and said it was early, how about going dancing?

"Dancing—sounds wonderful!"

"Belle Appleman, I like the way you second the motion!" The grin that made him look like a kid was back. "What if I suggested a moonlight swim?"

"Hoo-ha, that one I'd veto. Too chilly at night." And no bathing suits, neither—but that I didn't mention.

He gave a little wave of his hand, and like magic the bill appeared, sitting on a little silver tray. To the numbers at the bottom he added something, and signed it with a flourish. Then we were outside again at the car. No ticket on the windshield. He opened the door to usher me in, and a minute later we were off.

Where to? George didn't say and I didn't ask. But when we parked on Boylston Street in front of that high building, I knew. Dancing on the Lenox Roof, talk about fancy-shmancy.

It's like fairyland. From the Lenox Roof you can look down over the whole city. Across the Charles River, the M.I.T. dome glows in spotlights. Leading towards it, the Mass. Avenue Bridge becomes a string of lights with car headlights moving each way.

We were led to a little table with a candle burning inside a red glass chimney. The orchestra was already playing. George held out his hand and in a minute we were on the floor. The honey voice of the fellow singing said he should've known I was temptation, and George began to sing some of the words in my ear. Being way up there, on top of the world, moving easy and slow to the soft music put me into a kind of trance. We danced three numbers just smiling at each other now and then.

Back at the table sat two glasses of white wine that George had ordered. "Go ahead, try this, Belle, see if you don't like it better than Burgundy. . . ."

I took a teeny sip. Sweeter, not bad. Something familiar about the flavor. "What kind is it?"

"A Rhine wine. Called—"

"Goldtroepfschen!" A light went on my in brain when he said "Rhine wine." What another man ordered for me once.

George's eyebrows went up. "The things you come up with— boy, you're one surprise after another! Just when I thought I was getting to know you! Tell me—" He leaned forward, a lock of hair slid onto his forehead. "—which one is the real Belle?"

Who could answer that one? I gave him my secret Garbo smile. The orchestra started again, telling us it was easy to re- member but so hard to forget. Back on the floor we came to- gether cheek to cheek like Fred and Ginger. When I finally came to my senses and asked George what time it was I got a shock. Nearly midnight! I had to open the drugstore the next morning at eight, and he admitted he had to be at the hospital early. But who wanted to leave paradise?

Back in his car I snuggled into the folds of my cape and faced something else. What would saying goodnight bring? When George opened the car door in front of my apartment on Allen Street I told him I could go upstairs okay by myself, it was late. He inclined his head and said, "Different again! Most women want lots of attention. . . ." And added that a gentleman always sees a lady to her door.

So much for Appleman's how-to-end-dates-without-prob- lems plan. Up we went to the second floor. When I got out my key he took it away with one easy move of those long fingers and opened the door for me. When he handed it back the eyes had an extra gleam.

I couldn't resist telling him, "You're a terrific dancer, did you know that?" It was true, too. Anyway, I was tired of just daydreams, it would be so easy to ask him in. Should I?

"You're quite a partner," he murmured. His hand touched my cheek and stayed for a second, it made me quiver. "Goodnight, Lady Surprises," he breathed. "Parting is really sweet sorrow, isn't it? Shakespeare knew his stuff—"

His lips melted into mine, they tasted of wine, mm. My arms had no trouble finding their way around his neck. Wasn't the orchestra still playing out there?

Upstairs a door banged, we both jumped. George grinned, nuzzled my cheek, and headed downstairs. Before stepping into my apartment and closing the door I looked up at the third floor and sang out, "It's okay, Mrs. Wallenstein, he's a doctor!"

After I undressed and slipped on my nightie I stood a minute peering into the bedroom mirror. Slow down, Appleman, I told the flushed face staring back at me, don't get stars in your eyes so quick. He's a nifty dancer, what does that prove? You're on the trail of someone who's doing abortions around here and he's a doctor, remember. What do you know about him, after all?

And that reminded me of something I forgot all about asking him. Why was he buying those Ergotamine ampoules in our drugstore?

ten

"Wake up, Appleman!" screamed my alarm clock in my ear. Oh, swell, just what I wanted to hear. My hand reached up and slammed the button down to close its mouth.

My eyes were still pasted down from sleep, but it was worth lying for a minute to taste the pleasures of last night again. Dancing high up on the Lenox Roof, the lights winking from across the river and the stars up above, a man's arms holding me, a voice crooning songs full of promises.

Who wanted to jump out of bed so early on Sunday morning? But it was my Sunday to work till one o'clock. I managed to push the movie in my head aside and hop up. After all that food last night, who needed breakfast? But my mother had me trained, everyone's stomach needed fuel to start the day. *Nu*, the percolator with coffee, cornflakes with stewed prunes, a poppyseed roll with cream cheese. My appetite had me always ready for a meal.

Marcia was extra edgy this morning. When I asked her if there was anything new, she snapped no and clammed up. No is no, so I left her alone. I thought Harry might be interested to know nothing terrible happened to me on my date with George Parkland. But he was cross, too, and didn't say more than two words to me before ten o'clock.

Sunday was a newspaper day, people came in for the fat Sunday papers. The fattest was the *New York Times*, we put a bunch aside for our regulars. Nothing much doing on the fountain till after church. Of course, people still got sick on Sundays so pre-scriptions came in for Harry to fill.

So I kept busy with what Harry depended on me for—fill-ing in stock. It was important to write down when you were getting near the end of a shelf item—if you forgot, the item didn't get reordered. And it's like a law in the Talmud, the minute you run out of, say, Ipana toothpaste giant size, a customer comes in to ask for that.

I was stacking some Benson & Hedges cigarette packages in back of the tobacco counter when the door opened and lanky Dr. Somerville danced in with his nervous little step. He gave me a teeny wave as he headed for the back room. A couple minutes later one customer who didn't exactly tickle me pink arrived. Dr. Sam Revak.

"Belle, fresh as a daisy at this hour! On the level, you're a peach!" The man was certainly full of pep in the morning. I just gave him my high-toned Katherine Hepburn look. Marcia slammed down a metal pitcher on the fountain. He didn't turn a hair, only breezed toward the back room like he just won the Mr. USA contest. As he got there, Somerville came out.

"Hi, there, Haskell," Revak chirped.

Somerville didn't answer but for a second the expression on his face gave me the heebie-jeebies. Like he was looking at something so hideous it made him sick. Then the nervous mask went back on and he practically ran out the door. Revak only gave a shrug and went in back.

What was it with that creep that made Somerville so scared? Right away I went over to the back counter and got busy check-ing those shelves. Listen, those had to be done, too.

"Hey, Harry," Revak was saying, "didn't you give Haskell his fix this morning? Looked like death walking just now—"

"Cut it out, Sam," said Harry. "What are you talking about?"

"Come on, Harry, it's no secret about Haskell and his habit. Listen, it's no skin off my nose. You get those Ergotamine ampoules in yet?"

"Yeah, yeah. How many you want?"

"Six. Put 'em on my tab, will you? Oh, and Harry, let's not forget that little matter that's due. Maybe tomorrow morning at my place?" Harry gave a grunt that was kind of like a moan.

I moved quick over to cosmetics. Revak came out whistling and stopped in front of me. "Well, Lady Frosty, how's about that rain check? Dinner for two tonight—just name the place—"

A good thing the counter was between us. "No soap, Dr. Revak, you're ringing the wrong bell here."

He grinned, showing all those capped white teeth. "What's your problem? A peppy gal like you—be a sport!"

Marcia was right there behind the fountain, she could hear every word. "So long, Doctor, I've got a lot of work here—" I put on my Bette Davis glare, couldn't say too much to a customer, after all.

Revak wasn't the kind that gave up easy. He reached out to get my hand but I grabbed it away in time. "Come on, why play hard to get, you're all grown up!" he said. Then he gave a low whistle. "That's some build you've got!"

Why didn't Harry come out and help me get rid of him? He had plenty to say when George asked me out, and now he didn't even stick his nose out of the back room. Was he getting deaf?

"Get lost, Doctor, please." I spoke in a real polite voice and turned my back. Maybe Marcia would believe now that I wanted no part of that two-timing faker. Anyway, he must've given up because I could hear him whistling on his way out. Marcia just disappeared in back.

"'Morning, Mrs. Parkland," Revak's voice sang out, as he held the door open for her before he left. But she only raised her

chin and swept past him into the store. He looked after her for
a second, shrugged, and walked out.

What a relief to see Beatrice Parkland instead of that jerk.
"Morning, Mrs. Parkland, you're out early—" Did she know
who her son was with last night?

She was wearing a snappy pink silk shirtwaist dress and a
wide straw hat with a pink grosgrain band, like a page from
Vogue. "I was just passin' by when I remembered my face powder's
almost gone."

"What kind do you use?"

"Y'all—the woman here before you—sold me Coty's rachel."

"Coty's is the best." I inspected her skin, terrific for her age.
"But rachel I wouldn't recommend for your fair complexion.
Natural would be much more flattering, believe me. . . ." I gave
her a sample on a cotton ball to try.

She studied it. "You're just darlin'," she said. "I'll take it, the
natural, Mrs. Appleman—just charge it, please. . . ."

While I was wrapping it, I said, "Tell me, do you know that
Dr. Revak who just went out?"

She gave a shudder. "My dear, he's my next-door neighbor."

"With a neighbor like that you don't need enemies!" I handed
her the package. "You heard, maybe, it's possible some doctor
on the Hill is doing abortions?"

"Here? On Beacon Hill?" She stood open-mouthed for a second. "Goodness, are you sure?"

I shrugged. "A girl already died from it. The police are checking all the doctors."

"Is that a fact! Well, let them check up on Sam Revak. There's
some mighty peculiar goings-on in his place at night, if you ask
me."

"Peculiar? What do you mean?"

She leaned closer. "Lights on half the night. Visitors comin'
and goin' at all hours, a regular circus—"

So Beatrice Parkland was spying on Revak. Why was she so interested in what happened next door? Was she just another Mrs. Wallenstein under all that high-class polish?

Harry came up to us and gave my customer a big smile. "Good morning, Mrs. Parkland, Belle taking care of you okay?"

"She's adorable, Harry!" She smiled back at him and plopped the package in her bag. "Well, mornin', y'all."

Harry went into the back room and I followed him. Marcia was coming up the cellar stairs, carrying a gallon bottle crushed pineapple for the fountain. I tried to give her an "everything's okay" sign with my fingers, to stop her stewing over Sam Revak. But she brushed right by me and went out front.

Nu, so keep on stewing, Marcia, I thought, much good it'll do. I turned to Harry. "Listen, that stuff that Revak gets from you, that Ergotamine—is that like the stuff Daniel once told me can get rid of a pregnancy? That tincture of ergot?"

Harry nodded. "Something like that. But it's a different compound."

"But you wouldn't give it to a pregnant woman, would you?"

"No, I sure wouldn't. Why are you asking?"

"I was just wondering what Revak does with it. Maybe he's the—"

Harry cut me off. "I don't want to know about it! He's a doctor and he's the one that writes the prescriptions. I just fill them, that's it. So forget about the abortion business, Belle. Take care of business right here in the store, better! That's your job!" He went over to a side shelf to pick out a big bottle of pills.

Who could talk to such an itchy-pitchy guy? I went back into the store thinking about that Ergotamine. Appleman, you know darn well who else asked Harry for some before—Dr. George Parkland, the day he pulled me up from the floor. But could someone as nice as George be doing illegal botchwork like that? Impossible to believe. No, if anybody needed to be interviewed by Jim Connors, it was that no-goodnick Revak.

Luckily, I kept busy out front waiting on customers. Who wanted to be in back with that grumpy boss? Or near Marcia getting the cold shoulder?

But the back-room phone began to ring, and Harry didn't answer, must've gone downstairs. So I ran in and picked up the phone. "Charles Street Pharmacy—"

A kind of hoarse voice mumbled something.

"Excuse me, what did you say?"

The raspy voice mumbled a little louder. "—Eddie Plaut?"

"Eddie's coming in one o'clock. You want to leave a message, he'll call back?"

The voice muttered something.

"What? Listen, who's calling?"

The only answer was a click and the dial tone. *Nu*, the world's full of nuts, I thought, and hung up.

Only, why should someone who wants Eddie make like the mysterious Dr. Fu Manchu?

Wait a minute. Could it be that loud-mouth brother of Marcia's? And why would he want Eddie, anyway?

eleven

Who was George Parkland eating lunch with, I wondered, while scrambling a couple eggs with cottage cheese, slicing a ripe tomato, and putting some pumpernickel and sweet butter on my kitchen table. Did he eat in the hospital cafeteria with a lot of pretty nurses giving him the eye? *Nu*, I'd better be satisfied with Wayne King waltzes on the radio for now.

Right in the middle of my first swallow of milk I started to think about Revak being the abortionist and how to find out if he was. And that made me think about Clara and the Borofskys and the Plauts. So the minute I finished lunch, I went to the phone book, found the number under Leon Winkler, and dialed. A woman's voice said hello.

"This is Belle Appleman, you don't know me, but I'm a good friend of Sarah Siegel—she used to be your neighbor in the West End?"

"Sarah Siegel?" said the voice. "Oh, goodness, it's been years—"

"What I'm calling about, Mrs. Winkler, Sarah said you used to live in the same building with Jennie Borofsky and Hilda Plaut—"

"When we were first married—Sarah's right, that's where we lived—"

"You maybe heard what happened with Jennie's youngest, Clara?"

"Oh, God, I couldn't believe it!" She gave a cluck of sympathy. "The notice in the paper. What a tragedy! What on earth happened, such a young girl?"

"It's a long story," I said, "and maybe you could help clear things up a little—if you wouldn't mind—"

"Me? But I haven't seen any of those people in years! I've been meaning to send Jennie a note, I'll do it first thing tomorrow—"

"Listen, Mrs. Winkler, I know it's Sunday and you maybe got plans. But if you're going to be home, could I come over for a few minutes to talk to you?"

"Well—I guess so—we're going out for dinner, but not till six—"

"So, is it okay if I stop by in a little while to talk? I'll take the streetcar right away?"

No answer for a second. Then she said, "Well—why not? A friend of Sarah's—sure, come—Mrs.—uh—"

I told her my name and she gave me the address and said she'd be expecting me. Polite as she was, her voice sounded as if she couldn't figure out what I was talking about. *Nu*, a little mystery maybe helps to get people involved.

The Charles Street Circle El took me to Park Street and a Commonwealth-Brighton streetcar, to the Babcock Street stop. It's a funny thing, the first minute I ever walked on a Brookline Street, it felt like I was in a different country. If you only made a little better living, you moved from the West End out to Dorchester. Brookline was where you moved when you were in the money. One look at the apartment house where the Winklers lived told me they already moved way past their West End days.

Fay Winkler was a bird-like little woman wearing ruffled lounging pyjamas and armfuls of silver bracelets that clanked as she darted about. She treated me like an invited guest, took me in the den and insisted on getting a cup tea. Her husband poked his nose in for a minute to introduce himself, told me to call him Leon, and poked out again. A giant of a man, twice as high as his wife, which was maybe why he walked kind of bent over. Sarah told me they made their money in dry cleaning.

The den was small but sparkling with mirrored walls that doubled the matching velvet loveseats. It had French doors open to a porch with white wicker furniture. Fay came in with the tea and some fancy tarts topped with glazed cherries. Reminded me of what they served at the Kleins' wedding last year. I bit into one, mmm.

"These are Leon's favorites." Fay settled herself opposite me.

"He's got good taste."

"Frankly, for me they're a little too rich. And he's supposed to watch his weight, but he won't listen—you know men—"

I gave her my what-men-are look and wiped cherry stains from my fingers.

She put down her cup on the marble-top coffee table. "Tell me—uh, Belle—what is it you want to talk about? I'm dying of curiosity. . . ."

I swallowed the rest of the little cake and leaned forward. "Well, then—uh, Fay—you maybe heard about Clara Borofsky and Eddie Plaut?

"No—you mean the girl that just died?"

"That's right," I told her. "She and the Plaut boy fell in love, wanted to get married—"

"And she died! Isn't that terrible! What happened to her? The papers didn't say. . . ."

I hesitated. "An appendix. Broke before they could do anything—"

"What do you know!" She shook her head. "The doctors couldn't figure it out? Didn't they have a specialist?"

Tell one lie, you got to tell ten more to cover up. "You know young people, she didn't let on anything was wrong till it was too late. Anyways, what really bothers me—" I stopped and gave her my Myrna Loy look. "Sarah told me you were a person could keep a secret, Fay."

She straightened up, her bracelets clanked. "Absolutely!" She leaned closer. "Me you can trust, don't worry!"

"Good. The funny part is, both families were dead set against the marriage. Crazy, no? Two nice young people—"

"Let me tell you, Hilda's being against the match, I would expect." She waved her hands with more jangling. "Back even then she was standoffish. *Nu, Deutschen*, enough said."

"But the Borofskys were against, also," I pointed out. "And Eddie Plaut is a professional man, a pharmacist. Works with me in the Charles Street Pharmacy. A clean-cut type. And crazy in love with Clara, dying to marry her! You can imagine how he feels now."

She nodded in sympathy. "Poor boy—"

"So I'm trying to help him stop blaming himself. Was there maybe something between the Borofskys and the Plauts a long time ago? That made the families sore at each other? So the Borofskys weren't only mad at just him, but the whole family, I mean."

She gave a sigh. "That Plaut boy, he must be suffering enough."

"He's a changed person. I'm afraid it could even affect his work. It would be awful if he got fired on account of something that happened years ago. Could you think of anything between the two families?"

"So far back, who can remember—" Fay knit her brows. "Lemme think. Seems to me they got along fine. In fact," she nodded her head, "one time one of Jennie's little girls fell down in the street and Marcus Plaut brought her upstairs to the Borofskys'. I was on the first floor and I saw him coming up with the child crying in his arms. 'She fell down,' he said, 'got a nasty bump on the head.'"

"Where was the father—where was Sol?"

"It was in the daytime, he must've been at work. Why Marcus was home that day I can't remember, only he worked evenings sometimes. But see what I mean by good neighbors? Marcus was helping."

"It must be scary," I said, "for your kid to get hurt when you're all by yourself—"

"Of course, what mother wouldn't worry? You always think, maybe it's worse than it looks, a concussion or something. And in those days we didn't call doctors so quick, who could afford to?"

"Anything else you remember? What about the Plauts?"

"They didn't have two cents to their name, like the rest of us. But they spoke beautiful English. Marcus you could talk to, Hilda was the type kept to herself. She wanted to get away from that section, didn't like to be with that bunch from the old country. From Eastern Europe, know what I mean? For instance, we all used to go upstairs and sit together on the roof those hot summer nights, remember?"

"Who doesn't? What other spot could you get a breath of air in summer?"

"How did we stand it!" Fay rolled her eyes. "Not even a porch for the kids to play! Had to get them all dressed up and *shlep* them to the Esplanade for fresh air. It was no picnic, believe me." She ran a hand over the velvet of the love seat. "Thank God, we got away."

"So when did the Plauts stop this coming upstairs to the roof?"

Fay shrugged. "I can't remember—they just stopped, that's all."

"Was it after that business with the Borofsky child?"

"Maybe—maybe Hilda was mad that Marcus was getting in with the neighbors, who knows? It didn't take long before she found a place where more of their type lived, so they moved out. I can't even remember her going around to say goodbye, imagine, everybody did that."

"You never saw them again?"

Fay smoothed the back of her hair, the bracelets jiggled down her arms. "Never. Who missed them? Well, Marcus was a different story, he was a gentleman. But we women were relieved to see Hilda leave. No style at all but she was too good for the rest of us! And that's the whole story."

"Fay, you really helped a lot." I stood and she jumped up. We shook hands. "It was so nice of you to let me come. And having tea was a pleasure, you treated me like a friend."

"Drop in any time," she said. "And bring Sarah, we'll have a tea party!"

But as I walked along toward the streetcar stop, no light went on in my head about what Fay told me. A kind neighbor helping with a hurt child—how could that make two families into the Capulets and the Montagues?

Nu, I had plenty to think about. Last night I didn't get a lot of sleep, so this was a good evening to go to bed early and stretch out just dreaming about the date with George. But that nagging question kept poking itself into my brain.

What could have started such bitter feeling between the Borofskys and the Plauts?

twelve

When I got home the next day, I wondered did I have enough figured out to go calling Jim.

Not yet, Appleman, you still got puzzles plenty. I thought maybe I could hash things out with Sarah, so I picked up the phone and dialed.

"Plans?" she echoed in answer to my question. "What plans? If you mean is Cary Grant taking me to dinner—"

"No, but I am. Right here, give me about an hour, okay? What could Cary Grant give you as good as Mr. Schecter's lamb chops?"

"That I wouldn't answer, but I'll be there with bells on."

In the kitchen I put on the radio and out came that crazy song from last year, about the music going round and round. That trumpet player with the hoarse voice was singing it, what was his name, Louis? Louis Armstrong. His voice reminded me of the phone call for Eddie in the store. Someone trying to hide his real voice?

Cabbage and carrots for coleslaw, potatoes for baking, and stringbeans to slice up. The lambchops didn't need trimming, Mr. Schechter always gave me the best. So with all the peeling and slicing and checking to see nothing burned, the doorbell was ringing before I knew it. Sarah came puffing in, bringing a jar in a brown bag.

"You brought chopped liver? You made our dinner fancier, now we'll have an appetizer—Cary Grant should eat so well!"

Sarah enjoys good food, too. So while we ate we put our minds on it and I didn't bring up serious stuff. When we were finally sipping our hot tea and nibbling some of the coffee cake from Mr. Danberg's bakery, I said, "Sarah, were you wondering why I asked you for Fay Winkler's address?"

Sarah's brow wrinkled. "I couldn't figure out what you wanted it for—but I didn't ask, I know you already—"

"After I mentioned your name, she couldn't do enough for me."

Sarah leaned forward. "You went already? So what's it like where she lives?"

"Some difference from the West End! And she gave me tea, answered all my questions." I repeated what Fay told me about the Plauts and the Borofskys.

Sarah made a pout. "So what's that? Don't mean a thing, a neighbor helps out—"

I shrugged. "Who knows? But I maybe have a clue to who's doing the abortions on the Hill. Remember I talked about that doctor, Sam Revak? One of those doctors who comes in the store, a gynecologist, besides. He was going with Marcia, our fountain girl. *Nu*, wait till I tell you what happened with her. . . ." Sarah's eyes widened as I told the story about Marcia and how Revak tried to date me in front of her.

"A doctor yet!" She gave a shudder. "If that doesn't take the cake!"

"Wait, that's not all." I told her how he came in to get those Ergotamine ampoules all the time. "Not exactly good for a pregnant woman, Harry says."

"You mean it could bring on an abortion? But that's against the law, why would Harry give them out for that—"

"Sure. But maybe they're good for something else?"

Sarah shrugged. "Anyway, you can't prove a thing just because this doctor gets the stuff at your store. . . ."

"No, I can't, but I got a feeling—"

"You and your feelings, Belle! Watch out, they get you in all kinds trouble!" She put down her teacup. "Guess who asked me out to the movies last night?"

"Oh? Jimmy Cagney, right?"

"Even better. Nate Becker, can you believe it?" She had a big smile on her face, Sarah's really pretty, with that wavy blonde hair always so perfect. A smart dresser, too.

The minute she said his name, a little pang went through me. Appleman, you turned him down, remember. And then you went out for dinner and dancing. Ten times more exciting! Still, it gave me a funny feeling. *Nu*, you can't have your cake and eat it, too. "That's nice, Sarah. So what did you see?"

"We went to the Scollay Square Theater. *Charge of the Light Brigade*, with Errol Flynn."

"Errol Flynn—how was it?"

She shrugged. "Too much shooting. More horses than people." Her mouth widened in a smile. "But it was a double feature with Clark Gable and Claudette Gable, *It Happened One Night*. Wonderful!"

"But we saw that last year," I reminded her.

"*Nu*, it was even better this time. Nate and I laughed all through it. Then we went for ice cream sodas." She was still smiling. "I heard you had a date last night, also?"

"I was going to tell you about it. He's a doctor, a real gentleman. Comes in the store all the time. Wait'll you meet him, a regular Gary Cooper."

"A doctor, no kidding!" She finished her cake. "So what's his name?

"George Parkland."

Sarah put her cup down and looked me in the eye. "Parkland? What kind name is that?"

"From an old blue-blood family on the Hill, came over on the Mayflower, maybe."

She didn't smile. "But he's not your kind, Belle!"

"So what? Sixteen years old I'm not. Besides, who would know better about abortions on Beacon Hill than a doctor who lives there? We went to dinner at Locke-Ober's and then dancing on the Lenox Roof—you can't imagine how gorgeous it was up there—"

"Locke-Ober's," Sarah repeated slowly. "I was never there. But the Lenox Roof I know. So how was the food?"

"Swell. You should see the prices on the Locke-Ober's menu!"

She pursed her lips. "What do you need it for? Making whoopee, that's not your type—"

"Listen, something's wrong with having a good time?" Time to change the subject. "Guess what—I found out about that Revak character. Mrs. Parkland, the doctor's mother, comes in the store a lot—told me he lives right next door to them on Mount Vernon Street! Wait'll you hear—" I filled her in.

"So you didn't find out from your date, you heard it from his mother!" She frowned at me. "So why don't you call Jim at the Joy Street Station and tell him?"

"No, he'll say, where's the real evidence. Sarah, we're missing Fibber McGee—"

I switched the radio on to hear the *tararam* of everything falling out of Fibber McGee's closet. Then on WEEI came the Voice of Firestone—Nelson Eddy, who else!

So we listened to him sing and dreamed about being Jeanette McDonald. Then we started talking recipes until all of a sudden Sarah jumped up. "Belle, I got to get going! It's after ten-thirty—"

The phone rang. When I picked up, a surprise, it was Marcia. She was excited and babbling.

"Slow down, Marcia," I told her, "I can't understand what you're saying. Where are you?"

"I'm in the store. Wait'll you hear, Belle, Eddie just got a phone call and started running around here like a crazy man. Then he threw me his keys, yelled over I should close up the store, and ran out!"

I couldn't believe what I heard. "He ran out? He left you all by yourself and it wasn't even eleven yet?"

"Yeah, he left me absolutely alone, c'n you beat it?"

"Did he say who called?"

"No, after he hung up, he said some swear words about that rat Revak. Belle, what'll I do?"

"Do? Do what he said, Marcia. Close up, put out the lights, and go home. Remember to leave the night light on in the back room. You're opening tomorrow with Harry, no? So give him Eddie's keys and tell him what happened."

I hung up and turned to Sarah. Her eyes were big with questions.

"That was Marcia, at the store." I shook my head. "Imagine, Eddie got a phone call and ran out before eleven, even. Left her to close up. A kid like Marcia."

"So what's wrong with Eddie? Who called him?"

"Marcia didn't know. But, listen, Sarah, we got to do something to keep Eddie from getting into real trouble. It doesn't sound good, Eddie leaving the store like that, before closing time. It could make real trouble for the pharmacy."

Sarah shrugged. "*Nu*, there's nothing you can do about it."

"Wait." I pictured Eddie busting into Revak's house and slugging him on the jaw. Or worse. Revak was thick around the middle, he was no match for young Eddie. "Listen, Sarah, we got to do something to keep Eddie from maybe wrecking his life."

"Do? What could we do?"

"Go over to Mount Vernon Street and watch to see if Eddie shows up at Revak's place."

Sarah's jaw dropped. "We should go parading in the streets at night? That's *meshugah*! For crying out loud, Belle, it gives me the heebie-jeebies just thinking about it!" She shuddered.

"Okay, if that's how you feel, don't come. I'll go myself."

Sarah knew when she was licked, she gave a sigh. "*Nu*, okay, long as you aren't gonna break into that doctor's house."

I gave her my innocent Loretta Young look. "Who, me?" We both got a fit of laughing, remembering the time I once did break into an apartment to get evidence.

Sarah started to put on lipstick and then stopped. "Who needs makeup? Who's gonna see us?" She put the lipstick in her bag. "Are we nuts, running around this hour of night? What about dogs, or drunks, you never know who's out there—"

"Listen, it'll be an adventure."

So we went downstairs. A little salty breeze, but still warm. Not much traffic on Cambridge Street, it was easy to cross. Down Charles Street past the drugstore where Eddie was on tonight. I sneaked a look but couldn't see much. At Mount Vernon we turned left and started up the hill.

Kind of spooky out, because the street lights were far apart and not too bright. They were the old gas lights but now they had small electric-light bulbs in them. Traffic noises and a dog barking somewhere, some people out walking. Every sound gave Sarah a start.

Revak's townhouse was halfway up the hill, between West Cedar Street and Louisburg Square. I took Sarah's arm and she gave a jump. "Let's cross here. We'll watch from the other side."

Across the street we found a doorway without steps, looked like it used to be a garage. We crossed and stood there in the shadow. We could see the front of Revak's house. A few steps with an iron handrail led up to his door. No light in any of the front windows, or else they were covered by heavy drapes. So maybe it was a waste of time, he was out. Or asleep already? Right next door was George's townhouse. Which was his room? I pictured him in a fancy bathrobe reading in a big velvet chair. It was a nice way to pass the time waiting for Eddie to show up.

Suddenly my heart gave a jump up to my mouth. Someone was coming right up toward us, a long shadow in the dim lamplight. Was it Revak himself, watching us spying on his house? Or was it Eddie coming to do something we had to stop him from doing?

A masculine voice said, "Good evening, ladies. See anything exciting yet?"

"Nate, Nate Becker!" My heart sank back where it belonged. "You scared us! What're you doing here?"

"It's my fault," said Sarah in a small voice. "When you went in the bathroom I went to the phone and called Nate. I figured if we were going to do something dippy, with Nate along, at least—"

"That's swell," I said. Did Sarah think we couldn't even go around the corner by ourselves? But I looked at my two friends and decided maybe an extra pair eyes couldn't hurt. "Nate, thanks for coming. We need all the help we can get." He smiled.

"Wait!" hissed Sarah. "Somebody's coming!"

A shadow was moving down the street from Louisburg Square. The shadow turned into a man. Too dark to see the face under the hat. Could it be Eddie? I opened my mouth to call his name. But Nate stopped me with a "Shhh!" in my ear. "We don't know that's Eddie, and you could get us mixed up with some trouble. Let's see what he does," he whispered.

While we watched, the figure stopped at Revak's house, looked at it a second, and went up the stairs. A few soft taps, like he was knocking on the door. Then the door opened and the house swallowed him up. The door closed behind him.

"Was that Eddie?" Sarah whispered in my ear.

"I don't know, maybe it was. Didn't seem like him, but . . . I don't want Eddie to get into any trouble." I started to head up to the house, but Nate's arm blocked me.

"Look," hissed Nate, "someone's coming from the other way—"

We shrank back into the cover of our doorway and peered out. Another figure, also a man, hurried up the hill to stop in front of Revak's house a minute. Again the same business, knocking, waiting, then the door opening with him going in.

"For crying out loud," said Nate. "You claim this doctor is doing abortions. So why are men trooping in there instead of women?"

"Who knows?" I bit my lip. "Maybe some other kind funny business is going on, also—"

"Some imagination you got," said Nate. "Me, I hope no cop comes along. Go explain what we're doing here at this hour of night—"

"Look!" Sarah almost yelled.

"Shh," Nate and I whispered at the same time.

"The door's opening!" Sarah pointed.

She was right. Out came one of the figures that went in before, slamming the door closed. Next he started running back up the hill toward Louisburg Square. "That's the one came in first," I whispered. We stood there and watched him disappear into the night.

"What could be going on in there?" Nate said, half to himself.

Just then my ears caught a noise coming from Revak's place. At least, it seemed to come from there. A kind of muffled bang, like somebody shooting off a Fourth-of-July two-incher inside. We waited.

The dark silence like when we first came settled down on Mount Vernon Street again.

thirteen

The three of us stopped staring at Revak's house and stared at each other.

"*Gottenyu*, what's going on inside?" Nate burst out.

"It's not the Fourth of July!" I snapped. "Come on, let's go see!"

We dashed across the street to the door of Revak's place. Locked. *Nu*, there was a bell button to push, so I pushed it. We could hear the ring inside but nobody came to answer. I pushed again. Nothing happened.

"Maybe we should better go home?" asked Sarah in a breathless way. "God knows what we could be getting into—"

"Now? Run away? Nothing doing! We got to get in and see what's what." I rang the bell again, pushing hard as anything.

Nate tapped me on the shoulder. "Here, let me." His hand went up to something in the middle of the door. One of those brass knockers, you see them on fancy-shmancy houses. He gave a couple bangs you could've heard in the Public Garden blocks away. Nothing happened.

"*Nu*, nobody's home," whispered Sarah. "Let's go!"

Down the street shrilled a siren, blasting the silence. A second later a car pulled up to the curb. Out stepped two men. Who could miss that old fedora hat? My friend Jim, with his helper, Rafferty. They came up the steps and stopped dead in front of us. Three red-faced citizens stared back at the two policemen.

"That you, Belle? And your chums? What on earth—"

"Listen, Jim," I said, talking fast, "this is Dr. Revak's house, he's the one I got suspicious about, that he's the abortionist who killed poor Clara Borofsky, so I got Sarah and Nate to come see—"

"Whoa, hold your horses!" Jim stopped me. "You say this doc might be doing illegal abortions here? Got any *real* evidence?"

"Well, not exactly. But I thought—"

"Yeah, I know what you think, Belle." Jim took a flashlight out of his pocket and shone it on the door. "This is the number, all right," he told Rafferty.

"What? What number?" I asked.

"We got a phone call about gunshots at this address."

"Aha, you see, I knew there was funny business going on here. Of course there was a shot, we heard it!"

"We'd better go in," said Jim.

"Forget it," I told him. "We already rang the bell and banged the knocker. Nobody answers. And the door's locked."

"Maybe we'd better shoot it open, Rafferty," Jim said. "If you people will please move back across the street—we don't want anyone hurt by a ricochet—"

"Wait, Jim, I got a better idea." While he was talking about shooting, my hand poked into my pocketbook and pulled out something I brought along just in case. I showed it to Jim, and he shined his light on it.

"My God, a set of picklocks! Where on earth did you get them, Belle?"

"Oh, from a locksmith friend, and he showed me how to use them. Shine your light on the door, okay?"

A Yale lock. Took me only a second to find the right pick and I went to work. A twist here and a twist there, and the big front door swung open.

"I sure hope you're planning to use those for legitimate pur-
poses, Belle," said Jim, absolutely dead-pan. Rafferty's eyes
bulged like he was seeing the Messiah coming to Beacon Hill.

Jim took out his handkerchief. "If you're thinking about fingerprints on the doorknob, forget it," I told him. "I had to twist
it a few times, probably rubbed them off." Jim had his revolver
out. After all, if someone there was shooting, no use taking
chances. We tiptoed after Jim and Rafferty.

The hall was dark but I could see a light down at the end, a
back room. Jim came to the doorway and stopped, so we all
did. Then, holding his gun in front with both hands, he edged
around into the room and stopped.

"Hold it there—police!" he yelled real loud.

Who was he yelling at? I peeked around Rafferty. It only
took a minute for my eyes to get used to the light. Standing
right there was Eddie, our Eddie from the drugstore, head
turned sideways to look in our direction. Even in that poor
light he seemed lost, his face had no more expression than a
mannequin in a department store window. His right hand was
holding a gun.

Right on the carpet at his feet was a body. I didn't need no
fingerprints to identify it.

Dr. Sam Revak, that's who.

fourteen

Even if you paid two dollars to sit in the first row orchestra to see a Yiddish play at the Boston Opera House on Dover Street, you wouldn't see a more dramatic scene.

Eddie standing over the crumpled body like he was half asleep, gun in hand, swaying a little. And us all in a circle around him.

"Saints preserve us!" That was Jim.

"Eddie!" That was me.

"*Gottenyu!*" That was Nate and Sarah at the same time.

Rafferty just sucked in his breath in a whistle, but his eyes were popping.

Eddie moved his head a little, like he saw us, but he didn't say a thing.

"Eddie, give me the gun." Jim moved closer, reached out, and lifted the gun from Eddie's hand. Eddie still stood there like a statue, only his hand dropped down.

Jim put his own gun away in the holster under his jacket. He bent down and touched a finger to a spot on Revak's neck. "Dead, all right."

Revak was wearing a fancy paisley robe, the kind they call a dressing gown, open so the pajamas underneath showed. I went over for a closer look—maroon silk. On the chest part, a small hole. If there was any blood, you couldn't see the stain on the dark red fabric.

Jim straightened up, held Eddie's gun to his nose and sniffed. "Fired recently. Sorry, lad, but I'll have to take you in."

Eddie's forehead wrinkled. "Take me in?"

"Why'd you do it, Eddie?" asked Jim. "Kill him, I mean—"

"Kill?" Eddie shook his head like he was trying to shake something out. "I don't know—I didn't—" He stopped and looked at us as if he was seeing us for the first time.

"Rafferty," Jim said, "put in a call for the M.E. pronto! On the car phone—we don't want to touch these phones—" Rafferty dashed out like he was in the Boston Marathon.

Jim reached in his back pocket and pulled out handcuffs. "Put your hands out, Eddie, please."

"These you need?" I asked Jim. "He's not running away, he's hardly moving—"

"Standard procedure. He's a murder suspect now."

"But he barely knows what's going on—look at him—"

Jim was already snapping on the cuffs. "Yeah, he's in shock, probably. Sometimes happens to people after they kill, especially the first time—"

"Eddie, tell us what happened," I begged. "Tell us, come on—"

But all he said was, "My head hurts."

Nate crossed over and peered through his thick glasses at Eddie's head. "Looks like there's maybe a bump there."

"Listen," I said to Jim, "could be Eddie got into a fight first and got whacked on the head—" Jim shrugged.

Rafferty came back. "M.E.'s on the way."

"Take this one down to the station, Rafferty," Jim said, "and book him as a murder suspect. Edward Plaut, P-l-a-u-t, got it?"

"Got it, sir," said Rafferty, his eyes still popping. I guessed it was the first time he saw a murderer and a victim at the same time. He grabbed Eddie's arm.

"Take it easy, Rafferty, he's not going to run away."

Rafferty loosened his grip and led Eddie out.

"Now, ladies and gentleman," Jim said, "I'd like to hear all about everything." He took a pencil and his little black notebook out of an inside pocket. "Suppose you start, Belle."

I could hardly wait to tell Jim the whole story, starting with Marcia's phone call and how I talked Sarah into coming and she got Nate to join us. Jim groaned. Then Nate put in his two cents about the two figures that went into the house except only one came out. Sarah added the part about the firecracker bang.

"You're sure? You heard a shot?"

"Not a thing wrong with my ears," she said.

Jim licked the point of his pencil and scribbled in the notebook. "Well, I guess that wraps it up." He pushed his brown fedora back. "Belle, you sure get some wild ideas. But it's lucky you were all here to be witnesses."

Sarah sighed. "Oy, it's so late, I wish I was home instead."

"You folks can all leave now," Jim said, "I'll have to wait for the doc."

"Thank God," said Sarah. "Come on, Belle, Nate, let's go—"

"Sarah, you go on with Nate—he'll walk you home, won't you, Nate? Jim, I want to hear what the M.E. says."

Jim gave a snort and Sarah snapped, "Are you nuts, Belle? It's good and late, why should you hang around here?"

"Sarah, don't you know already?" Nate asked. "When Belle Appleman makes up her mind to mix in, wild horses couldn't shlep her away!"

Jim rolled his eyes toward heaven. "Remember, Jim," I said, "who got you inside here in the first place—"

Nate gave a shrug, Sarah a sigh, and they left together.

Jim looked down at Revak's body. "Never know how long you have to wait for Doc Barrett—"

"I don't have to be in till one o'clock. Oh, my God! Harry! He'll have to be told Eddie won't be opening tomorrow!"

"Right." Jim thought a minute. "Guess I can give him a ring from here." He looked at his watch. "Probably wake him up, though."

"Wake him, wake him! Better than if he should have a heart attack tomorrow because there's no pharmacist there."

Jim went to the phone on a rolltop desk and lifted the receiver with a handkerchief. "Know Harry's number?"

I gave it to him and he dialed, but it took a while before anyone answered, so they were asleep, all right. Jim kept his voice low, telling Harry what happened. I could hear the squawking of Harry's answer all the way across the room.

"No, I've no idea how long Eddie'll be away from the store," Jim was saying. "It's a murder rap, Harry, he might not even get out on bail. Sure, I'll fill you in on the details tomorrow. 'Night." He put the receiver back. "Boy, was he upset."

Meanwhile I was looking around. A rich man's furnishings, no question, the kind pine-panelled room they call a study. A maroon sofa, a couple leather wing chairs. One wall filled with books, a fireplace with a marble mantelpiece. Windows on the back wall hung with heavy velvet drapes, pulled closed. Paintings with elaborate carved frames. A dressy floor lamp—I spotted a light switch, went over and flooded the room with brightness.

"Hey, what're you doing?" asked Jim.

"So we can see Revak's body better," I explained.

Jim bent over Revak, unbuttoned the pajama top, and took a good look. "A bullet hole in his chest, all right."

The doorbell rang and we both jumped. "Don't touch anything, remember," Jim warned and went to answer the door.

A minute later he came back followed by four men. The first one was stocky, with salt-and-pepper hair, holding a little black bag. The M.E. Two of the others were carrying a stretcher, and the third had a camera.

"There's the stiff, Doc," said Jim. "Oh, you know Mrs. Appleman, she's giving me a hand here."

The M.E. grunted something that sounded like hello and bent over Revak's body. Then he straightened up. "Better let Mac take some pictures first."

The man with the camera stepped over and began snapping away. Each time he took a picture, a bright flash made me blink. When he finished, I could see little lights dancing around the room.

The doctor took a piece chalk out of his pocket and drew a line on the carpet all around the body. "Looks pretty cut-and-dried, bullet through the heart." He leaned over and squinted close up. "Powder burns here. Somebody held the gun pretty close."

"Any idea how long he's been dead?"

"My guess is only an hour or so. I can pinpoint it better at the autopsy."

"What time did you get here, Belle?" asked Jim.

"Hmmm—it was already after ten-thirty when Marcia called me about Eddie running out of the store like a wild man. And the store was already dark when Sarah and I went past. So when Sarah and I stopped across the street from this house, it must've been—well, at least eleven o'clock."

Jim looked at his watch. "And you heard the shot about when?"

"Let's see—first we talked about Nate being there . . . then the first figure went in . . . then the second . . . then the one that came out . . . then the bang. Who could check the time—too much going on!"

"And the call about hearing the shots came at about twenty-five past." Jim checked his watch again. "So he must've been shot between eleven-fifteen and eleven-twenty-five. About thirty-five minutes ago."

"Yup," said the M.E. "Rigor hasn't really gotten started yet."

"Doc, can you check to see if the bullet's inside?"

"Easy," said the M.E. He bent down and turned the body over. "See there?" He pointed to the hole in the back of Revak's robe. "Bullet went right through. Might be in the wall somewhere."

"Yeah, we'll check it out." Jim took off his hat, scratched his head, and put his hat back.

"Anything else before we take him out?" asked the M.E. Jim shook his head.

"Wait, Doctor," I said. "Why isn't there more blood on the clothes?"

"In this type of wound," he explained, "bleeding tends to be internal. Most of the blood lands in the chest cavity." He grinned at me. "Been reading *Black Mask*?"

"Don't sell her short," Jim put in. "She's the one solved the Classic Clothing murders—"

Doc Barrett got up from the floor and held out his hand to me. "By golly, you're Belle Appleman! We heard a lot about you at the coroner's office." He shook my hand. "How do you rate such attractive help, Jim?"

"Luck o' the Irish, Doc," said Jim with a straight face.

"Okay, boys, take him out." The two unfolded the stretcher, put the body on it, covered it with a blanket, and the four of them left.

Jim pulled at his ear. "Come on, Belle, I'll drive you home. Then I'll have to get back and have this house sealed."

"Just a second, Jim." I was thinking about the business of so little blood on the pajamas. "Let's take a look at the carpet."

The carpet was carved wool pile, must've cost a bundle. There was a small patch of brownish red against the beige. I bent down to study it. What I was looking for I didn't know.

A minute later I yelled, "Jim, come take a look! Right here in the middle of the stain!"

He hurried over and bent down. "Where?" My finger showed him. "By all the saints! A hole!"

He got the penknife out and started digging. Before very long, out came a little lump.

We stared at each other.

"So, one thing's settled," I said. " But something's bothering me—"

"Are you thinking what I'm thinking, friend?" Jim's eyes had a twinkle, he was giving me a test in detectiving.

An electric light bulb switched on in my head. "Revak was already lying on the floor when Eddie shot him!"

fifteen

We waited for Rafferty under Revak's white portico. Jim kept glancing at his watch. "What's taking him so long? You chilly, Belle?"

The whole street had put out its lights and gone to bed. The Parkland house poked a dark shadow into the night sky. Except for a cat yowling somewhere and that city-traffic hum, you could hardly hear a sound.

I sneezed and buttoned my cardigan. "Poor Eddie. It wasn't bad enough what happened with Clara, now he's in jail for murder, yet. Think he'll get any sleep tonight? All from two young people in love, can you beat it?"

Before anyone could answer that one, Rafferty drove up with a squeal of tires and stopped. We got in, me in the back.

Jim turned his head. "Take it easy, Rafferty, some people are in their beds asleep, remember."

"So you don't think I see things clear, about Eddie?" I asked. "But sometime you got to trust your own feelings, never mind evidence—" We sat there without talking while Rafferty drove fast. Soon we were right in front of my house.

Jim got out to open the door of the police car on my side. "Belle, you did some good work tonight. But that's it. The way you feel about Eddie—"

"He didn't do it." I climbed out.

"Maybe not. But this whole case is pretty messy. Somebody's out there hatching trouble and I don't fancy your getting into it. So can you let me take over for now?"

"You know me, Jim." I fished for my key. "Belle Appleman always minds her—"

"It's near midnight, friend," he broke in, "so let's dispense with the blarney. I'm responsible, after all, so have a heart, will you?"

"Jim, I'll do my best. Goodnight and sleep well."

"'Night, Mrs. Appleman," Rafferty called. Jim gave me his don't-give-me-that-stuff look as he said goodnight and got back in the car. As it roared away I looked up at my apartment house. No Mrs. Wallenstein at the window, thank God, she must be asleep. But as I climbed to the second floor, a door on the third clicked. I looked up to see a frizzy head disappear. Goodnight, Mrs. W. How many other neighbors came home this hour in a police car?

Who could fall asleep right away, tonight was too exciting. So after tossing around for a while, I went in the bathroom and poured myself a small glass Mogen David wine. What better way to get sleepy? I sat on the wicker stool and sipped and thought about the whole business with Revak.

Eddie with a smoking gun in his hand, imagine, could anything be worse? But somehow the way he looked and sounded, to me it didn't make sense that he did it. Or was I prejudiced, like Jim was warning me? The wine began to make my limbs feel heavy, so I stumbled back into the bedroom and got between the sheets.

A hole in the floor. Somehow those words went round and round in my head till it turned into a pinwheel spinning like crazy. Funny dreams all night long that I didn't remember in the morning.

Nine o'clock, bright sun hit my pillow and forced my eyes open. I got out of bed still feeling mixed-up so I took a quick shower ending with ice-cold needles that pepped me up. But in the icebox, not even an orange to eat. No wonder, I didn't go shopping for days already, a woman alone forgets. So I ate a black-spotted banana, wriggled into my clothes, grabbed my shoulder bag and a shopping bag, and ran downstairs.

There's no other place like Spring Street in the whole West End of Boston. You could start naked and hungry at one end of the street and be clothed and fed by the time you got to the other end. And even find a little peace for your soul in the Spring Street Synagogue halfway down. When I got to the corner, the sidewalks were already filled with women carrying shopping bags, pushing baby carriages, or shlepping crying children by the hand. A regular circus.

The street is so narrow you could spit across it without trying, imagine what it's like with fruit and vegetable trucks trying to get through. Some of the old-timers still use a horse and wagon to bring stuff, and they scream at the truck drivers for getting too close and scaring the horses. Naturally, the truck drivers shout back at them. So between the sobbing children and the scolding mothers and the teamsters, talk about noise, don't ask!

I started at Mr. Schechter's butcher shop. By now I didn't worry about eating kosher in restaurants but somehow wanted kosher meat for my own kitchen. The smell of fresh sawdust on the floor greeted me, along with a wide smile from Mr. Schechter, a short man with a neat little beard, trimming a roast for a woman ahead of me.

"Nice brisket today, Mrs. Appleman," he said, finishing with the roast.

I gave him my Mae West eyelash flutter. "How much meat do you expect a woman alone to buy? You maybe got one giant-size chicken wing?"

His eyes lit up and he chortled as he rang up the sale and gave the woman her change. "Listen, you want to hear a good

one? Mrs. Singer comes in early today, asks how much is calves'
liver. Thirty-nine cents, I tell her. Ha, she says, across the street
by Kranz's shop it's only twenty-nine cents! So I say, do me a
favor, go buy your liver from Kranz. Oh, she says, he's all out of
calves' liver. Naturally, I say, when I'm out, I charge only twenty-
nine cents a pound, also!"

It was an old joke but a smart woman keeps her butcher
happy so I laughed. To show he appreciated, he cut me a couple
nice lambchops from under the counter and picked out a plump
spring chicken. My mother, may she rest in peace, taught me
always to ask for a piece *fin hinten*, from underneath the counter,
where they keep the best cuts.

Another pleasure of Spring Street is the wonderful smells
that float right out from the shops. Mr. Danberg's bakery made
me almost faint with pleasure as I walked in. Everything they
bake right in the back. "A fine morning," sang out Mr. Danberg,
his eyes crinkling under his bushy eyebrows, "how about some
poppyseed rolls? Just out of the oven, still hot—" He knew my
favorites.

"Wrap up half a dozen," I told him. "And—let's see—a sliced
pumpernickel. It's warm out—a good day for business?"

"From your mouth to God's ear!" He had an elfish grin. "Listen, Mrs. Appleman, today I got something special—wait'll you
try it—"

I groaned. "From your specials, Mr. Danberg, I could maybe
become the fat lady in the sideshow!"

"You? Fat? Never!" He went to the back counter and came
back with a slice on a doily. "Taste—a new kind coffee cake—"

One bite was enough. "Who could say no to this? Okay, but
a small piece only—"

He cut me enough for a week and I paid him. Luckily, the
store was filling up, so I could hurry out before he talked me
into more stuff to *nosh*.

Schipper's fruit and vegetable market was a big place with everything in wooden boxes. Now it was filled with women poking and squeezing to make sure what they got was ripe but not rotten. Mr. Schipper was a skinny little man, a shrimp, while his son weighed maybe three hundred pounds and threw sacks of potatoes around like they were little pillows. How could so much come from so little?

Here you had to work your way or you'd never get a thing. A polite push here, a teeny shove there, and I was by the tomatoes, picking out nice firm ones. A small cabbage for cole slaw (you paid by the pound), a big solid head lettuce (you paid by the head), greenish bananas, some oranges. I asked Mr. Schipper to put the tomatoes and bananas in a separate bag, they shouldn't get squashed.

All these sights reminded me there was nothing for a quick bite in the house, so I headed for Barney's Delicatessen. Even this early the place was filled with people sitting at the tables eating. I went to the counter and ordered a quarter pound lean corned beef and a quarter pound tongue. Red-haired Barney twisted a cone from a piece wrapping paper and put in a glop mustard free of charge. "A half-sour pickle to go along?"

"Who can say no to a pickle? So pick one out."

While he was fishing around in the tray and I was sniffing all those wonderful delicatessen smells, a hand tapped me on the shoulder. "Sure and if it isn't the lovely Belle herself standing there!"

"Jim! Here so early?" I figured he'd be home asleep after being on night duty.

"Well, by the time I got the house sealed and the paperwork on Eddie done, it was breakfast time. Come on, I'll spring for a cup of Jamoke."

"Jamoke?"

He laughed. "That's what they call coffee in the Marines."
So I followed Jim to a table, dying to hear what was what with
Eddie. Jamoke. So Jim was once in the Marines. Must've been
a kid in the World War. Another layer of the onion of who-
Jim-was peeled away. Barney came with orange juice and coffee for two, a tray of kaiser rolls and Danish, and some cream
cheese.

"A whole breakfast, Jim! I haven't had breakfast in a restaurant since—I don't remember when. You're a real sport. So tell
me what happened." I sipped my juice, it was fresh-squeezed.
After running around grocery shopping, it felt ritzy to be sitting down getting waited on for breakfast.

"Well, for openers, you'd better make up your mind that from
the looks of things, Eddie is guilty as hell. He says he remembers going to Revak's house. Got a phone call telling him Revak
did the abortion on Clara. He got out his twenty-two-caliber
pistol, told Marcia to close up at eleven and hot-footed it over
to Mount Vernon Street." He drank his juice and spread cream
cheese on a roll.

"But, Jim, Eddie was the *second* one who came to the house,
he came from the Charles Street end. Someone else came *first*
from Louisburg Square down to Revak's house! We were there
watching, we saw it all!"

He nodded. "Right. But Eddie himself remembers ringing
the bell and the door opening. After that it's all hazy, he says,
till we found him standing over the body. Claims over and over
he doesn't recall either holding the gun or firing it."

"So who made that phone call to Eddie's house?" I tried a
roll, nice and fresh.

"Anonymous. A raspy voice."

"Raspy? Listen, someone called the store the day before to
ask for Eddie, sounded hoarse. Wouldn't say who."

"That so?" Jim got out his notebook and pencil and wrote. Meanwhile he chewed a piece of roll.

"Look, what about the other man who ran out of the house up toward Louisburg Square? Maybe he did it!"

"Maybe he did. But who was he? Can you give me any description of the person at all? No? How can you prove anything if you can't identify him? But we'll ask around. Maybe somebody out last night saw him." He finished the roll and started on a Danish. "By the way, they'll be doing the autopsy on Revak this afternoon. Maybe that'll tell us something we don't know."

"Tell-shmell! What I'm telling you is, Eddie didn't kill Revak."

"Oh? And it wouldn't be your sympathetic heart telling you that?"

"Sometimes you got to trust your feelings, you just know it. Like when you decide to get married, you don't ask your friends did you pick right, you don't have to, Jim."

He looked at me for a long moment. "Ah, you were the lucky one, weren't you. Even if you lost him so young, at least you had the best of all worlds." He put his coffee mug down. "Face it, friend, they gave Eddie's hand the paraffin test. He was holding that gun when it was fired, no question."

I started on a Danish, mmm, almost as good as Mr. Danberg's. But no use arguing, what was there left to say? Even a smart lawyer couldn't help Eddie now.

"Belle, I know how you feel." Jim bit into a Danish, too. "Don't you think I want to believe he didn't do it? But let's face facts. One, we found him standing over the body holding a gun. Two, the gun was in his hand when it was fired. Both add up the same, no way around it. Guilty!"

The last part of the Danish seemed to stick in my throat, I washed it down with coffee. "Let me pay for my own breakfast, Jim, we'll go Dutch—"

"Nothing doing, it's my pleasure. And it's little enough." He was quiet for a minute, eating and drinking his coffee. "You've been a big help, think I don't know? But, Belle, maybe you should stay away from this from now on. After all, Eddie's someone you work with day in and day out, and I don't want you to get hurt, know what I mean?"

"Jim, it's so good of you, to worry over my feelings." I finished my coffee and gave him my Jean Arthur grin. "Don't I always do what you say?"

"Seems to me I've heard that song before." His gray eyes crinkled.

"You just told me I was the lucky one, with my marriage," I said. Was I being nosey? "But now I only have memories. What about your family—you have a wife and kids, no?"

"That I do." He sat quiet for a minute. "Sounds great, right? But things aren't always what they seem." He looked away, and drummed his fingers on the table.

"What's wrong? Is one of them sick?"

"Well, you could say that, it's a kind of sickness. My wife Mavis hasn't been what you'd call blooming for some time now. You see, when we got married she'd scarcely been here from Ireland a year. And she got terribly homesick, comes from a big family, she'd never been more than a few miles from home before."

I gave a sigh. "It's not easy to come across an ocean, I did it, so I know."

"But we both thought that when the babies came, Patty and Sean, things would be altogether different. This would be her home then, you see, with her children around her."

"Healthy children must be a joy, Daniel and I could never have any. . . ."

"The whole thing was my fault entirely. She was so young,

and I always worked such rotten hours. She was left alone entirely too much, fretting over the little ones. Sean came before Patty was out of diapers, it was too much for her, she's not strong." He cleared his throat and took a sip of coffee.

"So is she all right now?"

"I hope to God she is, but it's not easy to tell a lot from letters."

"Letters?"

"Yup, I brought them all back to the old country to have a whole summer's visit with her family. They're still there." He loosened the collar of his shirt. "I'll be going to bring them home before cold weather sets in." He smiled. "I'm missing my kids like anything, I can hardly wait!" He jumped up and grabbed hold of my shopping bag. "Come on, I'll take you home."

When I walked into the drugstore at one o'clock, the first thing that caught my eye was the headline in the top copy of the afternoon *Globe* sitting on the magazine rack: PROMINENT DOCTOR SLAIN. The smaller print said: Pharmacist Held for Murder.

Marcia was behind the fountain making a soda for a customer.

In the back room Harry was on the phone. "What do you mean you don't have anyone better? There've gotta be dozens of pharmacists out hunting jobs! What kind of agency are you!" He slammed down the receiver.

"What's the matter, Harry?" I asked.

"Matter?" His face was beet-colored. "I'll tell you what!" His fist banged down on the front page of the *Globe* on his desk. "Look what that crazy kid went and did! How'm I gonna get a decent registered man on such short notice?" The phone book was open to the yellow pages. "You should've seen the guys they sent me—wouldn't trust 'em within a mile of my cash register!"

"Slow down, Harry. Look, why not call some of your pharmacist friends? They might just know somebody willing to fill in. What about that breezy guy, that Parke-Davis detailer, what's his name? Those guys get around—"

He nodded. "Gee, Belle, that's using your bean." He closed the phone book. "Well, I can stay all day today, and I'll give Charlie Johnson a call tonight, those drug detailers are up on the latest dirt." He held up the newspaper. "So what do you make of this whole affair?"

I was putting on my smock. "Harry, I was there last night."

He shot up out of his chair. "No kidding! You saw Eddie kill Revak?"

"No, of course not! But I was there when Jim Connors found Eddie in Revak's study. I'll tell you right now, Harry, Eddie didn't do it."

"But the paper says—"

"Paper-shmaper, what do they know. And it looks bad for Eddie, all right. But believe me, Harry, something mighty funny happened in that house, and I'm going to find out what. Eddie'll be back in the store, wait and see."

"What're you talking about?" Harry stared at me. "What is it with you nowadays? First you go making a date with that ritzy Parkland, even when I warn you not to. Now you know more than the cops about this Revak murder?"

"They've got their ways, I've got mine. Between you and me, it was Revak did the abortion that killed Clara."

"Oh? You got proof?"

"No, not yet. Am I right, nobody around here is sorry Revak is gone?"

Harry shrugged. "You can say that again!"

I started out front. "Harry, I've got to find out who really killed him. For Eddie's sake, at least."

"Belle, I thought you were smart. How can you get such nutty ideas?"

"Simple." I counted off on my fingers. "First Clara. Then Revak. Now Eddie in jail. And the paper says Eddie killed him. Well, my mother, may she rest in peace, used to say: truth has a lot of faces."

"So what?" asked Harry. "What're you getting at?"

"So I've got an itch to find out which truth is the real one!"

sixteen

To make Harry happy I promised to work the late shift at the store again. If he got a replacement for Eddie by then, he said, I could have the day after off. Sounded like a fair trade.

All the rest of the day I kept hoping George Parkland would come in, just to pep me up, but he didn't. At six, Jerry came in to relieve Marcia. Harry said he was going out for a little air, after all, he'd been cooped up all day, and I made myself an egg salad sandwich with a hot chocolate. One scoop of maple walnut ice cream for dessert.

When Harry was at the door ready to leave I asked him was it okay for the store to be without a pharmacist. He gave a wave of his hand. "Oh, they never check at night, don't worry. Besides, I won't be long, you know how to handle things. If a doctor calls, get the number and say I'll call right back."

No doctors called but Jim Connors walked in. I thought he came to have a game of cribbage. "Harry went out, said he won't be long."

But Jim said he came to see me, so we sat at one of the little round tables. "Thought you'd like to hear about the autopsy report."

"Who, me? You wanted me to forget the case . . ." I dropped my eyelashes like Claudette Colbert.

He groaned. "Fat chance! Take a hurricane to pry you off it, friend. Anyways, here's what happened. Doc Barrett found two bullet holes in Revak's back. Only one in front! Looks like two bullets took the same path through the body, can you beat it?"

"The same path—"

"Yeah, but one got deflected just a bit by hitting a rib. Now ballistics has checked the slug we found. It was definitely fired from Eddie's gun."

A good thing I was sitting down. One hole in front and two in back! And we found only one bullet in the room. "Wait. One thing still bothers me, that we found that bullet in the floor—"

Jim took off his fedora and rubbed his head. "Belle, Eddie was pretty steamed up about his girl dying. He could have done anything crazy. Maybe he shot Revak a second time after he was already down."

I gave up for the moment. "Listen, Jim, you could maybe arrange for me to see Eddie in jail?"

He nodded. "Sure thing. What time?"

"I'm working tomorrow late, like today. So maybe I could drop in around half-past twelve?"

"Done," he said. "And Belle, see if you can get him to talk. Maybe he'll think of something he hasn't told us. For his own good, you know."

"On the level, a bunch of people hated Revak . . ."

He jammed his hat back on. "Yeah, but they weren't caught standing over his body with guns. But we're still checking, keep in touch . . ." He stood up. "Can't keep playing hearts and flowers in this business, friend, gets you noplace." He gave a wave and walked out, moving always so light and easy for a big man.

I sat at the table thinking about what happened at Revak's. A real puzzle this time, all right. One bullet and three holes, what did it mean? Appleman, you're going to need all your *saichel,* to figure this one out.

In the first place, somebody wanted real bad to get Eddie over to Revak's house that night. Bad enough to telephone Eddie and tell him first, that Revak was the abortionist, and second, that Revak was at home that night. Somebody who knew that to hear that message would make Eddie mad enough to grab a gun right off.

But how did the caller know he had a gun, what if he came with a baseball bat? Whoever called wanted Revak dead, for sure. So was the caller the real killer, who wanted to pin the murder on Eddie? How did the caller know that Revak was the abortionist?

Wait a minute, what about the hoarse voice that asked for Eddie on the phone in the store? Now that I thought of it, that voice did sound kind of like Marcia's brother John. And when he came in the store and tried to scare me, he sure acted like a person who could kill someone in a flash without worrying over it.

Suddenly Jerry was calling my name and the store was full of customers. I jumped up and went to take a prescription from one lady and handed one already filled to another. Appleman, better remember your regular job comes first. A good thing Harry didn't get back while you were sitting chewing over facts.

When Harry did come in, finally, he sure looked happier than when he went out. I glanced up at the clock, gone over an hour. The fresh air sure did wonders for him. I gave him the prescription and told him he didn't have to call any doctor back.

"Got hold of Charlie." He glanced at the prescription. "He's got someone on tap, an older man. Coming in tomorrow."

"Thank God. But if I have anything to do with it, he won't be working here long. So tell him it's temporary till Eddie gets back."

Harry gave me his are-you-starting-again look and began getting bottles down. So I went out to do my usual, fill up stock. Meanwhile my head was trying to line up some facts. About the other part of the puzzle, Clara herself.

It was impossible to imagine parents of a daughter who got pregnant by a man who longed to marry her telling her not to marry him. So the parents couldn't have known about the pregnancy. But it was a fact, she broke off the engagement and went to have an abortion. Not a word to Eddie. How come? The girl in the library told me those two were crazy about each other. So what could've made her do it?

Could she have maybe fallen for another man, and this was the only way to make a fresh start? Such things happen. No, Appleman, maybe in movies or books, but not in real life. Not with a girl like Clara. It didn't make sense.

And then there was another part of the puzzle, Clara's mother Jennie. Wouldn't a girl in that kind of trouble confide in her mother? I remember when I first met Daniel, may he rest in peace, how we both felt right away, with sparks flying. I came home and told my mother that same night. "Ma, I just met the man I'm going to marry."

And my mother, may she rest in peace, only needed one look at my excited face. We talked for a long time about love and being married, and how different it was with her mother in the old country, where a girl had everything arranged by the family, not by love. Her mother really liked a young furrier but the family married her to the village teacher—learning counted for more, even though the teacher could barely make a living.

But for Eddie and Clara it wasn't easy, neither. From what Eddie told me, they had to fight both sets of parents. Must've been arguments plenty. Eddie's mother would never give in. And that Sol Borofsky, with such a temper! Was Clara so afraid her father would find out that she didn't dare tell her mother what happened?

My back was to the front of the counter when I heard a throat being cleared and a quiet voice saying, "Excuse me . . ."

I turned around. A man with dark eyes behind horned-rimmed glasses. Right away I recognized him. "Oh, Mr. Plaut—"

He nodded and cleared his throat again. "You're Mrs. Appleman . . ."

"Belle." The eyes were just like Eddie's, and the jaw-line. He smiled. "Then you must call me Marcus."

"I'm sorry about what's happening to Eddie."

"It's hard to believe, he's always been such a good boy . . ."

"You got a lawyer for him yet?" He nodded. "Listen, I hope you got a good one. Eddie's in a bad spot." I motioned for him to come closer and lowered my voice. "I'm not supposed to tell anyone, but I was at Revak's house when the police came, so I'm helping my detective friend on the case."

Plaut's eyebrows went up. "You are?"

"I helped with the Classic Clothing murders—you maybe read about that in the papers?"

"Oh?" He gave a sigh. "It's altogether different when it's a headline about your own son, believe me." He shook his head. "Well, I just came in to get Eddie's watch, he said he left it here the night he—he—"

I knew where it was. "Just one second, Mr. Plaut, I'll get it."

In the back room I said to Harry, "Eddie's father is here to get his watch—in the capsule drawer." Harry pulled open the drawer. "Want to talk to him?" He shook his head no, so I just took the watch and brought it out to his father. "Look, Mr. Plaut, for my money, Eddie didn't do it. But proving that is no cinch. Tomorrow I'm going to the Charles Street Jail to talk to him. But there's a lot of things that need to be cleared up, I mean what was going on between him and Clara. Could I ask you a couple questions? To maybe help Eddie?"

Plaut put the watch in his pocket. "Of course—ask me about anything—I'll try to answer." Such a refined man, with that quiet way of talking. But such a tired look.

I decided to jump right in. "Tell me, what did your wife have against Clara Borofsky?"

The question seemed to surprise him, he blinked a couple times. "It's hard to explain," he said after a minute. "But you must know how mothers worry, they think no girl's quite good enough for a son. She felt their backgrounds—they weren't really suited . . ." His voice trailed away.

"That I understand. But one thing I can't figure out."

"What's that?"

"Why was Jennie Borofsky so strong against her daughter marrying Eddie? Such a fine boy, the kind you can depend on. Wouldn't a mother want him for a son-in-law, a steady worker with a nice job?"

He shifted from one foot to the other. "Uh—well, these things start from nothing. But then they build up, you see, between families, the arguments take on a life of their own. It's true, Hilda did try to discourage the romance—she thought they were too young altogether, didn't want Eddie tied down. And—uh—Sol Borofsky got the feeling that his daughter was being snubbed, I'm afraid. Unfortunately, he's a very strong-minded person." He hesitated.

"Strong-minded, no question," I said.

"The whole thing just got out of hand." He straightened his shoulders, started to leave, then turned back. "Thank you for the watch—and for going to see our Eddie at the jail, that's very kind of you, I appreciate it. I hope you can cheer him up, Belle."

I was going to tell him I'd do my best but he was practically out the door already.

seventeen

Jails don't change much. The Charles Street Jail was the same as when I was there once before to see Nate that time he got arrested for the factory boss's murder. The clanging of the steel doors, the checking to see you didn't hide something in your purse to help a prisoner escape, the bare little room where you did your talking with a guard standing there watching and listening.

Eddie looked terrible, like he slept in his clothes. I brought him a couple magazines to read, and he smiled when he saw me in that room.

"Belle, you came!"

"A wild horse couldn't keep me away!" I went over and gave him a big hug. "How are you feeling?"

He rubbed the back of his head. "Better. But my head still aches all the time."

We sat down in the two hard chairs that faced each other. "Listen, Eddie, you got lots of time to think now. You remember anything more than what you told the police?"

He shook his head. "Only getting the phone call. Then going in that door and then standing over Revak's body. In between—" He gave a sigh. "—nothing."

"You're positive?"

His mouth drooped. "Nothing. I go over and over it, but it's an absolute blank."

I reached out and took his hand. "Eddie, it's my feeling you didn't do it. Hear what I'm saying? Something smells fishy about the whole business, believe me. So don't worry too much, you hear?"

"Worry?" he asked with a lopsided smile. "Caught standing over a dead body holding a gun in my hand that I fired? Nothing much to worry about there, huh?" He gave me the old Eddie grin.

Eddie had guts, all right, able to make a joke even in jail. I gave him my Claudette Colbert smile. "Free room and board! But we got to get you out fast, we miss you in the store. Something you need I can bring you next time? Chicken soup with matzo balls, maybe?"

He actually laughed. "Wish you could! No, thanks, my folks brought me stuff."

"You're getting enough to eat?"

He shrugged. "No chicken soup, and they don't even have the recipe for matzo balls!"

We both laughed, it was a good way to end the visit. I hugged him again and told him I'd make him chicken soup to celebrate when he got out.

Outside an east wind was blowing, bringing that salty smell from the ocean straight to my nostrils. To me it was the smell of Boston, I could almost taste it. In front of me a young man and a girl were walking hand in hand, smiling at each other, her cotton skirt was blowing in the wind. A traffic jam at the corner had a lot of drivers blowing their horns, but even that couldn't spoil the blue of the July sky or the relief of being outdoors.

Walking back along Charles Street on my way to the drugstore, I tried not to worry. Maybe Eddie didn't do it, but where could I begin digging up evidence?

In the store, a new face. Older, grayish hair, weathered skin. But he seemed someone you could depend on. He introduced

himself as Milt Cutter. Retired about two years ago and tried
to take it easy. No soap. Now he was enjoying life, filling in for
emergencies. "Everybody loves a temporary, they need you," he
told me. "Something new every time, never had it so good!"

I liked him right away, a sunny type. "Harry must be tickled
pink he got you." He grinned and went back to mixing a messy
ointment on the slab. I went out front to where Marcia was
cleaning up after the lunch rush and told her about seeing Eddie.

"Poor kid," she said. Her jaw shot up. "But that s.o.b. deserved just what he got!" Hate screwed up her features.

"Marcia , do you know yet whether—what about—"

"Oh, that!" She popped her gum. "I got the curse okay, it was
just nerves. On account of that creep, c'n ya beat it!" Her eyes
flashed. "He won't be playing games any more, will he!" She
giggled.

"Belle, my love! You're looking peachy these days!" My favorite doctor, Arnie Silverstein, slid onto a stool. "Marcia, baby,
how about my usual?" Marcia perked up, everybody liked Arnie,
and began making up a double banana split in a glass gondola
dish. When it was ready I told Arnie to bring it over to a table.
Meanwhile I got a cup coffee and joined him.

"Listen, Arnie," I said, "you heard already about that Revak
murder and Eddie, no?" He was too busy spooning whipped
cream into his mouth to talk, but he nodded yes. "Well, I just
came back from visiting Eddie in jail. Arnie, he doesn't remember one thing that happened! Could it be the same story we
had in that factory murder with you-know-who?"

He swallowed a cherry. "Factory? Oh, yeah, I remember, that
business about the guy having a fugue."

"That's it." I took a sip coffee. "Maybe it could be the same
business with Eddie? So whatever went on caused the fugue—
so he really can't tell the cops what happened?"

"That's true." Arnie was polishing off the second scoop ice

cream already. "Sometimes, if a person commits or witnesses a horrendous act, the mind can just close up—" He stopped to attack the third scoop for a minute. "—form a block just to keep from recalling."

"In that case, the person could maybe just be afraid to tell the truth, no? Especially if bad things might happen to him, like maybe the electric chair?" Arnie could say it so much better— of course, he was a psychiatrist, I just read about it in his book one time.

He looked up, the little lines around his eyes crinkling with his grin. "Absolutely correct, Mrs. Appleman. Now why did I waste so many years studying Freud and Jung when I could have come to you for all the answers?"

I gave him a poke. "Cut it out, Arnie, I'm serious. So it's possible that either Eddie knows what happened and doesn't want to say, or that his brain doesn't want him to know, right?"

"Absolutely right." He scraped up the last little puddle of syrup and ice cream. "Say, Belle, what about that dinner date we talked about? How about this weekend?"

"Oh, Arnie, you're a great guy." I reached over and patted his arm. "Honest, one day soon I'll take you up on it. But right now, with all this Eddie business, my mind is just too mixed up. Know what I mean? As soon as I figure out this puzzle, I promise we'll go. Is that okay?"

He sighed, pushed back his chair, and got up. "That's my Belle. The intrepid sleuth! Okay, we'll do it your way. But don't take too long!" Waving goodbye to Marcia, he strolled out. A real doll.

It got busy, customers in and out, new faces and familiar faces like Mrs. Parkland. Seeing her always made me wonder if she knew George took me out. And those two spooky doctors, Herlihy and Somerville. I guess Harry told Milt about

Somerville because I didn't hear no argument when he went in back.

A surprise, George Parkland himself came in to get some medicine. He stopped in front of my cosmetic case with a broad smile. "Hello, Belle." The sky-blue eyes met mine.

My heart gave a hop. I said hello and waited.

"I've been wondering when we can get together again," he said. "Maybe this weekend?"

"Maybe."

"I've got a heavy schedule, have to check my calendar. All right if I let you know tomorrow?"

"Tomorrow I'm off," I told him. "But you could call me at home—I'm in the book."

"Don't worry, I'll find you." His forehead creased. "Tell me, Belle, what's the scoop with Eddie shooting Sam Revak? Couldn't believe my eyes when I saw it in the paper."

"Believe it, Revak's dead and Eddie's in jail. But Eddie didn't do it. I'm going to find out who did."

"You?" His eyebrows went up. "Why should you—"

"George, remember when I asked you if you knew about the abortion—the one that killed Clara Borofsky?" He nodded. "Well, I think it was Revak who did it. And I also think somebody set things up to make it look like Eddie was the killer."

George gave me an admiring look. "Lady Surprise does it again!" He glanced at his watch. "Holy Moses, I'm late! Got to get some stuff in back—"

"The new pharmacist is Milt Cutter. Till Eddie gets back."

George reached over and gave my hand a squeeze before dashing to the back room. Was he going to get some more of those Ergotamine ampoules? Naturally, I didn't tell him he was still on my list as a possible.

My general plan was already at work. I was spreading the

news to all the people I knew hated Revak. News that I was going to find the real killer and get Eddie out. Somerville just shrugged when I told him. And Mrs. Parkland said what I expected: "But it's all in the paper, my dear, you have to face facts." Herlihy threw back his head and recited: "The mills of the gods grind slowly, but they grind exceedingly fine!" So the man had a brain when he was sober.

The new pharmacist knew his onions, all right, and I didn't have to help him find things too many times. At suppertime I took my tuna sandwich and frappe in back to eat at Harry's desk.

"Say, Belle," Milt said, "Harry didn't have much to say about the fellow I'm replacing, this Eddie Plaut. What's the story on him?"

"Eddie's a great kid." I gave him a short version.

"Gee whiz, a pharmacist killing a doctor! What'll they think of next?" He took a bite of his sandwich, a pastrami on rye from Rubin's Delicatessen down the street. "Sounds just like the Lux Radio Theater. But who'd believe it?"

We finished our suppers and I went out front to relieve Marcia so she could eat. While filling in the cigarette cubbyholes, I thought about what the autopsy on Revak showed. One hole in, two out. And we found only one bullet in the room. So where was the second bullet?

I decided to check in with Jim and went in the back room. "Listen, Milt, watch the front a minute, okay? Got to make a call right away." He said sure and went out. I dialed the Joy Street Station and got Jim.

"And who else would be calling me the minute I come on duty?"

"Listen, what are you going to do about that second bullet?"

"Why, go back to Revak's place and hunt for it."

"When, right this minute?"

"No can do. Too much other stuff. Tomorrow afternoon, probably . . ."

"Jim, I'm off tomorrow! How about—"

He cut me off. "How did I guess you were going to say that?
Sure, come along, I'll need all the help I can get."

It was swell, we'd meet at four. I hung up feeling a kind of
excitement. Milt and Marcia were out front, so I decided to
stop in the rest room and fix my lipstick. I opened the right-
hand bottom drawer under the prescription bench to get the
cosmetic case from my pocketbook. Marcia's bag, half-open,
lay next to mine.

Something shiny in there, was it what it looked like? Sure
enough, my hand reached in and felt cold metal. When I took
the thing out, it was a gun. Holding it, I peeked out front. Marcia
was still eating and gabbing with Milt. So I went back, put on
the rest-room light, and looked the gun over.

It wasn't the kind cowboys have in the movies, with the round
thing holding the bullets sticking out on both sides. This gun
was dark and flat. When I tipped it just the right way, I could
make out the word COLT and the number .22 on it. I heard a
scraping sound like Marcia was getting up from her chair, so I
quick ran back to stick the gun in her purse and close the drawer.

Aha, Appleman, something to chew over. Marcia with a gun,
imagine. Was she the one who shot Revak? Was it the bullet
from that gun that was missing? And that look of hate on her
face tonight. Even though she knew now she wasn't pregnant,
she was more bitter than ever over the way he treated her. And
didn't she tell me her brother taught her how to shoot? Marcia
a killer, imagine.

Her brother. Maybe it was her brother John who got into
Revak's house and shot him before Eddie came. We all saw the
figure running back up toward Louisburg Square. And that
funny phone call. And the way John acted here in the store. He

knew guns, all right. And he was crazy mad over what Revak did to his sister. Was he brainy enough to set Eddie up?

I tried to go over that night on the Hill again. Those two bangs came *after* the first guy ran out. So how to figure it?

Why just John? Marcia and Revak were once lovey-dovey, she must've visited the townhouse. As far as the bedroom, anyway. So she knew the layout of the place, no question. Was she already there that night of the murder, waiting for John to come? Maybe Marcia and John hatched out some scheme together.

After all, two not-so-extra-smart heads are better than one.

eighteen

In the middle of my biting a piece of Mr. Danberg's coffee cake, the phone rang. I swallowed and picked up the receiver.

"Belle?" It was Sarah. "Tell me, what's going on? I saw in the paper they're charging Eddie Plaut with the murder—"

"It's true, all right, I visited him already in the Charles Street Jail, imagine. Yesterday—I tried to tell him not to worry, he looks terrible."

"Poor kid, that's trouble, all right. Listen, you're working today?"

"No, Harry gave me off for staying late yesterday."

"How's about we go downtown? Filene's Basement has a big ad in the paper . . . summer dresses . . ."

"Sounds good, I could use something new."

You've never been in Filene's Basement, you don't know what you're missing. End-of-season bargains from places like Saks Fifth Avenue in New York or Collins Avenue in Miami Beach. The markdowns are automatic, twenty-five percent off after twelve selling days, fifty after six more, seventy-five percent off after twenty-four. What isn't sold after a month they give to charity. Where else in the world is there a store like a regular treasure hunt?

When we got downstairs to dresses on the lower level, a mob of women were already pushing to get closer to the tables with big SPECIAL! $3.99 signs. Sarah and I were old hands at the game. I saw a flash of snappy blue stripes, got a sleeve, and yanked. Across the table a woman tried to grab the other sleeve but I snatched faster. When I saw the tag it said size 20, would go around me twice. So I threw it back over to her. Two other women pounced on it, one had the neck and the other the skirt hem.

Can you believe there's no dressing rooms to try on things? You find a dress you like, you pull off your own dress right there and pull the new one over your slip. Nobody's bashful. Husbands stand on the stairway above watching the free show. But I found a way to fool them. To the Basement I wear a thin knit that's easy to pull another dress over. But today I forgot, my mind wasn't exactly on shopping. I really went to keep Sarah company.

"Look!" Sarah showed me a pure silk dress, plain like a shirtwaist, a beautiful stained-glass print. "A size 10, but it's an expensive one, you can see it runs big. Look at the price tag, $39.95, from Marshall Field's, that's in Chicago. Go ahead, try it on!"

"Sarah, you've got some eye." I bought it right off without trying it on. Anything there can be returned in forty-eight hours for a cash refund.

Sarah bought a nifty navy outfit for $6.95, she sells dresses, she knows how to pick. We went upstairs to the shoes, piled high on tables, each pair tied together. You had to laugh watching women dragging one shoe behind trying to see if they fit. Pretty soon we had enough, an hour there can wear you out.

So we left the Basement and went upstairs to the main store, fancy-shmancy. Whiffs of flowery smells were floating out from the cosmetic counters.

"Belle! What a pleasant surprise, I usually hate shopping!"

A pleasant surprise, all right. Gary Cooper coming out of the Men's Wear section. Sarah was all eyes as I introduced them.

"Oh, Dr. Parkland, Belle mentioned you."

"Ah," said George, taking her hand, "she didn't mention to me what attractive friends she has." Oh boy, did he turn on the charm for her. It worked, Sarah dimpled and turned pink.

George looked at his watch. "Ladies, how about joining me for lunch? It would be a pleasure to have such attractive company . . ."

Sarah hesitated, then she shook her head. "No, no, you two go ahead, I have to be at work a little early today. But thank you, Doctor." A flash of her dimpled smile and she was gone.

So I never had to answer yes or no, there I was on Washington Street with George taking my hand and saying, "How does Pieroni's sound to you?"

Pieroni's Seafood Restaurant is tip-top. In one of the two windows on Washington Street they always have a lobster big enough to fight a whale. The headwaiter there knew George also, just like the one in Locke-Ober's. This doctor sure got around.

"I'm having the Seafood Newburg," said George, without even a glance at the menu. "How about you?"

"No, that doesn't appeal." What would be in it? Something I did know about caught my eye. "The broiled flounder, please."

After the waiter left George looked straight at me and said, "This is my lucky day, running into you!" He took my hands in his. "You think fate is trying to send us a message?"

It was hard to think straight with his hands pressing mine, that athletic grip of his made me shivery. "Maybe. 'The mills of the gods grind slowly . . .'" That was the only part of Herlihy's words I could remember.

George stared. "Don't tell me you're a student of Greek mythology!"

I gave him my mysterious Garbo look and changed the subject fast. "Remember I told you I thought Revak was the one did the abortion on Clara?" He nodded. "Well, what I didn't mention was, every time he came in the store he ordered ampoules of Ergotamine. My husband Daniel was a pharmacist, and I remember him telling me about how ergot could cause an abortion."

George let go of my hands. Did his forehead crease? "That's right, but Ergotamine is used mostly for the treatment of migraine headaches. My mother is subject to them, so I get Ergotamine for her, it's the only drug that helps. Revak might have been using it for exactly the same purpose."

So now I knew what else that drug was used for.

The waiter arrived with the order. Big plates, hot, filled with the huge helpings you always got in Pieroni's. George speared a pink lump out of his creamy sauce and I squeezed lemon over my flounder. We ate without talking for a few minutes, sampling and smiling at each other. I buttered a crusty roll—my heart was feeling lighter, knowing why George got that medicine. If he was telling the truth, that is. I wanted terribly to believe him.

Should I tell him about the autopsy and the funny business with the bullet holes? No, better keep that between me and the cops. So I talked about Eddie and how I was trying to get him free.

"Shouldn't you leave that up to the police, Belle?" he asked, his head tilted in that way he had.

I sipped some coffee. Delicious, almost as good as what came out of my percolator at home. "No, it takes them forever! If you could see Eddie—he looks awful."

"Of course you feel sorry for him, you worked side by side, I can understand that. But, Belle, fooling around with murder, that's playing with fire! People who commit crimes like that don't have a conscience, anybody could be watching you . . ."

I pushed my fork into my salad. "That's the advice everyone gives me."

He opened his mouth and closed it again. Were his feelings hurt? With bluebloods you can't tell so easy, they don't yell at you, they're too polite. I reached over and touched his hand. "Listen, George, it makes me feel good to have you worry over me. And I don't take foolish chances, honest—"

He smiled. "Got an idea. Tell me, have you ever been to a professional baseball game?"

"What? Baseball?"

"The Red Sox are playing the Yankees this afternoon. I'm free as a bird today and the game starts at one o'clock." He stuck his wristwatch in front of his eyes. "We can make it . . ."

"But baseball—I don't know a thing about it—" Watch it, Appleman, you almost said a double negative. "I did go a couple times but I didn't know what was going on."

"I'll teach you! It's a great game! What do you say? Are you free this afternoon?"

"It's my day off." Suddenly I remembered. "But I got to be somewhere at four o'clock—"

"No problem, we'll leave whenever you say. Come on, I haven't been to a game in a dog's age!"

So pretty soon we were getting off the streetcar at Kenmore Square. There was Appleman, hanging on to a handsome doctor's arm, going to a ball game at Fenway Park. Near the entrance a wispy little man was calling out to get your souvenir pennants now, he had them hung along the fence, red felt with big white letters that said: RED SOX.

George turned to me. "You've got to have a souvenir if you're going to be a fan," he said, and winked. So he bought me a pennant and then got our tickets at the box office. We went in giggling, me shoving the pennant into my Filene's bag. We sat in front, in what George called box seats, on the first-base line. "Best seats in the house," he said, ushering me in from the aisle.

The sun was hot, it burned through my sleeves, so I rolled them up. George did the same and loosened his tie. Vendors were calling to get your hot dogs and root beer and peanuts, but we weren't exactly hungry after Pieroni's. He did buy a score card. There wasn't much of a breeze, but at least my big straw hat helped, the sun always makes my light skin turn beet red.

A bunch of players were out on the green grass of the park, throwing baseballs back and forth. I liked their uniforms, gray with little white stripes, and knickers that tied below the knee. Cute caps, also. I could see the letters NY on the front of their uniforms. They were the Yankees, George said. When they finished warming up, the game would start.

"See, there are three bases and the home plate where the batter stands," he pointed out, "that's why it's called a diamond. The player who throws the ball stands out there in that round sandy place in the middle, it's called the pitcher's mound."

As he talked the sun glinting on his sandy hair turned it to gold, and his blue eyes shone. He wasn't Dr. George Parkland no more—any more. He was a boy with flushed cheeks, all excited by a game he loved.

"That's what I was at college—a pitcher. He's the most important player on the field." He explained why, telling me the difference between a strike and a ball, and what an "out" was. Then both teams lined up on the base lines and George motioned we should stand up. The organ played *The Star Spangled Banner* and we all sang along, it gave me shivers like always. A voice over the microphone called out, "Play ball!" and the game started.

"So who's the better team?" I asked.

"Oh, the Yankees, they're on their way to the Pennant." The look in my eye told him he'd better explain what that meant.

He told me what year the Red Sox won the Pennant before. When that happened I was only eighteen years old.

I wanted him to think I knew a little about the game. "Isn't one of the players Babe Ruth?"

He laughed. "Sure, he's the home-run king. Watch, he's up at bat right now. Two outs and a man on first. Let's see what he can do."

I saw a pretty fat player standing at the plate making big swings with his bat. A lefty. He hit the first pitch and the ball went over our heads and into the stands. There was a rush to find it, and a happy yell. It was a foul ball, George said, that meant one strike. You could keep any ball that went out of the field. "When I was a kid I'd scramble to get a foul ball and after the game I'd run onto the field and get one of the players to autograph it for me." He touched my arm. "Let's see what Ruth does now."

What Babe Ruth did was to give the ball such a whack it sailed straight out over all the players' heads and landed in the right field bleachers. George and almost everybody else was out of his seat, jumping up and down and yelling. I got the feeling that for the first time I was seeing the real George Parkland. A kid let out of school.

Suddenly I sat up straight and asked what time it was. Quarter past three already.

"George, I've got to go." I stood up. "But why don't you stay and see the end of the game?"

He was on his feet. "Oh, no, nothing doing. You know that song, 'I'm Gonna Dance with the Guy what Brung Me'? Well, I brung you, Belle, and I'm gonna bring you back."

He sounded so funny, like someone from the wrong side of the Hill, that I giggled. "Anyway, with the score eight to nothing, the Sox don't have a chance to take this one." He ushered me into the aisle, and we strolled out of Fenway Park back to

Kenmore Square. We held hands and he told me about his base-ball days. While we waited for a car to Park Street, he asked, "Going back to your place?"

"No, I'm meeting someone on the Hill—Mount Vernon Street—"

"Oh? That's where I live. Anyone I know? Or shouldn't I ask—"

I put on my Myrna Loy face. "He's on the force—Detective Connors, an old buddy, I'm helping out with the Revak case."

His eyebrows went up. "No kidding! An amateur sleuth, and the police take you seriously!" He shook his head. "I never know whether I'm talking to Belle, the woman, or Belle, the—what else do you do?"

"Go to baseball games with handsome doctors?" In the middle of our giggling the streetcar came. After we sat down he glanced at his watch again and drew in his breath.

"Something wrong?"

He sighed. "Only that I told mother I'd be home early this afternoon and I forgot to call about going to the game."

"Nobody's perfect. Why would she worry, a nice afternoon like this?"

"Oh well, my mother's funny that way . . ."

Did his mother know how lucky she was? Most men his age phone their mothers once a week, it's a lot. One thing bothered me. If they were such pals, did she know about me? But no grownup man would talk over dates with mama.

"Let's get off at Arlington Street and I'll get my car," he said. "And I'll call my message service."

He came back from the phone booth with a serious face. "Belle, I can't drive you back, I'm afraid. Emergency with a patient at the Peter Bent Brigham—it's up at the other end of Huntington Avenue, you know."

"You go right ahead, George, don't worry, I love to walk. Thanks for a wonderful day—a real adventure—"

He leaned over. Was he actually going to kiss me right in public? He did, a tasty smack on my cheek. Then he loped away real quick across Boylston Street and I sauntered into the Public Garden.

Was George truly serious about me? He was treating me a little bit like I was one of those Greek lady statues. I never knew a man like him before, so this was strange country for me. But it gave me a nice feeling that he seemed really worried about my working on a murder case. Or did he maybe not want me to find out too much?

It was nice to be strolling along thinking about him. I came out of the Garden at the corner of Beacon and Charles, across the street from the Hampshire House. While I was waiting for the light to change, a stocky man came around the corner from Charles Street and walked down Beacon. It was Harry White, no question.

Where was he going? I remembered Rosalie claiming that Harry had another woman someplace. *Nu*, maybe I could find out for her. I trailed him, staying on the Garden side of Beacon. A little further down, just before Arlington, he stopped and went up the steps of a brownstone house. He rang the bell, the door opened, and he disappeared inside.

Who let him in, I couldn't see. I walked over to a bench across the street and sat down. Behind me, some men were working on the flowers in one of the big circular beds. A squirrel ran over and sat up in front of me asking did I have a peanut. When I told him no, he gave me a dirty look and ran away. Across the street a fancy-shmancy lady in a white suit was walking her fluffy little dog. Did the dog have on a diamond-studded collar?

When the traffic slowed up I crossed over and walked up the steps of the brownstone. Number 126. Was Harry in there with some woman? What if I rang and he came to the door? My finger didn't wait for my brain to answer, it pushed the bell.

The door opened. A big man with a squashed nose stood there, I mean he was tall and wide and wearing the kind of tux people only wore at night. He looked down at me with lips that were smiling but eyes that weren't and said, "Yes?"

Think fast, Appleman. "Good afternoon, I'm a checker for the Fuller Brush Company. Did one of our salesmen call here today and leave a sample?"

Meanwhile I was trying to see past his big body into the hall. There was a tall white vase on the gray carpet with some umbrellas in it. I could hear the sound of voices, but not what they were saying.

"I'm sorry, madam, but no such person has called here." The eyes told me our business was finished.

"Thank you for your help." I walked down the steps as the door closed behind me. So what did I learn that I didn't know five minutes before? They had umbrellas in the front hall. But that told me one thing, an apartment house it wasn't. More like a townhouse, like Revak's. But what was going on inside? Could this be one of those houses that people never talked about? That men visited to be in a room with a girl? I sure didn't have good news for Rosalie, no news at all.

Now I was late, so I rushed back to Charles Street and up Mount Vernon. When I rang Revak's bell, Jim answered right away. "Just about given you up."

"Sorry—stayed a little too long at the ball game—" I was nearly out of breath.

That stopped him in his tracks. "Ball game?"

"Fenway Park. Babe Ruth hit a home run." I showed him my Red Sox pennant.

"Will wonders never cease! Belle, the baseball fan. What next?"

I waved my hand to show it was all old business to me. "The Sox didn't win the Pennant since 1918."

Jim groaned. "Spare me the details, let's get to work."

We walked down the hall to the study, and he turned on the ceiling light and all the lamps. On the carpet was the white chalk line of Revak's body, made goose pimples start on my arms. The small brown blood stain was still there.

I looked around the walls. "Jim, we went over everything before. You think we'll find that bullet?"

He shrugged. "If we don't—"

It was plain what he meant. If we didn't, Eddie was headed for the electric chair.

nineteen

"Guess we're on a wild goose chase." Jim shoved his ancient fedora to the back of his head. I started walking around the room real slow, examining the walls. Pine is full of knotholes, to find a little hole wouldn't be easy. Too bad Revak didn't like wallpaper.

Jim poked around the other way. Let's see, Revak was lying with his head toward the wall with books. Oy, I thought, looking at all those bindings, who could find anything in there? Jim was studying the wall with pictures, so I started with the bookshelves. The first two, nothing. Number three, also nothing.

"Find anything, Belle?" Jim was standing behind me.

"Not yet. You?"

He shook his head.

"So help with the books. The one below the top. I'll start on this side, you on that one, okay?"

We started moving slowly toward each other like we were doing some kind of slow dance. We met in the middle, looked at each other, shook our heads. No holes in the walls. No holes in the books.

A good half hour gone already. "A wild goose chase, all right," said Jim.

"Goose-shmoose, that other bullet's got to be here somewhere, it didn't fly up to the sky. Maybe something on the wall's hiding it. Wait—" I moved over to where a fancy piece of tapestry was hanging. It showed a scene with ladies dressed in those old long frilly gowns flirting with knights in tin suits. A tapestry big as my kitchen table. When I looked the other time, I didn't spot a thing wrong. But this time, as I was kind of on the side, the light fell on a teeny bump in the heavy cloth.

I quick rubbed the threads. Sure enough, the cloth had a little tear. It wasn't fastened at the bottom, so I lifted the whole thing away from the wall.

There was the hole, all right. "Hey, look! Here, under this tapestry—"

Jim rushed over and peered at it. "Nice work, Belle!" He got his knife out ready to dig. "However did you spot it, among all those sporty ladies—"

"That was the style then . . ." I was examining the tapestry and right away I could see what happened. The bullet went through but the material was stiff and the torn part just flipped back in place, so you couldn't see the tear on that patterned fabric. I sent up a prayer of thanks, for Eddie's sake.

Next I took a look at the polished wood desk, the nifty old kind with a top cover that rolled down. It had a lot of little cubbyholes to store stuff, something like what we put cigarette packages in at the store. "Jim, you found anything worthwhile in Revak's desk here?"

He kept digging away. "Nah, nothing that amounted to much . . ."

Still, the desk looked like a place to store secrets, with all those tiny compartments. There was nothing to do till Jim pried that bullet out, anyway, so I started poking around in it, reaching into this cubicle and that one. All of a sudden one of the cubicles came loose in my hand. Did I break something? I pulled it out. Right in back was a little drawer with a built-in lock.

"Say, Jim, did Revak have any keys on him?"

"Yeah, they're at the station, with his wallet and stuff. Why?"

"Something I just found, never mind." I fished in my bag

and found the set of picklocks. In a minute the drawer was open. Inside was one of those little metal boxes you can keep cards in, and when I opened it, sure enough, it was full of cards. Cards with names. And dates. And numbers with dollar signs. "Jim, look—"

"Hey, got it!" Jim came over grinning and showed me the little lump of lead between his thumb and forefinger. He took a small cellophane bag out of his pocket and set the bullet in it real careful.

"Jim, wait'll you see—there was a drawer in back . . ." I held out the cards.

He flipped through them. "Holy mackerel!"

"Do you see those names—Herlihy, Somerville, even Harry! He was getting money from all of them! And take a peek—" I showed him the metal box. "Some more cards in here—"

He riffled through them. "All names of women." He stopped. "Can you beat it? Clara Borofsky—$100."

We stared at the card and then at each other, I shivered. One hundred dollars. I saw again the fringe of dark lashes on Clara's pale cheek.

The gold clock on the mantel gave a bong. "So it was Revak did the abortions, after all."

"Yup, looks that way."

A stone fell from my heart, thank God it wasn't George! "Jim, can I see those cards with the doctors' names?" He handed them over and I checked. No card with George's name. Good.

"Swell guy. A blackmailer *and* an abortionist," said Jim, glancing around at the velvet and leather and marble.

"Oh yeah, swell. What about the bullet?"

"Well, if the ballistics show it came from a different gun, we've got a whole new ball game. One funny thing, though. No cartridge cases lying around. Somebody was real careful about cleaning up."

I waved the cards at him. "And plenty new suspects, no?"

"Now don't get all worked up, friend, there's a killer out there, maybe closer than we know—"

"Never mind with the lectures, Jim, just listen. If this bullet did come from a different gun, then I got things figured out. The way it had to happen was that somebody killed Revak first with this new bullet. When Eddie came in, the killer knocked him out, took Eddie's gun, and fired it into the same hole in Revak's chest. So the bullet that went through the tapestry must be the one that killed Revak while he was standing up."

"Begorra," Jim sang out with that fake Irish brogue he could put on and take off like a hat, "beautiful and brainy, too! An absolute peach, by jingo!" He put the cards back in the box and snapped it shut, then he took my arm. "First we'll have to see what ballistics says. Only way we'll know for sure."

"And then they'll let Eddie out of jail?"

Jim nodded. "If that bullet behind the tapestry is from a different gun, he probably won't be indicted for murder." He looked at me. "But he still isn't completely in the clear."

"So you'll start right away checking out those names on the cards? Every one of them must've wanted Revak dead! To wipe out their debts to him!"

"You bet." He examined his watch. "We'd better be getting out of here, it's after five already. Come on, I'll see you home."

In the car I asked him if he knew anything about that doctor who was a drunk.

"Herlihy? Why him?"

"Well, he's one of the names on those cards. But I heard his practice is shot, hardly any patients. So why would Revak blackmail such a person? You can't get blood out of a stone. So I wondered . . ."

He pulled the car up in front of my house, took off his fedora and rubbed the back of his head. "Seems to me I did hear he was mixed up in some kind of shady deal years ago. Can't remember what it was about."

"So that's worth checking out."

He gave me a sharp look. "We'll be looking into it, don't worry."

"Sure, sure. But answer me one question, okay?" He groaned. "There's a house on Beacon Street I'd like to know about. Number 126. You maybe know something about it?"

Jim stared at me. "Boy, one thing after another. Where'd you hear about that place?"

Aha, Appleman, I said to myself, so you found something. I gave him my innocent Claudette Colbert look. "Someone that comes in the store went in there—"

"Oh? It's a gambling joint."

"Gambling? But I thought—"

"Yeah, been trying to close it up for a long time. Somebody high-up's got the finger in. Can't touch 'em. Too much protection."

"Big money, you mean?"

"You said it. Listen, Belle, if we sit here any longer, the neighbors'll talk."

"I'm going, I've got Evening English." I opened the car door. "Thanks, Jim, a lot of things got straightened out."

He grinned. "You're the one should be thanked." His gray eyes rolled. "For minding your own business . . ."

"Naturally." I got out. Somewhere above a window banged open.

"Hold on," Jim called, "you forgot something—" He got out and brought me the Filene's bag with the dress and the pennant. For a minute he stood facing me, his gray eyes narrowed as if the daylight was too bright. "You've sure got moxie. Now why didn't I meet the likes of you when I was young and fancy-free?" He bent over and gave me a little smack on one cheek and got back into the car.

The second time today my cheek got kissed by a man. At least Mrs. Wallenstein wasn't around the first time.

Going up the stairs and into my apartment, I was thankful I learned two new things. First, George wasn't the abortionist. Also, his name wasn't on that list being blackmailed. But a little voice nagged at me, maybe his name wasn't there because he was Revak's partner?

Second, now I knew what was wrong with Harry. He'd become a gambler, Rosalie was worrying about the wrong thing. What worried me more was the card with Harry's name on it. Was Revak blackmailing him on account of the gambling? But how would he know about that?

No, that wasn't it. I stuck my Red Sox pennant over my bedroom mirror and stepped back to admire the effect. As Jerry would say, it looked snazzy.

So what did Revak have on Harry?

twenty

When I got to the McClean Street School classroom Sarah and Nate were busy talking to each other. Did he call for her and they came together? Again I felt that nasty pinprick of jealousy. They looked up to greet me and I filled them in on the latest about Eddie and the two bullets.

Sarah gave a sigh of relief. "See, Eddie didn't do it."

"Jim's got a whole bunch of new suspects, Revak was sucking money from them." I waited for Nate to say something about my mixing in but he didn't say a word, just rearranged those long legs of his under the desk.

"And that terrible doctor was the one killed poor Clara Borofsky. So God punished him all right," Sarah said.

"What did God have to do with it?" Nate sat up. "This fool had the *chutzpah* to try blackmail on top of that other illegal business! So he got what was coming to him, that's all."

"But most doctors aren't like that. Look at that lovely Dr. Parkland you introduced me to in Filene's," Sarah said.

"That's the one took you out to dinner? Big deal!" Nate glared at me.

At her desk Miss Wallace was rapping for attention, she was going to read a piece by an Illinois poet who died not long ago. None of us had ever been in that state, but the Polish janitor, Mr. Misnewicz, said he had a cousin in Chicago.

The poet was Vachel Lindsay, and Miss Wallace told us that his poetry sounded like music. As she read "The Chinese Nightingale," I closed my eyes and drifted into another world:

> I remember, I remember
> That Spring came on forever,
> That Spring came on forever,
> Said the Chinese nightingale.

Somehow I thought of George Parkland during the part where the Chinese lady talked to her sweetheart. How did he really feel about me? And I about him? We never talked about the differences in where we came from and how we lived. Was he taking me out because I wasn't from his world and so he felt safer with me, I wouldn't be expecting marriage? If he did get serious, what would I do? What would his sweet-talking mother say about a Belle Appleman coming into her high-toned world?

Everyone was surprised when Lee Fong raised his hand, he was very shy. "All words very nice, like you say, like music." He hesitated. "But not about China I know, just about rich people."

"Oh, but didn't you hear that Chang in the poem is a laundryman, just like you?" asked Miss Wallace. "He's not rich, he's just dreaming about China of the past, of long ago . . ."

I raised my hand. "Isn't this poem about love? It's the same in China or America or anywhere—when two people love each other, they can be happy no matter what."

Miss Wallace beamed. "That's good, Mrs. Appleman. Poems can have different meanings for different readers, they can speak to each one of us."

While she talked, I was far away in that magic Chinese tapestry with George, dancing while the nightingale told us it would go on forever. All my worries that he could have been Revak's partner in crime were forgotten.

Nate and I left Sarah at her door on Blossom Street, then Nate walked me home as usual. We had to cross Allen Street to get to my apartment house on the other side. Nate was complaining that Miss Wallace didn't pick out poems about working class problems.

Suddenly there was a kind of roar in my ears. I glanced sideways and saw something shadowy and dark moving toward me down the middle of the street. A second later the light from a lamppost showed me it was a car. No headlights. And it was coming right at us. Fast.

What happened to my feet? They got frozen in the middle of the road. Just like in a nightmare, I couldn't seem to move. But Nate gave a quick jump and yanked me hard by the hand toward the other side. He stumbled and fell down and I fell on top of him with the roar of the engine in my ears. Would we get run over?

The car missed us by inches. The wheels gave an awful screech as it went out of sight around the corner. The smell of exhaust fumes drifted over us. My cheek was against Nate's bristly chin.

I breathed hard and rolled over. "Nate, are you all right?"

"Wait, I'll take inventory." He got up slowly and pulled me up. It took me a minute to remember where I was.

"Your glasses—where are they?" I spotted them, picked them up from the street, and gave them to him.

He examined them. "They're okay, too." He put them back on. "Come on, let's get off the street!" He took my hand and pulled me over to the sidewalk.

My legs stopped wobbling. "Nate, did you make out who was driving that car?"

He shook his head. "Who had time to look?"

"Me, neither, so we don't even have a license number."

"Without the lights on? No way." He took my arm and walked me right up to the front door. "You sure you're okay, Belle? I'm sorry I gave you such a yank."

"Sorry? Are you kidding? You were wonderful, you saved me, I'll never forget—"

"Forget? You forget all the time what I'm saying! You see what can happen when you go mixing in? You could've been killed!"

"You're right. But now I know for sure Eddie didn't kill Revak. Also, whoever was driving that car figures I know too much. So when I find out who was the driver, it'll be the murderer. And Eddie'll really be off the hook!"

"*Gottenyu!*" Nate exploded. "How can a woman so smart act so dumb! Real life isn't like that baloney you read in *True Detective!* Tell me, how many people did you already tell you're going to find a murderer? Six? Twenty? A hundred? Why didn't you put it on WBZ?"

Words began to boil up inside me, ready to pop out of my mouth at him. Always telling me how not to live my life, a regular Mussolini. But I choked the words back. How could I scream nasty things at the man who just saved my life? Appleman, the way you acted when you saw that car, frozen like Lot's wife in Sodom, you wouldn't be here enjoying the evening breeze now. It was Nate who had the wits to move fast.

So what Appleman did instead was to say, "Nate, you're absolutely right. And I didn't even thank you for saving me. From now on I'll tell you and Jim everything I do." I moved close and gave him a big hug.

Nate didn't just stand there like a statue. His arms went around me and hugged me back. Just then I heard a little cough. We were standing there blocking the front door so that Mr. and Mrs. Wallenstein couldn't get in.

Nate and I jumped back quick like bunnies. But Mrs. Wallenstein gave her husband a what-did-I-tell-you look as they went in.

Nate shrugged and turned back to me. "Don't you see, Belle, the reason I nag so much, I just don't want you dead."

I gave him my very best Loretta Young understanding smile. "And tonight you were a regular hero." I reached up and gave him a big smack on the cheek.

twenty-one

A surprise. When I opened the front door of the store in the morning, Eddie Plaut was standing behind the back counter register. I ran up and gave him a big hug. "You're back! They let you out!"

He hugged me also. "Yes, and Jim Connors told me who was responsible!"

I stepped back and gave him my Fay Bainter look. "Oh, I knew all along you didn't kill Revak. Whoever hit you on the head, that's the murderer. And we'll catch him, don't worry." I walked in back and he followed. By the time we got in the back room, though, Eddie's smiling face looked drawn, the jaw tight.

I put on my smock. "Isn't being let out of jail enough to keep you feeling good for at least five minutes?"

He took down the money can and started counting out change. "Boy, it's really something to be away from that place."

"I knew the bullet we found wouldn't match."

Eddie sighed. "Connors said I have to stay in town. I'm not really off the hook till they find the other gun."

"That's only a matter of time, they'll find it. You just have to snap out of it, Eddie."

He shrugged. "Easy to say. But how can I ever forget what happened? She didn't even tell me—*me*—she was pregnant. Clara, the girl I loved. It goes 'round and 'round in my head day and night, night and day. Sleeping's worse, nightmares you can't even imagine . . ." He rubbed his forehead.

"Listen, Eddie, solving a mystery is sort of like a jigsaw puzzle. A lot of pieces don't fit together, you can't make sense of it. Then one piece fits over here, another over there. You got to have patience."

"How can you be so close to a girl and know so little about her!"

"*Nu*, you can't make yourself sick worrying it was all your fault. She loved you, she wouldn't want you to destroy yourself."

"But that's just it, don't you see? It *was* my fault! Somewhere along the line I missed a cue. Something got by me, something I should've caught." He swallowed, his voice was tight with misery.

Marcia sauntered in, saw Eddie, gave a little scream and ran over to hug him. Everybody liked Eddie except Eddie himself.

"Marcia," I said to her out front, "it's nice to have Eddie back. But that means the cops are checking out everyone else might've had a reason to kill Revak. That means you, also. So—"

"Waddaya getting at?" She started the coffee.

"They know you went out with him. And Jim Connors knows you were sore at him."

She stared at me. "So you snitched on me! Anyway, being sore don't mean I bumped him off!"

"You sure sounded like you wanted to, lots of times. And the cops're going to ask you where you were the night he got shot. Better have a good alibi."

She bent over and yanked out the milk can with a bang. "What do you mean alibi?"

"Don't you know? Means you got to prove you weren't anywhere near Revak's house the night he was killed. So where were you Sunday night?"

"Who died and left you boss?" she snapped, pouring the milk into the milk pump. "Well, if you're so nosey, I started feeling

kinda rocky in the afternoon. So I went right home from work
at six. Ask Eddie, I told him I had one of my headaches."

"And you didn't go out after?"

"Nope, didn't even feel like eating. Took some aspirin and
went right to bed. Say, what is this, the third degree?"

"Your mother didn't make you eat something?"

"She was out. At a church supper."

"And your brother?"

"Not home. They must've come home late, both of them, I
never even heard them come in."

"Marcia, have you any idea where your brother was that
night?"

She looked up from pouring. "John? Who wants to know? I
don't mind his business and he don't mind mine. Who're you, a
G-man?"

I thought about the gun in her bag. And no alibi at all. And
brother John out that night, also. Sure didn't sound good, Jim
better know.

"Oh, Belle?" Eddie came out of the back room. "I almost
forgot. Harry wanted to know if you could work a split day
today. Said he'd make it up to you."

"Why not, I got nothing special on tonight."

Eddie smiled at me. "You really should. I ought to take you
out on the town to pay you back for all you did."

"*Nu*, you can pay me back in smiles, how about that!"

He nodded and went in the back room. A lady came in with
a prescription, some of our breakfast regulars climbed on the
fountain stools, and the Charles Street Pharmacy routine started.

Later Dr. Somerville showed up, gave me the same jerky hello,
and went in back. I heard him greeting Eddie, saying how good
it was to have him back. When he came out I stopped him.
"Listen, Doctor, I'd like to talk to you."

He frowned. "About what?"

"Not here. But it's important. About Sam Revak. You'll be in your office this afternoon?"

The minute I mentioned Revak's name, some little muscles on Somerville's cheek began to twitch. Still, he nodded. "Five hundred Beacon Street, third floor. Around three o'clock."

"Thanks, I'll be there."

At lunch time I helped Marcia with the noon-hour crowd. She had a long face and hardly said a word except to call out when a sandwich order was ready. Finally I said, "Marcia, don't be mad at me. Sure I told Jim, I had to, we're working together. But wasn't it better he should hear it from me than from some nosey people who might've seen Revak pick you up at home? This way the cops won't come to your house and start asking your mother a million questions and get you in trouble with her."

"Gee whiz." She studied her magenta fingernails. "You're right." Her head swung up. "Okay, pals again." But she ate lunch by herself while I was busy with customers.

There was enough left over from the lobster-salad special for a sandwich for me, and I treated myself to a strawberry ice cream soda for dessert, fun to make. First you put in the strawberry syrup and a squirt of cream and mix it up with a long-handled spoon. Then you push the soda-water handle back instead of down, so a thin stream of seltzer crashes into the glass, fuzzing it all up. Then a scoop strawberry ice cream and soda water to fill up the glass. Mmm.

A cloudy afternoon with a little salty breeze from the east wind, so I didn't mind the walk down Charles Street to the Public Garden and up Beacon Street to Somerville's office. A nice new doctors' building, with the names and office numbers on a board next to the elevator, high-class.

Looking for his name, I noticed another name: Dr. George Parkland, 205. My heart gave a little hop. When I got in the elevator I couldn't help it, my finger pressed the 2 button. Somerville, 315, could wait.

What are you doing, Appleman, I asked myself in front of George's office door. But my hand just turned the knob and pushed the door open partway. Two people, a man and a woman, sitting reading magazines. A cute young girl with dark hair in a page-boy sitting at a desk, she looked at me with a question in her eyes. I shook my head like I was in the wrong place and closed the door. My dress stuck to me, it was pretty warm in this building. The elevator came, I jumped in and went up to 3.

Why did you do such a crazy thing, Appleman? What if he stepped into the waiting room right then? Did you want to see if he's really a doctor? Or if he has any patients? You're as bad as a teenager with a crush.

When I opened the door of Somerville's office a white-haired woman was just leaving, but there was no one in his waiting room. He came out and motioned I should come in. He looked different in a white coat. But the same nervous fidgeting— *shpilkes*. He didn't ask me to sit down, but I did. Right then the phone on his desk rang, he answered it, made an appointment for the next day, and turned to me.

"Well, Mrs. Appleman?" He moved some papers around on his desk. The white coat made it harder to say what I had to, usually it's the doctor does the talking.

"Excuse me, Dr. Somerville, what I need to know is—where were you the Sunday night when Sam Revak got shot?"

He sat bolt upright. "What?"

"It's important, the night of the murder. Where were you around eleven o'clock?"

A dark flush came over his long, thin face. "What business is that of yours, may I ask?" Even upset, he stayed polite.

"Look, Doctor, I was with the police when they found Revak dead. And I know what they found in his study—a card with your name on it. He was blackmailing you—robbing you, no? What was it, he knew about the pills you get from Harry?"

His mouth opened and a little bit of spit rolled out of one corner, he licked it away with his tongue. "H-how—how—" he stuttered, but the words wouldn't come.

"Revak had cards with other names, too," I told him. "So each person he was blackmailing is a suspect. The police are checking everyone out, they'll be coming here, asking questions. Now, I'm helping Detective Connors with the case. It wouldn't look good for a doctor if people see police coming in his office. So if you tell me, they won't come to bother you, it'll be better, see?"

He kept staring at me like I was a ghost or something that came to haunt him. Finally he swallowed and said, "Very well. I was home that night. Read a while and went to bed early, I lead a quiet life."

"You got any proof? Did anyone call you on the phone, or did you call somebody?"

He pursed his lips for a minute, then shook his head.

"And you live right on Mount Vernon Street, right? So what's to keep the police from figuring you did it?"

He gave a sudden pound with his fist on the desk that made me jump. "My dear young lady, I didn't kill him. But I wish I'd had the guts. If anyone deserved it—" He broke off, massaging the hand that pounded, his fingers were long and bony.

"He wasn't exactly popular. So he found out about your—uh—problem?"

"He threatened to expose me to the Medical Board. I'm a surgeon, it would've ruined me." He pulled a tissue out of a box on his desk and wiped his face.

"Tell me, Doctor, you're such an intelligent man. How did all that get started? With the pills, I mean."

He looked through the window at the skyline in the distance. "Not easy to talk about." He picked up a silver-framed photograph of a pretty woman in a long dress and studied it for a minute before setting it back. "Several years ago I arranged to meet my wife near Franklin Park in Roxbury. Helen loved the zoo. I drove up and parked the car near the corner of Seaver and Blue Hills Avenue—you know where that is?"

I nodded.

"Then I stood there watching the streetcar come to the stop where she was to get off. You know how the Mattapan car comes down Seaver next to the Park and makes a sharp right turn onto Blue Hills Avenue? Well, that day, the car didn't stop. Either the brakes failed or the motorman was going too fast. I watched it hit the turn and just go over on its side. Helen had been standing in the doorwell, ready to get off—"

He stopped. His hands were shaking, he began rubbing them together.

"Oh, no—"

He sat quiet. "You'd expect," he said slowly, "you'd think—" He stopped and cleared his throat. "You'd think a doctor, especially a surgeon, would be accustomed to the fact of death. But I couldn't get myself to believe that it had really happened to Helen. I stopped sleeping, couldn't get back to work for weeks. A surgeon can't work if his hands shake, you know. So I tried morphine and it helped. That's what keeps me going." His eyes were looking somewhere past my head.

"When I lost my husband, I couldn't sleep neither—nobody knows what it's like . . ." What else could I say? Tell a doctor pills are bad for him? It was time to change the subject. "Tell me, you maybe own a gun?"

"Why do you ask?"

"That's what the police are asking everyone on Revak's list."

He shrugged. "Yes, a twenty-two I keep at home, for target practice to help keep my hand steady."

I stood up. "Take my advice, bring it to the Joy Street Station to be checked. As long as you didn't use it to shoot Revak, you'll be cleared." I picked up my bag and slung it on my shoulder. "I'm sorry about what happened to your wife. To lose a life partner—only people that did, can understand."

He stood up and held out his hand, it seemed steadier now. "Thank you."

"Now that Revak's gone, I hope you'll sleep better—maybe you won't have to bother Harry for those pills—"

He patted my hand. "Maybe I won't."

As the elevator passed the second floor I couldn't help thinking about George's office and my quick visit. I decided to forget about it and think over my talk with Haskell Somerville. Was he telling me the whole truth? Would he really bring his gun to the police station? In any case, better tell Jim about that pistol.

Poor man, what misery Somerville had to face, how many times did that accident flash through his mind. A happy marriage, going to the zoo with his wife. A real gentleman, old-fashioned polite, even when I asked such nosey questions.

Still, he was a drug addict. A man with a terrible habit, a man who had to have money to take care of that habit. And to pay a blackmailer. And he was honest, said he hated Revak.

What would stop a person with such a habit from killing and lying about it after?

twenty-two

Sure enough, it began to rain right after I left the drugstore to walk home, already after eleven at night. I put up my umbrella and buttoned up my jacket, the wind was chilly, you could smell the ocean. Usually I love walking home after being cooped up indoors, what's a little rain. But somehow the back of my neck began to tickle like somebody was following me.

A lot of cars were whizzing by and horns blaring, but hardly a soul out walking. Should I just keep on going and pretend everything was okay? Maybe start to run? It began to rain harder, drumming on my umbrella. My stockings got so wet they felt plastered to my legs. Should I cross the street? No stores to dart into there, neither, they were all closed.

When I got to the Cambridge Street Circle I couldn't help it, I gave a whirl around to see. Nobody in sight. Or did a shadow sneak into that doorway back there? Stop imagining things, Appleman, it's that business with the car the other night. Nobody's following you. Still, I took a deep breath.

Heavy traffic, but instead of taking the tunnel underneath the street I walked fast to the other side of Charles. The walls and barred windows of the Charles Street Jail made me think of Eddie, thank God he got out. So I walked on and tried to think about the Eddie-Clara puzzle instead of bogeymen.

Funny how people always know what's best for their children. It was the parents I still couldn't understand. And what I saw and heard the night when the Borofskys were sitting *shiva*.

How thoughtful Marcus was, and how terrible Sol acted. Neighbors, imagine.

Still, it was worth following up on. Next day I called Sarah from the store and asked her to arrange we should visit the Borofskys after supper. When she asked me what for, I said it was busy in the store and I'd call her when I got home after six. If Sarah knew what was in my head, she'd never make the date. So when I did call her, she said yes, Jennie Borofsky said come about seven, she'd be glad to have our company, Sol would be away at a meeting.

"All the better," I said.

"Why? What do you mean?"

"Oh, for women's talk, that's all."

Sarah's voice changed. "Belle, something fishy I smell. What're you up to?"

"Sarah, I got something on the stove, I'll come by a quarter to seven."

When I picked up Sarah I began to tell her all about Harry and Rosalie, how worried she was he had another woman stashed away, and how I how found out he was gambling. Sarah knew them both so she was plenty curious, and pretty soon we were at the Borofskys'.

Jennie seemed thinner but she was glad to see us. I looked around the living room, seeing what I couldn't before with all that crowd there. A nice two-piece set, carved wood-framed sofa and chair in taupe mohair, and a tapestry Cogswell chair. Everything ship-shape and clean, showed a real *balebosteh*, a good homemaker. We sat down and talked over the weather, and Jennie went in the kitchen to put the kettle on.

The minute she came back and sat down, I jumped right into hot water. "Jennie, forgive me, I got to ask a couple questions. To try to figure it all out, to help Eddie, he's suffering something terrible, feels so guilty." I cleared my throat. "Did Clara tell you she was carrying Eddie's baby?"

"Belle, what're you saying!" Sarah shrieked in horror.

Jennie's face got paler but she waved her hand at Sarah. "It's all right, I understand. And no one wants Eddie to wreck his life, there's misery enough already." She swallowed. "The answer is no, she didn't tell me."

"*Nu*, so you didn't know." I took a deep breath. "But what I can't figure is why you and Sol were so strong against their getting married. After all, Eddie wasn't just some nogoodnick..."

Her chin went up. "It wasn't Eddie, it was his family. How would you like your daughter to have in-laws who treated her like she was from a lower class of human beings?"

"Okay, about the *Deutschen* I know. But what I'm wondering is, what if your daughter told you she was pregnant, what then? What would you do?"

I stopped, because Jennie's face crinkled up, she put her hand to her forehead and started to cry.

"Belle, stop already with those questions, you hear! The water's boiling, I'll make the tea." Sarah stomped off toward the kitchen.

I went over and touched Jennie's arm. "I'm so sorry. I never meant to hurt you, believe me—I'm only trying to help the best way I can."

She took out a handkerchief and wiped her eyes. "The least little thing, I cry buckets, what good does it do—"

"See, I work with Eddie every day, so I watch what's going on with him. He's not the same boy any more, believe me, he's half crazy. I'm afraid he could make a mistake with a prescription, says he can't sleep nights—"

"Poor boy." Jennie heaved a sigh. "Don't think I don't have feelings about him. But right now it's all I can do to live from day to day and help Sol."

Sarah came in with the tea things and we started sipping.

Suddenly the front door opened and Sol Borofsky came into the living room. Jennie gave a start that almost upset her teacup and began talking to Sarah a mile a minute, about what was the length of dresses for the fall.

"Well," he said, coming to a stop in front of us, "company tonight, that's nice. How are you, ladies?"

"Hello there, Sol!" Sarah put her cup down on the coffee table. "I'll go get another cup tea. You sit, Jennie—"

Sol sat down heavily in the Cogswell chair. "First we had so much company we didn't have room for them. Then, all of a sudden, nobody, an empty house, that's how it is." Sarah came back and handed him his tea.

"Company's good for Jennie, I'm glad you both came."

I put my cup down. "To tell you the truth, Mr.—Sol—, I was very glad to be with Jennie again. But I'm also trying hard to help Detective Connors figure out the whole Revak mess. You probably heard they let Eddie out of jail?"

Sol's mouth was open. "You mean they let him out, that murderer?"

I nodded. "It means somebody else killed Revak. I was there watching Revak's house the night it happened. And I saw Eddie go in. But before Eddie, another man—looked like a man—came down Mount Vernon Street and went in. Sarah was there, she saw him also, right, Sarah?"

Sarah's forehead wrinkled up. "Belle, what're you starting?"

"So—" I went on like I didn't hear. "—I got a funny feeling that first man was—maybe—you?"

Sarah got red, she looked around like she wanted to run out the door. Jennie's eyes got wider and she sucked in her breath. Sol put down his cup and stared at me. Then he gave a loud laugh. "You're kidding, right? Where did you get such a nutty idea?"

"I don't know," I said, "maybe my woman's intuition?"

"Then your *intuition* is telling you a *bubbe meisseh*, an old wives tale! Because I was right here that night, right in this chair! Ask Jennie, she'll tell you!"

"Remember, Sol, you're on Detective Connor's list of suspects. So he'll be coming around to ask questions. In the long run, you'll have to tell him the truth. For your own sake—"

Sol jumped up like my words lit a fire under him. He began to walk up and down, smacking his fist into the palm of his other hand. "If that doesn't take the cake! First that Plaut boy gets ahold of our Clara—how he talked her in, such a smart girl, the devil only knows. Then she had to crawl to some stinking butcher all by herself, nobody to even give her a hand! Next minute her life is over, she didn't begin to live yet!"

His face was mottled in purple, he stopped in front of me and jabbed a forefinger at my nose. "Eddie they found with a gun in his hand, him they let out of jail. But me you're trying to pin a murder on!"

Jennie sprang up and took his arm. "Sol, stop it, your blood pressure! Here, take it easy, sit." She got him settled in the big chair and she sat on the footstool. "Sol, listen. Clara's gone, but we still have two daughters and we have each other. You can't keep on like this, you'll destroy us all!"

She was almost in tears but she kept talking. "Sweetheart, it's not good to keep things hidden. Anything that has to be kept secret eats away at your insides, we pay for it, believe me. So let's start right now, maybe we'll feel better, okay? Tell her, Sol, tell her what you told me. You know, about that night—" She stroked his arm as if he was a child. "Tell her, go ahead, it's the only way."

Sol's mouth worked for a minute. Then he lifted his chin and looked right into Jennie's eyes. "You were always a softy, Jennie," he said with a sigh, "stuck with a roughneck like me.

But maybe you're right, maybe it's worth it to get rid of some of this lump in my chest.

"Mrs.—Belle, to tell you the truth, after they arrested Eddie, I was glad. Glad! I wanted him behind bars! All my Clara's misery started with that boy! Eddie Plaut is just as responsible for Clara dying as that greedy doctor!"

"Sol, take it easy," Jennie begged.

He nodded and patted her hand. "How could I forget what happened to my Clara? I had to do something. You're right, I was the one." His voice cracked, he sipped some tea. "Late that night, we were almost ready for bed, the phone rang. A funny voice told me Revak was the one killed Clara—and also said Revak was home that night. Even told me the address! How do you think I felt? Here was my chance to get revenge! Jennie tried to stop me but I was a crazy man. I got out my gun, I keep one around because I carry sometimes a lot of cash, and hopped in my truck."

"Your gun," I asked, "it's maybe a twenty-two?"

"Yes. So I parked on Pinckney Street, just to be on the safe side, and walked down from Louisburg Square. I guess that's when you saw me. First I rang the bell, then when nobody answered, I knocked. When I tried the knob the door was already open so I walked in. My heart was banging plenty, believe me. I saw a light in a room near the back, so I walked toward it—"

"Sol," Jennie interrupted, "stop and take a sip tea—"

He did what she said and then went on. "When I got there I saw a body on the floor. I didn't stop to see if he was dead or what, I got so scared I turned and ran back towards the door. All of a sudden I was in worse trouble, I left the front door open and a man was coming inside! It was dark, I couldn't tell who it was." He wiped his forehead with the back of his hand.

"What could I do? I didn't want anyone should know I was

there in the house with a dead body, they'd think I did it. I had to get out without anybody knowing. So I gave the man coming in a good crack on the head with my gun and he fell down. I jumped over him, slammed the door shut on the way out, and ran back up the street to my truck."

"So you didn't even know it was Eddie you hit?"

"No, not till I found out he was arrested. Then I wished I'd given him a harder hit on the head for what he did to Clara!"

"Excuse me," I said, "please don't be so quick to make Eddie the villain. I heard him on the phone with her, she was the one broke it off. She hung right up, wouldn't tell him where she was going. Remember, they would've been married already if everyone wasn't so set against it—"

Sol threw his hands in the air. "So now it's all our fault! All I know is my Clara, my beautiful Clara, is dead! And if she didn't get mixed up with those Plauts, those *Deutschen*, she'd still be alive today! We've lost her. And this we have to live with all the days of our lives. God, what did we do to deserve this!" He sank back in the chair and covered his face with his hands.

Jennie got up and bent over him, putting her arms around him. "Sol, it's not your fault, Clara would never want you to carry on like this, it's nobody's fault, it just happened . . ."

"Jennie?" I asked. "I'm so sorry, I never meant to upset you two, you've had so much—forgive me, I only wanted to clear things up, for everyone's sake. Come, Sarah, we'll let ourselves out."

Sarah got up and we tiptoed our way out trying not to see the two figures huddled together. A man sitting in a chair and crying without a sound and a woman kneeling on the floor holding him in her arms.

Out on the street Sarah glared at me. "Belle, how could you do that! It was cruel, you tortured them—"

Her words stabbed me, I began walking fast just to do something. "Look, it's like an abscessed tooth. I only did what was best for them. Got the truth out, that's all. It would've been worse if it was the police."

"That's the truth," Sarah spluttered. "More like the third degree!"

"Maybe. Think I enjoyed it? King Solomon himself couldn't figure this case! Can you imagine any girl not wanting to marry the man who was the father of the child she was carrying?"

"You still don't know that part," she said.

"*Nu*, look what happened when I asked Jennie if she knew Clara was pregnant. She started crying right away. Like she just couldn't stand to hear it. Did she cry because the truth was too hard to bear? No kidding, Sarah, even asking her that gave me the willies."

"Belle, you had some nerve!" We stopped in front of Sarah's house. "Losing a daughter that way, in one flash, does she even know what she's saying? Imagine how she felt when he went running out with a gun the other night! How she must've shivered till he came back, how did she stand it! And then you come sit with a cup tea in her living room and ask her such a question. I thought I'd die!"

"You're absolutely right, she looks terrible, thin as a rail," I said. "And she's got such *chayshik*, such courage, never complains. Sarah, tonight was the worst night of detecting I ever went through. This case cuts right inside people's hearts, maybe I should quit altogether—"

"Absolutely." Sarah nodded like anything. "Who needs such aggravation? You're not a dentist, paid to pull teeth, making a living from it. Where does it get you, tell me?"

"You're right." She was my best friend, after all. "And Eddie's out of jail. It's enough already. Tonight was too much, to hurt other people like that. I never want to do that again. On the level, I'm through."

Sarah turned around with her hand on the doorknob. "Swell. And tomorrow morning—" her eyes rolled "—the *Globe* headlines will say that Filene's Basement is giving away free mink coats!"

twenty-three

Who wants to be called the meanest person in the world? Jim Connors always tells me, a good detective never lets feelings get in the way. But in the drugstore all day long Sarah's words about the questions I threw at the Borofskys stuck in my head. Was I just butting in to people's private affairs and hurting them deep down in the bargain? Was it worth going on with?

Still, the facts spoke for themselves. A murderer was loose out there somewhere close by, no question. And all Jim had so far was a pile of scribbles in his notebook.

As to the Borofskys, who knew if Sol was really telling me the whole truth? Sure, the part about hitting Eddie over the head with the gun. But maybe he killed Revak first. Then when he saw Eddie walk in he saw a quick way to put the blame on a boy he hated plenty, and get off the hook himself. Maybe he didn't even tell Jennie that.

What about the big question: why did Clara break up with Eddie at such a time? Did anyone in either of the families have a glimmer of the reason?

So, Appleman, I told myself as I sold a woman a package Lanteen, that new contraceptive jelly, Sarah was right—it looks like Filene's Basement won't be giving away mink coats just yet.

Late in the afternoon when Eddie and Jerry were busy I took a minute to pick up the phone and call Jim.

"Listen, I got some things to tell you. You're coming by tonight to play cribbage with Harry?"

"Yeah, I'll drive you home, we'll talk then."

Next I dialed Rosalie White. After we chatted I asked her if Harry was home the night Revak was killed.

"When? That Sunday night? Who can remember?"

"You'll have to, the police are checking everybody that had any business with Revak at all—"

"So what's Harry got to do with all this?"

"Don't kid yourself, they know Revak used to come here and get drugs from Harry for abortions. I just want Harry to be ready with a good alibi for that night, hear what I'm saying?"

"Belle, have a heart, Harry's still my husband." I heard a sigh at the other end. "All right, truth is—he wasn't home. Didn't come in till almost midnight. And he wouldn't say where he was, just it was business. See, I was right, he's seeing some woman." She choked. "Belle, what should I do?"

I wanted to tell her where Harry went but I figured that news better come from his own mouth. "Listen, Rosalie, don't talk yourself in. Wait till I figure out what's what, okay?"

"Oh sure, wait, that's about all I do nowadays! The kids've grown up, but not Harry—"

I told her there'd be news for her soon, and hung up. Of course, Harry could've been in that Beacon Street gambling house that night. Or was he? Rosalie could be right, for all I knew, Harry certainly did a lot of wandering around. He wasn't paying attention to the drugstore the way he used to, for sure.

My eyes fell on the bottom drawer of the right-hand side of the desk, it was slightly open. I swear I bent down to push it shut but my hand didn't do what my brain said. It pulled the drawer open. Inside lay a gun.

I was learning fast about guns so I knew where to look for the caliber number. There it was, .22. I put the gun back and shut the drawer quick. Now I really had something to talk to Harry about.

He came in at six and Eddie went home. The new silent Eddie filled prescriptions and answered questions okay, but no more world-is-my-oyster snappy comebacks. I went out to the fountain and made myself a sandwich from the leftover tuna salad and Jerry whipped me up a chocolate frappe. I carried it all into the back room. Harry was mixing some powders in the big mortar, so I sat at the desk.

"Harry, the night Revak got shot, you were off, no?"

He grunted and worked the pestle harder.

"So where were you that night?"

He stopped mixing and turned around. "Where was I? What's it to you? Who're you, the F.B.I.?"

"Not me, the police want to know. You'll see, when Jim comes in tonight, he'll ask you."

"Big deal. What's to tell? I was home, so what."

I ate and drank for a minute while he stopped mixing and started counting out powder papers. "You're positive, Harry?"

"What do you mean, positive? You can go ask Rosalie."

"I already did. And she told me different."

He looked at me. "Oh, you know Rosalie, she gets all mixed up, never gets anything straight." He started making folds in each powder paper, then he laid them out on the counter.

"Listen, Harry. Jim knows about you and Revak. Your name was on a list of people Revak was blackmailing. So when he comes tonight, he'll ask questions. And I know something about you he doesn't—yet. I know about Number Twelve Six Beacon Street. It's where you go gambling, no? So what's the story? What did Revak have on you?"

Harry's face turned red. "You got a lot of moxie, you know that? Okay, you guessed it all right, I've been gambling. What did you do, tail me? Who cares, I don't give a hoot who knows."

"So why don't you tell Rosalie, Harry? Maybe it's none of my business, but—"

"You can say that again!"

To that I paid no attention. When people feel guilty, I notice they always try to make someone else feel crummy just to get their minds off their own messy affairs.

Harry went out to help Jerry while I finished eating. What was the real story with Harry? Used to be such a good husband, now look. Funny, he and Rosalie got along great when they were poor like us, no money to gamble then. But what was it that Revak knew about Harry bad enough to be able to blackmail him? If it was another woman, how on earth would Revak find out?

Harry came back with a couple new prescriptions. "Harry, was Revak threatening to tell Rosalie something?"

He picked up the spatula. "Forget it! Revak's gone, it's over now. And I don't tell Rosalie things that would worry her."

"But Harry, you're still going there?"

"Sure, I'm trying to make up what Revak sucked out of the business, see?"

I saw, all right. He wasn't telling me the whole story, he wasn't even looking me in the eye. "Come on, Harry, the gambling was no big deal. What was it Revak had on you?"

He groaned and laid down the spatula. "You're like the Canadian Mounties, you never give up! Okay, the gambling began because I was on Revak's list. It was to make up the money, I was going nuts."

Poor Harry, stuck like a fly on those paper streamers. "So what was the secret Revak knew?"

He gave a groan. "Something that happened a long time ago, something I did to help a good customer." He started working again.

"Like Somerville, for instance?"

"Nope, it was Herlihy. Ancient history now."

"So what happened with Herlihy?"

"Listen, enough with the true confessions for one day. You're through eating, go help Jerry."

He was the boss, I got up. "Anyway, better tell Jim about that twenty-two you got in your desk. That's the size bullet killed Revak."

He stopped folding the powder papers. "My God, Belle, you got a nose like a bloodhound!"

"Nose-shmose. It's Rosalie I'm worried about. Harry, if it was me I'd tell her right away tonight about the gambling. She's worried sick you're having an affair with some *nafke*." I went right out front without waiting for him to answer.

When Jim dropped in later I told him Harry might have something to show him. It was pretty busy, I waited on customers and shmoozed with Jerry about his getting ready to take the Pharmacy Board exam. Just before closing time, eleven, Harry came out to take the cash and change the register tapes and Jim to offer me a lift home.

After Jim got the car moving he said, "Well, Belle, looks like you've turned up enough twenty-two calibers to start a gunsmith shop."

"Somerville and Harry both gave you theirs?" He nodded. "Well, there's one more I didn't tell you about. You'll never guess. Marcia!"

"You're kidding!"

"On the level. I saw the gun right in her handbag in the store. And, look, after the way Revak played her for a sucker, she was sure mad enough to want him dead."

Jim was parking the car in front of my house. "Belle, if think-ing about murder was against the law, the jails would be loaded! But we'll talk to her."

"Something else about her. That brother of hers, John, taught her to shoot a gun. He came in the store one night, mad like anything, and said he'd get Revak. And Jim, he has a funny voice, kind of hoarse. So he maybe killed Revak and made those phone calls?"

"Hmm, sounds like we ought to talk to him, too." He opened the door and started to get out.

"Wait, something else. I found out who was the person went into Revak's house just before Eddie."

He sat back again. "Wow, you're a regular mine of informa-tion tonight, friend."

"Listen—it was Sol Borofsky, Clara's father." I told him what Sol said about finding the body and conking Eddie.

"Hmm—" Jim took off his fedora and rubbed his head. "If he's telling the truth, that'll clear Eddie, for sure."

"But it doesn't clear Sol, right?"

"Never fear." He put his fedora back on and got out of the car. "We'll check all that out, Belle."

Like a real gentleman he came around the car, opened the door on my side, and helped me out like he was bringing me back from a dance at the Copley-Plaza. "Thanks, Jim." I looked around, wondering whether to tell him. "Look, the last couple times I walked home from the store I got a funny feeling some-body was following me. Think I'm losing my marbles?"

He frowned and peered up and down Allen Street. "Doesn't look like there's anyone around now. If it happens again, give me a call quick, okay?"

"Okay." I took his hand and gave it a squeeze. "You're a real friend, Jim."

He squeezed back. "You can count on that, me beauty," he said with a grin.

Upstairs we heard a window bang open and we looked up. A dust mop was shoved out and shaken hard from the third floor. Jim's face had a question mark. "What's going on? Housework at night?"

"Only on Allen Street," I explained. "My upstairs neighbor always checks out who brings me home, the dustmop is her cover-up. Maybe she's giving the lowdown on me to J. Edgar Hoover, a list of all the men I see."

Jim winked at me. "After this I'll come in my sergeant's uniform!"

twenty-four

It was driving me nuts. What was the secret Revak knew about Harry? At the same time, jobs don't grow on trees these days. It wouldn't pay to push Harry too far. No wonder he was so grouchy, with the gambling and the investigation and God knows what else.

Nu, Appleman, what've you done about that Herlihy character? Jim told you he got in some kind trouble a long time ago. And even Harry admitted he did a big favor for him once. What did all that add up to?

Next day I was off after lunch. Hot and sticky, with swirls of greyish clouds but no rain, so I decided to take a walk and think everything over. Just to keep the showers away I carried my umbrella and headed for the Boston Common. By the time I got to the top of the Hill on Joy Street I got an idea.

Maybe Arnie Silverstein knew something about Herlihy, more than Jim Connors did. After all, doctors all belong to the same club, no? And Arnie already helped me before, he's one smart cookie. Here I was at the corner of Joy and Mount Vernon, why not take a chance he was home, it was Saturday.

Appleman's luck was operating. Arnie's voice answered my ring and the buzzer let me in. Arnie gave me a big hug and ushered me into his living room with the thick wall-to-wall carpet and the damask sofa you sank into up to your neck. Everywhere those dishes of nibbles. Chocolates, Jordan almonds, stuffed dates, raisins and walnuts. A huge bowl fruit. Name anything to chew, it was there.

"Surprise, surprise," he beamed, plumping down on the sofa

beside me. "What brings you to my humble dwelling today? Here, have a pear, just ripe enough—"

"No, thanks, Arnie, not this minute," I said, as he bit into one. "Look, Arnie, I'm maybe taking advantage of friendship. Could you give me some help on this Revak case?"

He finished the pear, put the core into an ashtray shaped like a fish, and grabbed a handful of raisins and walnuts. "Sure, Belle, my pleasure. You do all this work as a kind of public service, why shouldn't I help out."

"You know that Dr. Herlihy that comes in the store? Heavy drinker, purple nose?"

"Tom Herlihy? Sure, everybody on the Hill knows Tom." He finished with the raisin mixture and held out a plate with stuffed dates. I took one and nibbled. With Arnie you had to learn to make one goodie last as long as you could. Otherwise he could turn me into a pear shape in no time. "So what do you know about the trouble he got into?"

He rubbed his chin with his knuckles. "Let's see—oh, yeah, I remember. He used to be a member of the State Medical Board, and something happened that forced him to resign. Something kind of juicy, but right now, I just can't recall it." He jumped up, he moves fast even if he's heavy. "But I know someone who will. Let me call my friend, Joe McGinnis on the *Traveler*."

There was a telephone on a side table, he called and chatted a bit, then asked about Herlihy. It must've been a pretty long story, because Arnie mostly listened and put in "Ah—ha—" now and then.

When he came back to the sofa he handed me an ecru linen napkin, he wasn't the paper-napkin type. "So he knew the whole story?" I wiped my sticky fingers.

"Have a Jordan almond? Get this: Herlihy was asked to resign because a charge of accepting bribes had been made against him."

"Bribes? What could he do for someone who gave him a bribe?"

He bit his pink Jordan almond in half. "Are you kidding? For example, a member of the State Board could cover for someone who flunked the exam!"

"You mean he could get a license for a doctor who couldn't get one?"

"Exactly. Otherwise the doctor would never be able to practice. Not in Massachusetts, anyway."

"Even after going through medical school, imagine. No wonder they offered a bribe."

"You said it. Anyway, after his resignation Herlihy's practice fell apart. He gave up his Back Bay office and started drinking, poor guy. Now he's living in a run-down house on Myrtle Street. A few of his old patients still come to him. He used to be good, you know."

"From one mistake, imagine." I managed to work myself out of the sofa. "Arnie, you know all the right people. How can I thank you, you're a real pal."

"Wait a minute, Belle." He pulled me back down. "Don't rush off. Have some cashews. I want to talk to you, just sit back and relax, okay?"

I settled back. "What do psychiatrists do when *they* need advice?"

He smiled. "Gee, let me catch my breath—you're always in such a hurry, did you know that? Not good for you, Belle—"

"It's nice to know you're worrying about my health, Arnie. But what're you getting at?"

"For God's sake, Belle, I'm trying to talk about *us*." He reached over and grabbed my hand. "Look, my divorce is coming through this week. I'm a free man! And I've been thinking a lot about you and me. Every time I see you, it's like the sun coming out!

We'd make a swell pair. Don't you get it? I'm asking you to marry me!"

It was like lightning hit me on the head. Arnie Silverstein proposing to Belle Appleman? Just like that, bingo? Appleman only stared and said, "Honest? We never even got to have dinner together. You're serious?"

"Belle, you do like me, don't you?" He kept my hand in his.

"No question—"

"Truth is, I've had enough of these head-over-heels whirls. They're not much of a basis for a long-term relationship. On the other hand, you and I really get along, we're chums. Maybe that's what matters most in the long run, what d'you say?"

Say? I was too flabbergasted to talk even. He kept pressing my hand like it was his life-preserver.

"Belle, I'll give you anything you want. This townhouse—I'll put it in your name, okay? Anything your heart desires—name it—"

This house, imagine. I got my tongue untied. "Arnie, I'm flattered you're asking, you're tops in my book. But getting married, that's not something you make up your mind in two seconds. It takes time to get to know one another. Can't you wait a little while? I got to think about this—" My hand slid away from his, it was getting crushed, I had to rub it to get the circulation back.

His face fell. He grabbed a Milky Way and undressed it, then put it down. "Sure, Belle. All my fault, guess I sprang it too suddenly." He held his hand up. "But I meant what I said, every word. And we'll take it slow from now on—"

"Thanks, Arnie, you're really swell." I gave him the long look Greta Garbo gives Frederic March. It took all my strength to pull myself out of the sofa's clutch. "And I'll think about it, I promise."

He got up and walked me to the front hall, his arm on mine. I turned for one last look at that gorgeous living room. Appleman, it could be all yours. A doctor's wife, no more worry about jobs, rib steaks every day!

"Let me take care of you, Belle, you shouldn't be out there all by yourself." His bright brown Teddybear eyes looked into mine. He put his hands on my shoulders and gave me a big smack on my cheek.

A lovable roly-poly, I thought, and a real brain. A woman could sure do worse. And he wanted to take care of me, imagine. I reached up and gave him a big hug. "It's the nicest thing that's happened to me for a long time, Arnie."

"I'll be calling you," he said as I reached the door. "We'll go places and do things."

I gave him a wave goodbye and started walking back to Joy Street. Ah, Appleman, wait'll Sarah hears! First you begin having dates with a regular doctor. Now a specialist wants to marry you! Look what a drugstore job did already! It was a long time since any man ever wanted to take care of me, maybe that was better than all the fantasies.

Of course, a good detective can't let romance interfere with business. If I married Arnie, would he mind my detectiving? Or would he want me to just collapse on those tasselled cushions and nibble pink coconut bonbons?

No, he said my work was a special kind of service without pay, or something like that. So that was okay. I didn't tell him I'd be sure to cut down on his sweets, bad for his health.

What now? Maybe there was time to check out Herlihy's alibi. Myrtle Street wasn't far, only a block below Pinckney on the wrong side of the Hill. A street so narrow you could almost touch the other side. Beside the entrance to Number 74 a small brass sign said: THOMAS HERLIHY, M.D.

His office was on the first floor, an older woman and a young woman were just coming out. They left the door open so I went into the waiting room. No receptionist, kind of a musty air. Old-fashioned furniture, cushiony but shabby. On the wall, old medical prints the drug houses give free to doctors. I knocked on what I guessed was his office door and his whiskey-deep voice told me to come in. Somewhere a phone was ringing but nobody was answering.

Herlihy was sitting at a desk pushing one of the drawers shut with a bang. The strong smell of liquor told me he just had a quick drink after those two women left, probably he would still be at it except for my knock. Weren't his eyes a little bleary already? He straightened up. "Oh, it's you, Mrs. Appleman. What strange wind wafts you my way?"

I didn't waste no time, just sat down on a straight chair. "Dr. Herlihy, do you know that you're a suspect in Sam Revak's shooting?"

He straightened up even more. "Are you mad? Revak? I had nothing to do with him!"

His shaky hand pulled open a lower drawer and he took out a bottle Seven Crown whiskey and a glass. He filled the glass and gulped some down.

"Your name was on a list of people he was blackmailing."

"So what? I had plenty of company!"

"So maybe you killed him to make him stop."

"Hah! It's a rare sense of humor you've got." He gulped some more. "Nope, no need to. Sam stopped that business long ago, had to."

"Stopped? What do you mean stopped?"

"Because once all this happened—" he waved his hand at the walls "—there weren't any secrets left. Funny, huh?" His roaring laugh turned into a belch.

"You mean, after the scandal about the bribes?"

"What do you know about that?"

"Plenty. Listen, I'm working on this case with Detective Connors."

"Undercover cop, eh?" He pointed to the bottle. "Don't suppose you drink on duty?" It seemed to him a good joke and he laughed again. "Didn't know they had ladies on the force. Using the drugstore job as a cover?"

"Never mind, tell me about Revak, as long as it's all over. Was he getting money from you a long time?"

Herlihy slumped down in the chair. "That son-of-a-bitch. Found out I was taking a little on the side for getting some people licensed. For God's sake, I was helping out the poor devils! Never could say no to a sob story. That bastard had me on the hook for years. Then the scandal broke—oh, those reporters had a field day!" He stopped to hiccup.

"Most of my dough gone by then. But at least Sam was through bleeding me. I was home free! Free!" He picked up the bottle and waved it at me. "Jeez, I'm glad the louse went and got himself killed. Talk about poetic justice! Almost makes me a believer again—"

"Look, Doctor, Harry said something about Revak knowing some kind of secret, a secret between you and Harry."

He poured some more and drank. When he spoke, the words were getting kind of mixed up. "Harry? Yeah, I owed him one . . . favor f'r a friend over there . . ." He jabbed with his finger toward the other side of the Hill. "Got to help your friends, that's the only true religion . . . sure, why not . . . one f'r all 'n' all f'r one . . . good guy, Harry . . ."

Next thing I knew, his head sank down onto the desk. "What friend?" I asked. No use, he was out like a light.

I got up and went out, closing the office door behind me. Not one patient sitting in the waiting room. A good thing, the shape he was in.

So I still didn't know. What favor did Herlihy do for what friend on the Hill?

twenty-five

Marcia banged down the aluminum pitcher. "Say, listen, you got some crust, Belle Appleman! Why d'ja hafta go and squeal to the cops on me and John? What's the big idea, anyway?" She planted her feet apart behind the fountain, shoving back that tangle of hair that kept drooping on her forehead.

A swell way to start the day. I just walked right on in back to change. But she followed me in, yelling almost in my ear. "Account of you we coulda got hauled off to the cooler! Who d'ya think you are anyway, J. Edgar Hoover?"

Even Eddie noticed, he turned from counting out the register money on the counter. "Hey, what's going on?"

"Nothing, Eddie," I said.

"Whaddaya mean, nothing?" Marcia parked herself right in front of me. "They came and took every one of John's guns away! Now all his buddies in the Boston Patriots'll be laughing at him! And it's all your fault!"

"Wait, Marcia. The cops would've done it no matter what. They're looking for the gun that killed Revak, you know that. If John's guns don't fit, nothing's going to happen—"

"Says you!" She pointed a finger at my nose. "And you squealed to Connors about me and Sam Revak, I know it! Whaddaya wanna do, pin the murder on me?"

"Pin-shmin, it's better to have it all out in the open. They would've found out everything soon enough. Stop worrying—since you and John didn't do it, what've you got to worry about?"

She stood there glaring, hands on her hips. Finally she popped her gum, muttered "Aw, dry up!" under her breath, and marched out front.

"Gee." Eddie turned to me. "Did I hear right? Marcia packs a gun?"

"You remember the night her brother came in the store and made all that *tararam* about getting even with Revak?"

Eddie put the money can back on the shelf. "Yeah, I remember. What a sweet character he was."

"Well, I got him pegged as a good suspect. He's got a hoarse voice—like the voice that called you on the phone that time. And he shoots guns with a bunch of buddies that call themselves the Boston Patriots, imagine. Some patriots! Jim's going to check them out."

"What was that crack she made about her and Revak?"

"Oh, Revak made a play for her and she went for him in a big way. Thought he'd marry her, fat chance! So she was all burned up about it." Of course, I didn't tell Eddie about her being worried she was pregnant. "So that makes her a suspect, also."

"What a mess!" Eddie shrugged and went out front to distribute the cash. Marcia hardly spoke to me all morning, only when she had to for business. *Nu*, if she couldn't see I was only trying to help, that was her problem.

After the lunch rush I made my sandwich—tuna on toasted whole wheat—with a mocha ice cream soda. The *Globe* was lying nearby, so I grabbed a copy to read while I ate at one of the round tables. That way Marcia's set mouth wouldn't spoil my appetite.

It was on page 3. A small headline and a couple inches of story:

EL TRAIN KILLS LOCAL DOCTOR

Dr. Thomas Herlihy, 74 Myrtle Street, was killed instantly last night at about 7 p.m. after apparently falling into the path of an oncoming train at the Charles Street Station. Dr. Herlihy was 55 years old and had been a member of the State Medical Board in the past. The platform was crowded at the time and no one appears to have seen the accident occur. However, one witness stated that Herlihy had seemed to be unsteady on his feet shortly before the accident.

Herlihy dead, just like that! The words leapt out at me, but I just couldn't believe them. Where was he going at seven o'clock last night? When I left his office, he sure didn't look ready or able to go anywhere except to bed. And now maybe I'd never find out the whole story about Harry and the favor for that family on the Hill.

So who could've given poor Herlihy a shove? Was it the real murderer of Revak, trying to shut Herlihy up? But why kill him now? After all, the whole bribe business was a long time ago. Who would care about it any more?

Now there were three people dead—Clara, Revak, and Herlihy.

True, Herlihy could've been plenty unsteady on his feet. But he was too smart to go riding on subways when he was in that shape. Somehow I didn't believe he was trying to kill himself. If he was that type, wouldn't he have done it when the scandal broke?

Somebody sure didn't want him to do any more talking to me or anyone else.

twenty-six

While I searched like crazy through my bag for the key, the phone was ringing its head off. Turned out to be Sarah.

"Belle? Guess what, that movie we missed, the one with Bette Davis? It's at the Bowdoin Square Theater, how about it tonight?"

I got my breath back. "Sounds good, after supper—"

"Supper? Let's be sports and have a bite at Walton's, okay? It's right next door to the movie, we'll be ladies for once."

"Okay, no dishpan hands today!"

Inside Walton's Cafeteria we each took a ticket from the machine and went to the food counter. First a tray with silver and a napkin, then the hot food section for the big decision.

"What're you going to have?" Sarah asked, like always.

I looked things over. Pork chops with applesauce? Not on your life. Salisbury steak? Mr. Schechter's hamburger was the only kind I trusted. Fried chicken? That grease could kill. Crusty baked macaroni with cheese? Mmm, that was it. We gave the order and went to the dessert section after the clerk punched twenty cents on each ticket. Layer cakes, pies, cobblers swimming in sauce. I took a tall goblet of fruit salad. Sarah took something buried under a mountain of whipped cream.

"Sarah," I said, "that's five pounds extra—"

She shrugged. "So I'm living it up a little. Tomorrow I'll skip breakfast."

We each got coffee and a roll with butter and took our trays to a table near the window. Lucky to get it, the place was crowded. Not a bad meal for forty-five cents. Outside traffic roared past in Bowdoin Square, you could hardly hear it indoors. It was awfully warm inside, in spite of the big fans, but the smell of coffee in the air was nice.

The macaroni was delicious, I took my time over it. "Sarah, do you know a family named Green, live on the same street with the Borofskys?"

She stopped her fork halfway to her mouth and pursed her lips. Then she shook her head. "No, I don't think so. Why?"

"Well, Sol Borofsky mentioned that Clara used to go with their son. I think his name was Raymond? Studying to be a dentist?"

"So what could the Greens tell you?"

"Oh, not them, their son. Because one of the ideas I had about why Clara broke up with Eddie was maybe she realized she loved someone else, maybe that Raymond. He used to be crazy about her, Sol said. So then she had to get rid of Eddie's baby to make a fresh start—" I speared a pineapple chunk.

Sarah rolled her eyes. "A daughter of Jennie's? Sounds more like what you hear on 'John's Other Wife' on the radio!" Her brow wrinkled, she sipped her coffee. "But young people today, who knows? So she used to go steady with this Raymond?"

"Since kindergarten. Oh, listen, there's something else, it was in today's paper." I told her the story about Herlihy and how he got killed.

"Oy!" She shook her head. "You're not keeping the promise you made, to stay out of that whole mess. And look what happens! The minute you talk to somebody, he gets killed in such a horrible way!"

"Have a heart!" The macaroni began to feel heavy in my chest. "Let's just enjoy ourselves now."

Sarah raised her eyebrows and attacked the whipped cream mountain. It didn't take us long to finish and walk to the movie house.

The marquee said:

DOUBLE FEATURE DISH NIGHT

OF HUMAN BONDAGE

HOPALONG CASSIDY

We fished in our pocketbooks for the thirty-five cents admission and got our dishes, white soup bowls with a green border. I told Sarah I needed a soup bowl like a hole in the head.

"It's for free, what's to complain about? You can put fruit in it, or a plant."

We came right in the middle of the Hopalong Western, thank God, we didn't have to sit through the whole thing. An usher with a flashlight found us two nice seats in the orchestra. I sat the dish on my lap, clutching so it shouldn't fall.

Pretty soon Hopalong got all the bad guys and the picture ended. Then the Pathé News rooster gave a cackle. We watched Hitler making a speech to a bunch of *meshugeneh* Germans screaming and sticking their arms out. Mussolini told his soldiers how brave they were to shoot those Ethiopians that were fighting them with spears. A Japanese man said his country really didn't want to kill people in Manchuria, only Japan was too small so they needed room. Some news, who needed it! At last a Mickey Mouse cartoon, you could relax and laugh.

After Coming Attractions came the Bouncing Ball. The organ played and we all sang while the ball on the screen bounced from one word of the song to another to lead us. We sang "There'll be a Hot Time in the Old Town Tonight" and "Daisy, Daisy, Give Me your Answer True." Oldies but good fun.

Finally came Bette and that slim English actor, Leslie Howard. It sure wasn't a movie to make you laugh. Bette played a mean woman, a regular skunk. And Leslie was a *nebbish* who couldn't stop hanging around her, giving her money and whatever she wanted, making a mess of his life. But one funny thing happened.

When Bette said to Leslie, "Darling, I'm going to have a baby," at least six soup plates went crashing down on the floor. Finally, thank God, Bette died and Leslie met a nice girl who got him back on the right track. When we got outside it was starting to rain. "Look, Belle, we can cover our heads with our soup plates!" Sarah showed me and we ran home giggling.

The rain stopped by the time we got to Sarah's, it was barely misting as I walked up Blossom to Allen. A car was parked in front of my apartment house. Just as I got to the door a man jumped out, Marcia's brother John.

"Hey, I wanna talk to you," he said, coming close.

I edged away. "It's late, I got to work tomorrow, g'night—"

"Think you're smart, doncha. Marcia put me wise, told me who squawked to the cops about my guns. Boy, you sure loused everything up. Now they got all the guys in my club under investigation, how d'ya like that! Just when we was gonna get started checking out the Reds in City Hall—"

"Look, John—" I fished for my key. "I'm only trying—"

"You shut up! I don't give a hoot what you're—"

I didn't wait to hear his story, I jumped through the front door and dashed up the stairs. But when I got to my door and kept hunting for my key, he was right behind me.

I turned around. "You'd better go, or else I'll scream. Somebody'll call the cops!"

"Now get this—you better not scream if you know what's good for you." He held up his right hand and I saw the glitter of a knife blade. Maybe not the biggest knife, but right then it looked like one of Mr. Schechter's twelve-inch carvers. "Just get the door open, and we'll go inside nice and easy."

How can you argue with a nut? By now I had the key out and I got it in the lock and he followed me in. The front hall light was on, like I left it. He kicked the door shut with his foot. Oy, Mrs. Wallenstein, I thought, where are you when I need you?

Appleman, I told myself, this you got to handle like you're Arnie. After all, he talks to nutty people all the time.

"Look, John," I said, "I don't blame you for getting mad at that Dr. Revak. He was plenty mean to Marcia, no?"

"Mean? Are you kidding?" He waved the knife around. "That bastard took advantage of her, she's just a kid! He got just what he deserved!"

Did you do the killing, I wondered. And maybe you're the one tried to hit me and Nate with your car that night.

"So you got a right to be sore." I wanted to calm him down.

"You're damn tootin'!"

"Maybe I can help. Tell me, where were you the night Revak—you know—got killed? The police'll be asking—"

"Tough apples," he growled, moving closer to me. "They can't touch me!"

"How come?"

He gave a snort. "Every guy in the Patriots'll swear I was with 'em that night! How's them for apples, Mrs. Nosey Hogan?" He gave a wave of the knife under my nose, the metal gleamed. "A lulu like you hadda poke your nose in where it don't belong!"

Just then there was a loud knocking at the door. Hicks stopped waving the knife. "Who's that?"

The knocking changed to a loud banging.

"Okay, open up." Hicks made a motion with the knife. He moved over to one side so he would be in back of the door.

A surprise! Nate Becker rushed in. "Belle, are you okay? Where's that—"

John swung around from behind the door, shoved at Nate so hard we both toppled over, and ran down the stairs two at a time.

"Hey, you, come back here!" Nate yelled. He was on the floor, I was sitting on him, we were clutching each other. We heard the downstairs door slam shut. A second later a car roared away.

"You're all right, Belle?" Nate said in my ear.

"Oh, sure, some all right." To get up was no cinch, I was still catching my breath. But something made me turn my head. Mr. and Mrs. Wallenstein stood in the hall staring at us. That helped me get up quick. They went on up the stairs as I closed the door quick. "Thank God you came, Nate. Who knows what that nut was going to do next!"

"Who is that jerk?" Nate asked, scrambling to his feet.

"Marcia's brother, you know, the girl that works with me in the store." I looked at him. "Nate, it's so late, what were you doing on my street?"

He took off his glasses and polished them with his handkerchief. "I was just taking a little walk, helps me sleep better. From way down Allen Street, I saw him push in after you."

"Nate, you're a regular angel! Let me make you some coffee—"

He shook his head. "Thanks, no, it's pretty late. But Belle, you better tell Connors about this, that guy knows where you live—I don't want him to pay you any more visits—"

"Absolutely, don't worry—"

He put the glasses back on. "It's no laughing matter, you wouldn't forget?"

"Would I lie to an angel?"

He smiled, then he came close and gave me a kiss on my cheek. "Goodnight, then, sleep well."

"You, too. And thanks a million."

I made sure the door was locked tight before I went in the bedroom. I felt like I just finished acting in the Bette Davis movie myself. But maybe Nate was right, maybe I should call Jim right away.

"Anything wrong, Belle?"

"I'm okay, but listen—" I told him all about John.

"I'd better go right over and pick him up."

"That'll make Nate feel better—me too—"

"And, Belle? Remember what I warned you about? I don't want you getting hurt, it'll be on my head, remember . . ."

"Don't worry. With you and Nate around—" Imagine, Nate kissed me. Did he really worry about me?

Jim gave a snort. "I'm not kidding. Now lay off that Revak case, don't give me any headaches."

"You know me, Jim," I said.

"Yeah, that's the trouble," he growled, and banged down the receiver.

twenty-seven

Marcia threw me an Edward G. Robinson mad-gangster glare as she came dashing into work late, her hair flopping on her face. The minute the breakfast rush was over she stalked across to the cosmetic counter.

"Who died and left you in charge, Belle Appleman?"

"What?" I gave her my Loretta Young blank look.

"Don't hand me that malarkey! On accounta you, me and my mother didn't hardly get no sleep last night! That detective came over looking for John! Some baloney about assault with a deadly weapon—"

"That was no baloney, Marcia." I told her what John did to me.

Her mouth tightened. "Says you! John wouldn't do stuff like that!"

"Don't kid yourself, he did it, all right. So did the detective talk to him?"

Her eyes got teary. "John wasn't home. He didn't even come home last night, we don't know where he is. On accounta you, he's a fugitive from the law now! I hate you!" She stormed back to the fountain.

Nu, what can you do? I suppose it's hard to believe anything bad about your own brother. But I had other things to think about. Arnie, for example, was he really serious? And was marrying him what I wanted? That question would take plenty thinking.

What about that Raymond Green? Maybe he could tell me things about Clara I hadn't heard yet. It would be easy to ask his folks about him, maybe he still lived at home.

"What was that all about?" asked Harry as I came in the back room. He was shaking some stuff up in a bottle. I told him how John Hicks barged into my place.

"How come he ran away? After all, he really didn't lay a hand on you. He just made things worse for himself, that's all."

"Hey, what do you mean, didn't lay a hand on me! His knife was almost in my nose! Maybe he ran because he's the one killed Revak, he sure loves guns and knives. Anyways, it's that poor Herlihy I got to find out more about, and now he's gone. You never did tell me about the favor he did for you. What was it, Harry?"

He gave the bottle a last shake and reached for a prescription label that he rolled into the typewriter. His back was to me. "Listen, I don't want to talk about it, I want to forget it."

"Look, Harry," I said, "I talked to Herlihy only yesterday. Don't you think it's funny he should happen to fall under a train right away the very next day? What if he got pushed? And the pusher was the one who murdered Revak?"

Harry kept right on typing the label, didn't say a word.

"So that's why I got to know about this favor he did you. He said it was a family on the Hill. Who was it, Harry?"

He swung around, a scowl on his face. "You won't like it if I tell you, Belle. Some things are better left untouched, believe me—"

"I'll take a chance."

He just sat for a minute. "Don't say I didn't warn you. It was for a good customer." His eyes stared right into mine. "Wait'll you hear, you'll be sorry you ever started this." He was quiet for a minute, still studying me.

"Harry, for God's sake, spill the beans already—"

"Okay, okay. You won't like this story, but it'll be good for you to hear it and find out your snooty date is a faker. Yeah, it's the family of that high-class doctor you like so much, you rush to go out with him. Now do you see why I tried to keep it hushed-up?"

"What are you telling me?" So George was in this, after all.

"I'll start at the beginning. One night, just when I was closing, that Mrs. Parkland called me up. She needed a refill of a prescription, her son George wasn't home, could I bring it by after I closed. *Nu*, what do you say to a customer runs up a bill for thirty, forty dollars a month? So I said okay. But when I rang the bell she asked me to come in. She had a big problem on her hands, maybe I could give her some advice."

I had to smile. "So a doctor's mother needed to ask a good pharmacist for help!"

Harry didn't laugh. "It wasn't medical advice she needed. It was advice what to do about her son, George, he's the light of her life. He graduated from medical school, but had a hard time getting by, he's no great student—"

"He already told me that, said he really wanted to be a baseball player, but his mother wouldn't hear of it—"

"Oh, sure. But I'll bet he didn't tell you he flunked the State Board! Which meant he couldn't practice in Massachusetts. Or anyplace else, for that matter. So here was his mother, crying like anything that her baby boy was in such trouble, after all the time and money she spent getting him through med school. What could she do?"

"He told me he owed everything to his mother," I said. "So this is what he meant?" George was a cheat, his license was bought with a bribe, his whole career was a fake. A perfect gentleman.

"That's it, all right. I told Mrs. Parkland I knew somebody on the State Medical Board, I'd see what I could do, but it would cost her a pretty penny. Me, I didn't get one red cent out of it. But Tom Herlihy got a bundle from her. And your George Parkland got his certificate to practice."

"Herlihy claimed he really did it to help out guys he was sorry for. And that's why your name was on Revak's list?"

"That louse Revak! Somehow he got wind of what happened and started bleeding me!"

"And he was bleeding Herlihy, also. Till it all came out in the papers."

"Yeah, poor Tom, he took the rap. But the names of the candidates were never published, somehow, Beacon Hill bigshots carry a lot of clout. So Parkland was lucky, he stayed squeaky clean, and he's still sitting pretty." Harry turned back to the counter, wet the label, and slapped it on the bottle. "And that's the whole crummy story."

"So paying off Revak made you start gambling?"

"Yup. Feel better, now that you know how George became a doctor? Some hero—"

"Front!" Marcia's voice sang out.

As I went out to talk to a woman who wanted to know if that new contraceptive jelly really worked, everything Harry told me was tumbling around in my head like the popcorn bouncing behind glass in the pushcart parked in front of the Bowdoin Square Theater.

twenty-eight

George was a faker, imagine. Those clear blue eyes, that open gaze, that whole clean-cut look, it was just put on, like the hand-tailored jackets on his broad shoulders.

The customer handed me the money for the package Lanteen Jelly, we could hardly keep it in stock, it sold so fast. I pushed the buttons on the cash register automatically.

Nu, flipped the cash register, Harry warned you, you wouldn't like the story. So George with the Gary Cooper grin is a little crooked, why are you going around with a face so long you'll trip over it? You're thirty-six years old, not a kid like Marcia.

Listen, I snapped, everybody gets a little blue sometimes. Anyway, who cares if George Parkland cheated over his license? What's it to me? He's not going to take out my gall bladder!

So, clanked the register, how come you melted like strawberry ice cream in the sun when you danced with him? What kind detective are you, Appleman, making eyes at a maybe murderer?

Say, listen, detectives are only people, I shot back.

Pooh-pooh, enough with the sob stuff, croaked the register. Better you should get busy and figure what's going on already. Stop all that moaning over Dr. Gorgeous.

I slammed the drawer shut so hard my hand hurt. Plenty questions with no answers yet, all right. First, what part did John Hicks play? He had a topnotch reason to kill Revak, revenge for what that fast talker did to his sister. Second, was there a connection between the two killings, Revak's and Herlihy's? Third, a separate puzzle but at the core of everything, what soured the Plauts and the Borofskys enough to make all that unhappiness for their children? Come to think of it, did Shakespeare ever explain why the Capulets and the Montagues hated each other so?

All those questions at once, my brain couldn't handle them. So while I ate my lunch I thought about Herlihy. Let's see, Revak was blackmailing Harry and Herlihy for the same thing.

Just the same, George was getting Ergotamine from Harry, like Revak. So was George doing abortions, also, was he Revak's partner in that horrible business, even though he claimed the medicine was for his mother? Partners always get into fights about everything. And Revak was a regular *gonif,* some partner he'd be. So with Revak out of the way, George could run the business himself and take all the profits.

Thinking about this made me give a shudder.

Right then, George Parkland walked into the store. And he didn't head for the back room, neither. I was down on my knees cleaning the glass on the inside of the cosmetic case when his face appeared on the outside of the glass. One of his eyes was winking at me. I yanked my head out quick and stood up.

"Belle, I've been meaning to come by but somehow things just got in the way . . ."

"Don't worry—I didn't make you sign a contract you had to come in every day or else—"

That easy grin came over his face. "Tell me, are you free tomorrow night?"

I shook my head, no.

He snapped his fingers. "Darn, I wanted to take you out for dinner and dancing again, it was terrific last time—"

Appleman, I thought, if what Harry told you was true, here's your chance to break off with George. But then, here was my chance to find out what was what. Real evidence to show Jim that George was the one killed Revak and Herlihy. Maybe, maybe not.

"Well—perhaps I can fix it with Harry, let me see." I went in back.

Harry got that sour look on his face. "After what I told you? You're still fooling around with him?"

"Listen, you don't understand. Anyway, Marcia'll be on late. So is it okay if I open and work till six instead?"

He gave a snort.

"Harry, be a sport—"

He waved his hand. "Go, go, take the whole day off. But don't come crying to me afterwards!"

"Thanks, sport." I raced out front to tell George.

"Great," he said, those blue eyes all lit up, "what about the Copley-Plaza?"

An idea came into my head. "This time let's go to my type restaurant, okay? You ever been to Meltzer's?"

He shook his head. "Never even heard of it."

"Then you'll see a whole different side of Boston."

"You're the boss." He took my hand and gave it a couple soft strokes on the back. "What time shall I pick you up?"

"Seven o'clock. Excuse me now, George, I got to get back to work." I pulled my hand away.

"Of course, see you tomorrow at seven." He gave me that Gary Cooper grin again and walked out.

After he went out the door, Jerry called over from behind the fountain, "Hot diggity-dog! Woo-woo!" He rolled his eyes.

"Enough with the wolf whistling," I told him, but I couldn't help laughing. Another evening with George. I felt young and silly myself.

After supper I met Sarah and Nate at the McClean School for Evening English.

"Belle," Nate asked, "that guy who was waiting for you, did he ever show up again?"

"No, he ran away someplace. Jim's hunting for him."

"Thank God!" Sarah said. "Nate told me. They should only find him quick and shut him up in jail!"

"From your mouth to God's ear," I said.

"Aren't you scared he's still sore at you? And he'll maybe come back?" Sarah said.

"Belle," Nate said, "you think he's the one with the car that night?"

"Car, too?" asked Sarah. "So what else happened, you never told me!"

"*Nu*, some idiot almost hit Nate and me with his car on Allen Street. After the last Evening English class. Nothing happened—"

"Nothing, she says!" Nate eyed me. "A murderer maybe trying to kill her is nothing!"

"*Gottenyu!*" Sarah gasped.

Thank God, our teacher was talking already, so Sarah couldn't rave any more. Miss Wallace read a poem by a man named Robert Frost, about how the world would end in either fire or ice. The ice part was like hating someone.

How much icy hate was dripping out of the Revak case, I thought. Everybody hated Revak—Harry, Sol, Eddie, Herlihy. Sol hated Eddie, also. The Plauts and the Borofskys hated each other. John Hicks hated enough to kill—maybe me? And George, was it possible he hated Revak, too?

After all, Appleman, I told myself, even though Harry said George's name was kept out of the scandal, wasn't it possible Revak found out and started blackmailing George along with the others? And couldn't George, after shooting Revak, have found the card with his name on it and taken it out of the pack?

How many of these questions would I figure out by going out on a date with him? Look, men mix business with pleasure all the time, why shouldn't Appleman?

twenty-nine

My stomach gave a jump when the phone rang in the morning, just when I was finishing a cream-cheesed bagel. Could it be George? Maybe breaking our date?

"Belle, you're almost ready to leave for work?"

"Sarah, guess what—Harry gave me the whole day off! Because I've got a dinner date with George tonight, go figure—"

"Again tonight with that doctor? Belle, I've been thinking it over. Something tells me you shouldn't be seeing that man—he's not for you."

"What do you mean? You sound just like Harry! What's wrong with George? Because he comes from money?"

"So sue me, there's something fishy there. He's just not your type, can't you see that?"

"Type-shmype, am I marrying him or anything? Why, did Nate say something?"

"Only about that horrible man that followed you. It's maybe none of my business, but I'm worried. What about that car almost ran you down? And this ritzy doctor from the Hill, on the level—" She was silent for a minute. "—of course, it would be okay to see him for your gall bladder, but not like this!"

"There's nothing wrong with my gall bladder! Besides, you met him—"

"That's just it, I don't trust him. He's too perfect, I saw how the women in Filene's stared at him. Why isn't he out with one of those society debs that get their pictures in the paper at those charity affairs? What does he want from you?"

"Sarah, I got to go. Tell you what, soon as I get home tonight I'll call you, okay? Unless it's too late—"

"Never mind too late, even if it's after midnight, you call me! Promise me!"

So I promised. Now I had free time to find out about Raymond Green and Clara. The Greens' number was easy to find, a woman answered. I thought fast.

"Mrs. Green, I'm with the insurance company that's checking into the death of Clara Borofsky."

"What's with this checking?"

"Well, it's confidential, I'm talking to any friends Clara had. I heard your son Raymond knew her, is that true?"

"Oh, my Raymond knew her since they were kids."

"Good. Tell me, he's home now?"

"Now? No, he's working, he's a dentist."

"Oh, that's wonderful. And where's his office?"

"He didn't graduate yet. Today he's practicing at the Forsyth Clinic."

"Thanks, Mrs. Green, I hope you have lots of *naches* from your son."

Sure I knew about the Forsyth Dental Clinic. It was where you went to have your teeth fixed if you were poor. The fixers were dental students, with some regular dentists who walked around checking to see if the students were doing the right thing. My mother, may she rest in peace, used to take me there to get my teeth cleaned. If you got a smart student you were lucky.

When I got there, the Forsyth Clinic turned out to look just as it did when I was a girl holding my mother's hand tight. Big and busy, smelling of antiseptic. But since I wasn't going for a cleaning this time, I went right in like I owned the place. At the reception desk a bleached blonde was filing away at her nails with an emery board. She barely glanced at me as she asked if she could help me.

"Yes—you got a dental student working here, Raymond Green?"

"The place is full of students." She swivelled on her chair. "I can't tell one from the other."

Oh, a wise-guy type. I gave her my Constance Bennett sophisticated look. "Listen, it's important I talk to Mr. Green."

"Just a sec." She put down the emery board and dialed a number. "Dr. Scanlan? Can you come out here a minute?" To me she said, "You'll have to ask the supervisor."

Dr. Scanlan was a tall, white-haired man with a ruddy face. When he came to the desk the receptionist pointed her finger at me. So I explained that I was working on an insurance case and had to talk to Raymond Green for a few minutes. I gave him my Myrna Loy straight-shooter face.

Dr. Scanlan nodded. "Just a minute." He went back to his office. Oy, I thought, he's going to ask me to show him a badge or a card or something. Goodbye, Appleman.

He came back out and said to the receptionist, "Call Area Four and ask Mr. Green to come down as soon as he's finished with his patient." He pointed out a bench where I could wait.

For maybe twenty minutes I watched mothers dragging scared kids into the clinic and dragging tearful ones out. Poor dentists, nobody loves them. Finally a young man in a long white coat came over to the desk and spoke to the girl, who pointed to me.

Raymond Green was a chunky young man with curly red hair. Big ears, freckles, a cheerful air. "You wanted to see me?" A friendly type, he would've made me comfortable in his dentist's chair. "They said something about an insurance investigation?"

"From one redhead to another, I said that just to get you down here. It's about Clara Borofsky, I'd like to ask you some questions." His forehead wrinkled up. "There's someplace we can talk confidential?"

His smile gone, he motioned me to follow him to a little room off the main lobby, with some easy chairs. He motioned I should sit. "What's this about?"

"It's about Clara, like I said. I'm trying to clear things up. To find out why she broke off with Eddie Plaut all of a sudden just before she—she died."

He sat across from me and fixed me with his brown eyes. "What's it to you? Who are you, anyway? I don't recall Clara ever mentioning you—"

"Clara didn't know me and I never met her till the day before she died. I was the one who got Clara to the hospital with Detective Connors. She came into the store—the Charles Street Pharmacy—and collapsed on the floor. I'm Belle Appleman, I work there."

"Oh, so that's how it was." He leaned back and sighed. "Her appendix was ruptured—God, from such a small thing, I can't get over it—"

"You heard that story," I said. "Did you believe it? About the appendix?"

He gave a shrug. "There were rumors about something else—something ugly—"

I nodded. "The ugly something else, that was the truth." He sucked in his breath. "She went to a doctor on Beacon Hill that night and had an abortion. Only he botched it and she died from it. Then the doctor who did it got killed and Eddie Plaut was arrested . . ."

"I read all that." He passed a hand over his face. "My God, an abortion!"

"Raymond, was it your baby?"

His face got red to match his hair. "What in hell kind of question is that? Clara wasn't that kind of girl!"

"Oh, I know. But the whole business is mixed up with a police investigation, Raymond. So I'm trying to help figure it all out. The sooner the truth comes out, the better it'll be for everyone, especially Eddie."

"Eddie Plaut, what a louse he turned out to be," he said. "How could he let her do that, a girl like Clara—"

"So you were her boyfriend before Eddie?"

He moistened his lips. "If you'd known Clara—she was one in a million. Yes, she was my girl, it was understood—"

"So what happened?"

"Oh, we grew up together, passed notes to each other from the first grade on. Everybody expected us to get married after I finished dental school. But then she met Eddie at a party one night, and that was it. I never could figure out what she saw in him—" His mouth worked. "Funny, there was a storm that night, we almost didn't go to the party—"

I leaned forward. "What I'm trying to find out is—why Clara broke off with Eddie all of a sudden. The day she had the abortion, imagine." I put on my Mrs. Thin Man professional detective face. "Listen, did she say anything to you about it?"

He tugged at one ear. "What makes you think that?"

I gave a shrug. "Just guessing. After all, she knew you from way back. You still stayed friends after she went for Eddie, no?"

"Friends? Like hell, it hurt too much. But somehow—well, I kept hoping she'd change her mind. And we did run into each other from time to time—" He looked at his watch.

Talk faster, Appleman, he's getting itchy. "Listen, I know how it is. But the way I figure, Clara must've changed her mind at the last minute about Eddie. Who knows why? Eddie claims he's got no idea at all what was the reason. But maybe he's just not telling—"

"Eddie, who'd believe him!"

"Whatever happened, Clara all of a sudden decided to get rid of Eddie's baby and start over. Maybe to go back to you. Am I right?"

He sat bolt upright. "How—how the hell did you know?"

I pushed a little harder. "So how did she do it, Raymond? She gave you a call, maybe, and asked you to meet her? What did she say to you?"

He stared at a chart on the wall. Then he gave a long sigh. "Might as well tell you, it doesn't matter now. She wrote me a letter. It's the last thing I ever got from her. I keep it with me . . ."

He shoved his hand inside his white coat and took out a wallet. From it he pulled a folded piece of paper and handed it to me. The handwriting was a little careless, like the writer was in a big hurry.

> Dear Ray,
> You were right all along—I'm breaking up with Eddie. I'll call you as soon as I can. You're the only one I can talk to—
> Clara

"Came in the afternoon mail the day she—" His voice broke for a minute, he swallowed. "She was already gone. I didn't know till—till later—"

I handed him back the letter. "I'm sorry." His eyes were slits, like he was trying hard not to cry. "Thank you very much for your help. Something tells me you'll be a fine dentist."

"One thing you ought to know," he blurted, his voice rising. "Whatever happened to Clara wasn't her fault, I'll swear to it!"

I nodded and we shook hands. I watched the solid figure in

the white coat go out of the room and across the lobby to the stairway. It's hard to get over that shock, when someone close to you dies who isn't grandmother age. *Nu*, he was young.

So what happened that wasn't Clara's fault?

thirty

It was chilly standing in the front hall without a stitch of clothes on, I gave a sneeze.

"You caught me undressed, Sarah," I said into the phone, "I got back late from talking with that Green boy. You know, the dentist that was going with Clara before Eddie—"

"So what did he have to say?"

"Look, it's late, I'll call you tonight soon as I get in, okay?"

"Belle, you shouldn't be going out with that doctor, I'm telling you! Cancel him while there's still time, tell him you're down with a bad cold—listen to me, what do you need him for?"

"Sarah, don't be such a worry-wart. It's just dinner, what's the big deal?"

"You don't need his dinner, you don't need him for anything, you know that? *Nu*, have it your own way. You'll see—" The receiver slammed in my ear.

That Sarah, what got into her lately? So later on we'd laugh at the whole thing. Meanwhile I jumped in and out of the shower, rubbed my curly hair dry, and dabbed on makeup. What dress to wear? That was easy, I only had one fancy one—the ivory crepe de chine I bought last year for the Kline wedding. Size ten with a Saks Fifth Avenue label and a Filene's Basement price tag. I took it out and looked at it.

So what if it made me feel sort of undressed? It was that low-cut V-neckline, hard for me to get used to. Still, part of being a detective is dressing for the part, no? And it had a really slinky look, like for a private eye. You can't be a fraidy-cat, Appleman, if you want George to open up about the Herlihy business. This way he's more apt to spill the beans.

Then I put on the garnet earrings and necklace my Daniel, may he rest in peace, bought me for an anniversary present such a long time ago. What would he have thought about my going out with George? I barely finished snapping the catch on the necklace when the bell rang. A minute later, a knock on the door.

George was a knockout in a navy blue gabardine suit, looked tailor-made, not like the Classic Clothing Company off-the-rack stuff. Cream shirt, blue silk tie with narrow cream stripes slanting across. A regular Hart, Shaffner, and Marx advertisement.

His eyes crisscrossed every inch of me and he gave a low whistle. "Wow, a totally new Belle Appleman! Sophisticated lady!"

"That's me—" I batted my eyelashes and gave him my long, sexy Sylvia Sydney look as I picked up my cape and my bag. Outdoors I stopped for a minute and looked around.

"Anything wrong? Did you forget something?" George asked.

"No, but I had a funny feeling somebody was watching us." I peered up at the third floor. No Mrs. Wallenstein in sight.

George looked up and down the street. "Nary a spy on the horizon."

He ushered me into the front seat, closed the door, and got in the other side. "You'll have to tell me the way. I'm just putty in your hands tonight—" His blue eyes sent out sparks.

"Harrison Avenue, near the corner of Beach. You know where the garment district is?" Putty he wasn't, exactly. More like a small boy let out of school.

He nodded and off we went. But after he parked the car and we started up the steps to the restaurant, I suddenly got scared.

Maybe Sarah's hunch was right. Appleman, why didn't you tell Jim what you learned about George? Practicing medicine with a fake license. Some server of society! And if he could lie about that, couldn't he have killed Revak and lied, also?

The minute we stepped into Meltzer's the headwaiter got crosseyed trying to look at us and at the V in my dress at the same time. But he decided that George was a ritzy type and he took us over to one of the best tables. When me and Sarah ate there he always tried to put us near the kitchen door.

And somehow I felt better now. What could possibly happen to anybody in Meltzer's except a stomach-ache from overeating? The waiter showed up and handed us each a menu. George had a big grin on his face. "It's your party, you order for both of us."

"Okay, tonight you'll eat what Jewish mothers feed their families." To the waiter I said, "We'll have the mushroom-barley soup to start, then the *tsimmes*."

The waiter's eyebrows shot up. What kind of man lets a woman decide? It's not easy to deal with waiters in Jewish restaurants, they want to tell *you* what to order. So to keep this man from having a heart attack I asked, "The *tsimmes* is okay tonight, no?"

He woke up from his trance and nodded. "The best. If you ordered the fish I would've told you no. And what to drink?"

George would've ordered coffee, so I said, "Hot tea with lemon, in a glass." Tonight Dr. Parkland was going to get the works.

After the waiter left George took my hand in his. "Fascinating, absolutely fascinating! What's that dish you ordered—tsi—something?"

"*Tsimmes*. It's a kind of pot roast made with prunes and sweet potatoes. Wait'll you see."

Still holding my hand, George looked around. His forehead

crinkled. "Belle, are you trying to prove something by bringing me here?"

"Maybe. We're from two such different worlds. Your world I know something about. But what do you know about my world?"

"Not much, you're absolutely right. But you're willing to teach me, right? And I'm a very willing pupil." The blue eyes gleamed.

"We'll see. Well, most Jewish food is really the food of the country where the family came from. My mother cooked Russian style, my friend Sarah cooks Lithuanian style, that's where she's from."

"Of course. The Diaspora, the scattering, after the Romans conquered the Jews."

A surprise. "Where did you learn about that?"

He smiled. "Well, I did learn a few things at Harvard."

"But they never told you about *tsimmes*, did they?"

This time he laughed. "No, that's why I'm lucky I met you." He kept giving my hand little squeezes that made my heart miss a couple beats. George wasn't so shy like I thought. Appleman, was it a mistake to wear this dress?

By this time my stomach was starting to gurgle from hunger, so when the waiter brought our basket of hard rolls and rye bread I didn't wait. Right after, we were eating our way through the soup, thick with mushrooms and barley.

"So," I asked, after we let our spoons rest in empty soup plates, "how was it?"

He wiped his lips with his napkin. "Way better than the clam chowder in Durgin Park's! And these rolls, so crunchy, I'll never be satisfied with those mushy Parker House things again!"

I did an Al Jolson voice, "You ain't seen nothin' yet!" He grinned. "Al Jolson uses double negatives," I explained.

He leaned over the table toward me. "Belle, you can use triple negatives for all I care. I love the way you talk, that's what counts!"

"No, this is America and it's important to speak good English. I'm taking Evening English for the second year. We're learning poetry now, like . . .

>Spring came on forever,
>Spring came on forever,
>Said the Chinese nightingale . . ."

His face lit up. "That's beautiful. The way you say it, as though you relish every word—" My heart did a flip-flop. Watch it, Appleman, a woman could drown in those sea-blue eyes.

The *tsimmes* arrived so hot the steam was rising from the plates. George studied it as he picked up his fork.

"Don't worry, it won't bite you," I told him.

"Isn't the idea for me to bite *it*?" He started tasting. After a good swallow he looked at me, forehead wrinkled in surprise. "Belle, is this the kind of food you were brought up on? Manna from heaven! Food of the gods! Why hasn't anyone ever told me about this?"

"Oh, this is restaurant cooking. Wait, sometime I'll cook up a homemade one for you—"

His eyes opened wide. "Would you really do that?"

"Of course. Why—a home dinner—is that such a big deal?"

"In your home, yes, it would be." His words came slow and deliberate. "Because I keep getting the feeling that somehow—deep down—you can't get yourself to trust me."

What he said came as a shock. Appleman, maybe he can read you better than you can figure him. But I just raised my eyebrows and said, "See, I was married very young, so I only had one man in my life. Since then I haven't had much social life, the type that invited me just didn't appeal. Maybe I *am* a little afraid, you're absolutely right."

"And I'm nearly forty, and never married at all. Like you, the type that I've met hasn't appealed. Right now, I seem to be a little afraid, myself—"

"Afraid? You?" His words made me smile, he seemed so in charge of everything.

"Ah, but you see, with you I'm venturing into the unknown. Your background is so foreign to me, how do I know what you want, and what you expect?"

"Does that matter so much to you?" I asked.

"I've never met anyone like you, never. You're so full of life, it's contagious! I don't want to go too fast—to scare you off—but you matter a great deal to me . . ."

His words sounded so heartfelt, my head began to spin.

"You're different, too—a whole new world for me. It takes getting used to—" We stared into each other's eyes, then we both began to giggle.

Nu, Appleman, it was time to get down to business. "George, were you good friends with Sam Revak?"

"What?" He put his fork down. "Why on earth do you ask that?"

"Because it's important. Were you good friends with him?"

He shook his head. "No. But why waste a beautiful evening on him?"

I ate a forkful of my *tsimmes*. "Something's awfully funny about the way he was killed."

"Why bother your pretty head about it?"

I gave him my Myrna Loy professional look. "The same reason you're a baseball lover. It's like a puzzle I just can't give up on. And I care about Eddie Plaut, too, so I want to clear his name."

He put out his hand and covered mine with it. "No nasty items on the agenda tonight. Just moonlight and music, all right? We've had so little time together."

Was there something he was afraid to talk about? Or was he just tired from hospital rounds? We finished our main course and then the raspberry sherbet with hot tea and lemon in a glass without another mention of Revak. Peeking at each other from time to time. Smiling with our eyes and our lips, it wasn't hard for me to do. The waiter brought the check, George paid and we left.

I wanted to enjoy his eyes admiring me, the press of his hand on my arm as we sauntered out. But why did he clam up at the first mention of Revak's name? Could someone so sweet, so believable, be a murderer? One minute up, then down, my heart was on a seesaw.

In the car he turned to me, a boyish grin on his face. "Ever been to the Totem Pole?"

"Norumbega Park!" A bunch of memories exploded in my brain. Daniel and me in that big out-of-doors dance hall, the evening breeze blowing our hair, holding each other close. Daniel handing me an ice cream cone and then wiping the chocolate mustache off my face with his handkerchief.

"Jimmy Dorsey's band's there tonight. What do you say?"

Appleman, I thought, if this guy's a murderer and you're going to die, better to die dancing. What was the poem Miss Wallace read us the other night? "I say—" I made my voice deep like Garbo— "sail on! And on!"

George laughed and started the car, and before long we were in Norumbega Park. The dance hall was already crowded but George found us a little table. A blonde was singing "I Surrender, Dear" into the microphone on the stage. Appleman, watch it, you're not about to surrender to this doctor. He pulled me to my feet and we melted together on the dance floor.

It was time to become Detective Appleman. "George, I talked to Herlihy before he got killed," I said in his ear.

"Oh?" He missed a step, shuffled his feet, and we got back in step.

"He told me everything." I let that sink in. "The Board exam business, the bribe, how you got certified to practice."

The boyish light in his eyes went out, they were blue agates. We kept dancing but he wasn't holding me so close. "So you know." Now his words plopped like stones.

"And that's why Revak was blackmailing you?"

He looked down at me. "What? That's not true!"

"But he was blackmailing Herlihy and Harry on account of that . . ."

The music stopped. "We'd better sit down." He walked me back to the table without touching. "Now what's this all about? What are you getting at?"

We were two strangers. "It's about who had the best reason to kill Sam Revak," I said. "And yours was a good one."

"You throw a wicked curve, lady, but let's get some facts straight. Yes, Herlihy told you the truth. No, Revak was not blackmailing me. And I did not kill him." He was staring at me.

"But George, you're smart, don't say you're not. Why did you need the monkey business with Tom Herlihy?"

He rubbed his forehead with his hand. "Remember I told you that getting through Harvard Med was tough for me? All through college I had this hangup, I guess they call it exam anxiety. Even if I knew a professor was going to give a little quiz, I'd break out in a sweat. Didn't make any difference whether I knew the stuff by heart. You're so gutsy, probably you can't even understand—"

"Oh, yes I do. When I was a girl working in the sweatshop, I remember how scared I was that the seams I was sewing on the shirtwaists would be crooked. If they were bad too many times, tough apples, you got a pink slip in your pay envelope, fired. I cried plenty of times."

He gave a long sigh. "When I walked into that exam room to take the Board, I just panicked. Everything I ever learned about medicine fell out of my head. I answered the questions but God knows what I wrote. When the failing grade came back in the mail my mother got terribly upset. I told her I'd just keep taking the Board till I passed."

"Why didn't you?"

"Well, my mother made up her mind she would take care of it, and she found a way of getting to Herlihy. At first I was dead set against it, but she said no, I was a born doctor and that was that. Ever since then I've worked my head off, day and night. Trying to prove I belong at it." His mouth worked. "One little lie—"

That part must be true, it was what Beatrice Parkland said about him in the store, how hard he worked. Jimmy Dorsey's trumpet section gave a blare and George pulled me to my feet. "You *were* getting to be a habit with me," he sang in my ear. "But after what you found out, I probably don't have a chance of becoming a habit with you . . ."

"Oh, you still got a chance—if you still want to—"

"That's good to hear." We did a fancy dip. "What made you get onto this whole business?"

"Simple. I thought you were doing the same kind of abortions like Revak."

He moved me away a little in the middle of a swing and said, "I have never performed an illegal abortion in my life. You'd better believe that, Belle."

"And I kept thinking Revak was such a rat, maybe he found out about the Medical Board business and started blackmailing you, also. So I thought you maybe killed him to end it—"

"Murder, too? Is that all? And all the while I thought my manly charms were bewitching you!"

The orchestra swung into a waltz, "Falling in Love Again," that Marlene Dietrich sang in that skimpy outfit in "The Blue Angel." George's arms went around me again and we twirled into the crowd of dancers.

So while my feet were going one-two-three, something else was waltzing around in my head. Was I all wrong about George? Or were those Gary Cooper eyes taking me for a ride?

What was I doing here on the Totem Pole dance floor, getting whirled about in the arms of a murderer? What was his next move going to be?

thirty-one

Some moments are printed in your mind forever. Even while they're happening you say to yourself, did I dream this up or is this the real world?

That's the way I couldn't help feeling while George waltzed me around the Totem Pole floor. The breeze cooled my hot cheeks and the aroma of new-mown grass filled my nostrils. The dancing chased all the worries I had about him right out of my head.

The strains of the Dorsey band drifted to our ears, first a croon, then a wail. The little lights all around winked like fireflies circling. George's cheek was a little bristly as it grazed mine. He danced like the athlete that he was, full of playful swings and easy glides, a feather in the wind. In my ear he hummed that wonderful melody, that he was in the mood for love simply because I was near him.

His cheeks were flushed, his eyes partly shut, his lips curved in a half-smile. "This little dream could end," he sang, and the lock of sandy hair fell on his forehead. His problem was becoming my problem—it was Appleman who was being bewitched.

When the number was over, we started back to our table and I forced my brain back into business. "Excuse me, I have to stop at the ladies' room."

"Of course." I turned my head to watch him go back to our table.

What I really needed was a telephone. I put a nickel in the
pay phone on the wall of the ladies' lounge and dialed the Joy
Street Station. A voice I recognized answered. "Rafferty, this is
Belle Appleman. Jim's there?"

"No, he's out on a call, may not be back for a while."

"Listen, give him a message, will you? Tell him to call me at
home when he gets back, no matter how late. Okay?"

"Gotcha, Mrs. Appleman, okay."

Too bad, I wanted to fill Jim in on what Raymond told me.
And maybe about George, maybe not. *Nu,* it would have to
wait. Back at the table, George was sitting with two glasses.
"Have some lemonade."

"Mm, nice." We sat and sipped. Then Jimmy Dorsey blew a
few notes on his saxophone, who could resist? Time melted
away with me in George's arms, sniffing his aftershave lotion,
my feet moving happily in response to his lead. I forgot all about
Belle Appleman, detective. It was so much easier being just
Belle Appleman, woman.

During a break I remembered there was a tomorrow, and I
asked George the time. He glanced at his watch. "Quarter to
eleven."

"So late! I have to work tomorrow."

"Me, too. This evening's going so fast, I hate to see it end."
His eyes searched mine. "What do you say, shall we run away
to the South Seas? Become beachcombers?"

I put my hand on his arm. "Why not?" To be on an island
with him, no Harry scowling at me, sounded good.

The smile on his face disappeared. "Could you really care for
me, Belle? Seriously? For a lifetime?"

"A lifetime? You really want us to leave tonight for some
island? You're kidding!"

"About the South Seas, yes. But about going away together,
spending our lives together, I mean it. Let me explain." He

took my hands in his. "I have a close friend in Colorado, college roommate, family owns a big ranch. He's been after me for years to come out and help run the place. Cattle, horses, the works. A whole new life, real out-of-doors living. Mountains, it's God's country. Would you go with me? Get married, of course. What do you say?" He was holding my hands tight.

I caught my breath. "George, it's—well—we just don't know each other very well yet. Marriage, that's a big step. Colorado, I've never even been there—I can't even imagine it . . ."

He gave a sigh. "You're right, to drive off right now would be madness, perhaps. You'd be leaving your job and I'd be leaving mine. But if I don't do it tonight, without taking time to think, just cutting all my ties fast—" His eyes searched my face. "It's our whole lives, Belle. Look, we could know each other for ten years, would we still be one hundred per cent certain?"

My heart raced. Could I do it? Did I want to? Would it be foolhardy or the start of a great adventure? For once in her life Appleman was speechless.

He studied my face for a few seconds, then let my hands go. "It's too much to expect of you." He sighed and stood up. "I'm afraid I'll never make it to that ranch. Come on, let's get out of here." We walked to the car in silence.

While we were driving up Commonwealth Avenue he suddenly said, "Belle, if you won't run away to Colorado with me, how about coming up to my house for a little visit?"

His words took me by surprise. "Now? But, George, it's awfully late. Wouldn't we wake up your mother?"

"No chance. She somehow heard about—well, you and me—at the drugstore. So I told her I'd be bringing you. She's staying over at my aunt's house, but she's left a snack for us."

And his mother didn't object to Belle Appleman who sold cosmetics in a drugstore? Whoever told her about us at the store, anyway? "George, I don't know—"

What would Dorothy Dix advise? Say no, Appleman, don't go looking for trouble. Alone in his place, yet. But I was still itchy to learn more about him, who he really was. And I had to admit I was curious about how the Parklands lived. Besides, George said tonight he really wanted to marry me. And I felt bad about not taking his dare.

"After all, fair is fair. I've been to your place, now you should see how I live. My world, right?"

"All right, then, but just for a little while. I'm still a working girl, remember?"

As I stepped through the door of the Parkland townhouse on Mount Vernon Street, a little shiver went through me. Was it because deep down, I wasn't sure he was telling the whole truth? Or was it because I was still afraid to be alone with him like that? But it was time for me to act like a woman of the world. So I stepped inside and he closed the door behind me.

His world was different, no question. The foyer was all pan-elled wood with a long Oriental rug all the way down the cor-ridor. He took me by the hand through a door on the left. When he put the light switch on I gave a little gasp, thinking, wait till Sarah hears about this!

A living room as big as half my apartment. Pale gray wall-to-wall carpet your feet sank into. In the corner a grand piano, the kind they play in concerts. Furniture like in a Norma Shearer movie, everything in pale colors and gleaming wood. A fire-place with a marble mantelpiece. On the dove-gray walls, beau-tiful paintings.

"Like it?" George was studying me. He led me over to a stuffed loveseat covered with flower-garden chintz and sat me down. "Hold the fort, I'll be right back—"

I felt as though I was sitting in one of those rooms in the Art Museum from old times. Daniel, may he rest in peace, used to take me to see them. You know the kind I mean, where that

French king, Louis something, kept all those willing ladies. Only now I felt like the little girl in *The Wizard of Oz*, blown into the wrong country. What was I doing there? Was I there as a detective or as a woman?

George came back holding a silver tray. On it was a platter with crackers heaped around a bowl, two tall thin glasses with stems, and a bottle wrapped in a big white napkin. He held out the plate. "Have some caviar."

Caviar I tasted before, at weddings. I spread a cracker with it and munched. Salty, like pickled herring. He picked up the bottle, fooled around with the top till it made a loud pop, and poured something fizzy like seltzer into the glasses.

"Champagne?"

I took it and we clicked glasses. "To us," he said.

"*L'chaim*—to life!" I said, and gave a sip. Bubbles from the champagne went up my nose and made me give a little sneeze.

"To life, that's a great toast," he said. He put his glass down and took mine and put it on the tray. Suddenly he was seated beside me, holding me close, giving me a delicious champagne kiss, mmm. His arms stroked my shoulders, it was heaven. Then his lips moved lower, down my neck. Soon he was grazing in the deep V. I got shivery. Watch it, Appleman, better quit now. But who wanted to? It was like a daydream, only better . . .

Right in the middle, like an alarm clock going off, a high-pitched voice said, "Oh, would y'all pardon me?"

We jumped away from each other like guilty teenagers necking in a parked car and stared at Beatrice Parkland standing there in a blue silk outfit.

"Mother! I thought—you said you were staying over—" George's brow was knit.

"I know," she said quietly, but in a who's-boss-here-anyway voice, "only something came up, you know how things are. Forgive me for interruptin' your plans."

"Excuse me, Mrs. Parkland," I said, "but we didn't have no—
any plans." It was hard to remember double negatives, I was so
furious at her words. "George asked me to stop by for a minute
to see your house. I've already stayed too long, you'd better take
me home, George." I jumped up.

"Oh, heavens, no," she went on in that sugary voice, "why,
here's a chance for us to become better acquainted. My son has
told me such nice things about you, Mrs. Appleman—Belle,
isn't it? Sit down and have some more of that lovely caviar, it's
Beluga, from France. George, be a darlin' and get a glass for
me, please."

Oh boy, some cozy get-together. Who wants to chat with a
man's mother after she just found you in his arms? But George
brought her a glass and gave her champagne, so I had to sit
down again. She perched on the sofa across from me, he stood
by the fireplace with a long face.

"Now, George dear, your mother isn't one of those stuffy Pu-
ritans. Belle is a very attractive young woman and I certainly
don't blame you for wantin' to kiss her. I'd far rather you were
with her than with some schemin' little Junior Leaguer."

"Mother!" George stared at her as if he couldn't believe his
ears. I was sure my own ears were turning the same color as my
hair. Who ever heard of a mother talking like that right in front
of her son's date? What she meant was all too plain: a Junior
Leaguer he'd have to marry, but not me!

Meanwhile Beatrice was studying her watch, and now she
said, "It's after eleven. I suppose the drugstore is closed by now,
isn't it, Mrs.—uh—Belle?"

I just nodded.

"Well, in that case—" She got up and came over to me. "I
wonder if I could ask you for a little favor. Would you please
call Harry White at home—" She glanced at her watch again.

"—I think he should be home by now—and ask him to come back to the store?"

"What?" Was Beatrice Parkland going off her rocker?

"I'm askin' you to call Harry and tell him to come back to the store. You can make up some excuse. Tell him there's an emergency or somethin'—"

Gary Cooper woke up. "Mother! What in the world—"

"George," she said, "just stay out of this for the moment, please."

I stood up, I couldn't believe what she was asking me to do. "Oh, I couldn't bother Harry like that. He's probably in bed—"

Before I could even finish, she opened the little beaded clutch bag she never put down and took out something she pointed at me. A lipstick it wasn't.

A gun? That's right, a real, honest-to-goodness automatic.

What did Appleman do? Just what she did when she saw Dr. Fu Manchu on the screen. She froze.

"What're you doing, Mother?" George tried to step between us, but she waved him away with the gun. "What's come over you? Is this some sort of joke?"

"Joke? Perhaps. Just don't interfere, George," she said as if he was ten years old. "Some things have happened about which you know nothin'. And I have to take care of 'em. Just leave this all to my better judgment. Haven't all my decisions been the right ones for you?"

George looked at me. He seemed stunned. He opened his mouth and then closed it again.

I gave one more try. "Mrs. Parkland, it's foolish to try anything, you'll just make things worse—"

She gave the gun a wave. "That's enough, Belle. I know all about the little visit you paid Herlihy. Just do as I say, make that call."

What could I do? Gary Cooper sure wasn't whistling for his white horse to gallop us out. There was a telephone on an end table near the door. I walked over, Beatrice following with the gun, and dialed Harry's number. He answered with a grumpy hello.

"Harry," I said, "it's Belle. Listen, can you come back to the store right this minute?"

"What? Belle, where are you? What's wrong, tell me!"

"Harry, listen, it's a real emergency! I can't tell you on the phone. Just get in the car and hurry back."

"Wait a minute, is it a fire? What's going on?"

"Plenty, believe me!"

"Boy," he barked, "this better be good!"

"Harry," I said real quick, "who won at cribbage?" But I wasn't sure he heard that, he hung up so fast.

"What was that you told him?" Beatrice asked. "About a game?"

I thought fast. "It's a game he plays, I wanted him to think that all this was on the level—"

"Oh? Well, now we'll just sit down for a while and give Harry a chance to get there." With the gun she waved me over to a ladderback chair.

"George," I said, "what's going on? What does your mother want from me and Harry? Please get her to stop this craziness—please, before it's too late—"

George sat down like a child that learned to obey or be whipped. When he spoke, it seemed to me that the George who held and kissed me before wasn't there any more. He couldn't even look me in the eye. "We'd better do what my mother says," he said in a flat, tired voice, like he was a mechanical man somebody wound up with a key.

So I sat. The clock ticked. Oh, Appleman, I thought, why didn't you listen to Harry way back about George? Next time you want a handsome man around, go better to the Loew's Orpheum and watch Clark Gable. If there was even going to be a next time.

"George, dear?" Beatrice told him to go in the study and get her a shopping bag on the desk. He did just as she told him, then sat down again.

Finally he spoke. "Mother, what're you trying to do here? I can't see what Belle has to do with—"

"Trust me, darlin'," she crooned, "believe me, it's all for your own good, isn't it always?"

He slumped back in his chair. I just couldn't understand why he was doing exactly what his mother said. "Look, Mrs. Parkland," I said, "what if I did talk to Herlihy? He didn't tell me one thing about Revak getting killed."

She got up and waved the gun again. "That's enough, Belle, it's time to go. George, please take the bag."

He picked it up, still not looking at me, and we filed out of the house and into his car. He drove, while Beatrice sat next to me in back, keeping the gun stuck in my ribs. It didn't take us two minutes to park in front of the Charles Street Pharmacy. I looked out the window. Not a person in the street, just cars racing by. Why didn't I give Harry that hint sooner? Some detective you are, Appleman.

A car came down Charles Street and parked in back of us. The headlights went out and Harry opened the car door. Beatrice motioned for me to get out. She and George followed, him with the shopping bag.

Harry's mouth opened. "What's going on? What is this?" He stared at Beatrice. "I thought there was a robbery or something—"

"Good evenin', Harry," said Beatrice, like she was inviting him to a cocktail party. "Let's all go into the store, shall we?"

Aha, I thought, one thing she doesn't know. Harry has a gun in his desk drawer. So when we get into the back room, I'll—

Then I remembered. Harry's gun was in ballistics, getting tested for that second bullet. All because I told Jim about it.

Appleman, you did it again.

thirty-two

We stood in the light of a street lamp as a frowning Harry searched in his pocket for the store keys.

It was a warm, muggy night, with hardly a breeze at all, my fancy dress was sticking to me. Felt like rain, too bad it wasn't pouring cats and dogs, maybe Beatrice would've stayed at her sister's. If she even had a sister. By now everything the Parklands said seemed to be a pack of lies. She used Coty's Emeraude, must've bathed in it. I used to like that but now the aroma of it when she stood close to me made me feel sick.

Where were all the people in the neighborhood? No passersby at all, on a summer night? A siren gave a scream somewhere far away, a car whizzed by, and George's face in the shadows didn't tell me a thing. What if I tried to make a run for it? But where could I run to, in the open street? Would Gary Cooper stop his crazy mother from shooting me down? He didn't seem to have the energy to even think for himself.

Nu, Appleman, this time you took too long to figure things out. Some detective you are, wasting all that time on the other Revak-haters. Dope, why didn't you start with Herlihy? And then you had to go falling for George. Would Mrs. Thin Man let herself get bamboozled by a doctor that's scared of his own mother?

Harry finally got the key out, unlocked the door, pushed it open, and we all filed in behind him, George, me, and then Beatrice with her gun. "In the back room, Harry, please," she ordered us in her grand-lady style, and let the front door slam behind her. Harry always left on the back-room light for a night light, so we could see where we were going. Now he didn't even try to put on the big lights. Too bad, maybe somebody would notice.

"You," Beatrice snapped, waving the gun in my face, "sit!" She pointed to the desk chair. Where was the polite lady now? It was more like the way people talked to a doggie, I almost said bow-wow, but you don't swap jokes with a gun. I sat.

What was this *meshugeneh* going to do? Could Harry and I jump on her together and get the gun away? I tried to catch his eye, but his gaze was fixed on Beatrice like she put him under a spell, just like George. So neither man was going to be any help.

Harry's eyes bulged as he threw the keys down on the prescription counter. "Bea, for God's sake, what's going on? Tell me, what is it?"

Bea?

How come no gushing "Mrs. Parkland" this time? So, Harry, maybe your Rosalie wasn't so far off the beam like I thought. Oho, plenty must've gone on the night you went to Bea's house and she asked you for a little favor. What was she wearing, a sheer kimono that barely met?

Just a word or two with a guy on the State Medical Board, named Herlihy. You told me you didn't get a penny out of the deal, you sounded proud of that. Not money, no. But how often did you make visits to her afterwards, when George was working? No wonder you were always running out of the store for "a breath of fresh air"! And of course you tried to keep me from going out with George—I might find out about your love-nest.

"Harry," Beatrice answered in that Southern lilt (who knew if she was even from the South, maybe South Boston) "a li'l problem's come up that puts us all in jeopardy. So I've worked out a way to solve it, that's all."

Harry's jaw was working up and down. "Bea, for cryin' out loud, what's the gun for?" He moved toward her.

"Stay right where you are! Don't come one step closer!" she barked.

"Sweetheart, what're you saying? It's me, Harry, you can tell me anything—"

"Mother!" George woke up. "You mean to tell me that you and he—you and a married man—how could you? It's—it's disgusting!"

"You got a nerve, Parkland," Harry said. "Stay out of this! Your mother's a saint, she turned the world upside down just to pull your irons out of the fire! Why the hell couldn't you take your medicine like a man, everything got loused up just on account of saving your skin!"

"You bastard!" George practically spit at Harry. "A married man taking advantage of her!"

"She was worried sick over you!" Harry yelled back. "I stuck my neck out for you!"

"Now calm down, Harry," Beatrice said in her snooty way. "It wasn't George's fault at all. He's a born doctor and he's worked his head off. And no little buttinsky is going to wreck things now, Mrs. Applesnoop!" She glared at me. "George, darlin', please take that rope out of the bag." His brow wrinkled but he obeyed. "Now tie that foxy schemer up tight in the chair, dear."

Tie her up? She was talking about Appleman! "Say, listen—" I began.

"This is crazy!" Harry's head swiveled from Beatrice to George and back to me. "Crazy! You can't—"

"You're not serious, mother!" George's whole face shone with sweat.

"Oh, yes I am," she said quietly. "I have it all worked out. Trust me, it's the only way."

"Now just a minute, Bea, you can't—"

But she poked the gun in his face. "Quiet, Harry! Go ahead, George dear. Get it over with, get the job done."

"Harry!" I yelled. "Call Jim, don't just stand there, quick!"

Harry put his hand out toward the phone.

"Don't touch that phone, Harry!" Beatrice waved the gun again like an orchestra leader with a baton. "George, stop dawdling, hurry and do as I say!"

"But, Mother, can't you see, this is all wrong?" He was begging like a kid who's been told to do the supper dishes.

"Just do it, darlin', trust me." She giggled. "Y'all think I'm batty, don't you?" Was she on drugs of some kind, too? From George's bag, of course. But who tells people with guns that they're crazy?

Suddenly George was actually tying my arms to the back of the chair. "George! What're you doing? You know better, you went to Harvard!" He didn't say a word, just kept on tying. "George, you took an oath to help people, not hurt them, remember?"

Was Gary Cooper under a spell? He was an athlete, big and muscular, why didn't he grab the gun from his mother and put a stop to the nightmare? "George, look at me, it's Belle! What about Colorado, how can you do this to me!" But he just kept his eyes on what he was doing.

Into my mind flashed a memory of a play Daniel took me to see once at the Wilbur Theater, called *The Silver Cord*. About a widow with two sons who can't stand to give them up to any woman. One is married, so he gets away. But the younger one has to choose between his mother or going with the girl he loves. The mother nearly kills the girl by letting her ice-skate on their melting pond.

At the end, the son stays with the mother and loses the girl. And the actor who played the son seemed at the end of the play to be just like George was now. Blind to what was happening, deaf to me, only hearing and obeying what his mother told him.

Funny, you see something like that on the stage, you think, it's only a play, it couldn't really happen like that. Well, Belle Appleman has news for you, it happens.

Appleman, you got to keep this crazy woman talking, stall for time. "So, Beatrice, now I got it figured out. You got some head on you, all right. You killed Revak and fixed things so Eddie would be blamed. Shooting Eddie's gun into the same hole from your bullet, that was genius!"

Harry woke up. "Bea! How on earth did you learn to shoot like that?" He sounded proud of her, imagine.

Two men, George and Harry, now mush instead of men. They both gaped at Beatrice.

She smiled. "Southern ladies always learn to shoot and ride. Mah daddy taught me."

"Oh? One thing bothers me," I said, "the part about Eddie. How did you know he would come with a gun?"

She shrugged. "Well, I didn't, of course. But if he didn't bring the gun, I would've hit him on the head and put my gun in his hand."

She was no dope. "Pretty lucky that Sol Borofsky came along and did it for you," I said. Would Jim ever get the message from Rafferty that I called? A lot of good it would do, he'd just phone my apartment and get no answer. And Harry never heard my hint about playing cribbage, or didn't stop to figure out what I meant, he sure didn't call Jim.

"You're right, that was lucky." Beatrice smoothed back her ash-blonde hair with her free hand. "It made no difference which of the two came after I called them."

"So, you were the voice on the phone!" A little late you're putting things together, Appleman. "And you pulled the card with your name on it out of Revak's file—George never knew about the blackmail—"

George gave a gasp. "Mother, why didn't you tell me all this, why didn't you let me handle it?"

Harry snorted. "When did you ever handle anything? She shouldered all the burdens, all you had to do was play doctor. Why didn't you just take the stinking exam over again, for cryin' out loud!"

"George, I wanted to spare you the horrid details." Her voice poured syrup on him. "So you could put your mind on your work. That's why I'm doin' all this, don't you see? Now tie up her feet, darlin', it's got to be done, get it over with—"

"Mother!" George was half-sobbing. "You don't know what you're asking!"

"Bea," said Harry, "have a heart—"

"Now, George." Beatrice was commanding a regiment. "I'm gettin' one of my awful migraines. What're you doin' to me? Just do your job, we all have nasty jobs to do but it's our duty—"

A white-faced George began again to obey his mother.

"But you didn't plan to kill Herlihy," I said. Talking was helping to keep my mind off the rope he was tying around me.

"No, not till I followed you to his office. I knew that drunken sot wouldn't keep his mouth shut. See the trouble you caused? It's all your fault!"

"And I'm guessing," I went on, "that you drove the car that almost hit me on Allen Street—and my pal, too." How long could I stall her?

"A clear warnin'," she snapped, "when I found out you were stickin' your nose into Revak's death. But you didn't take it seriously, did you. Too bad. That was *your* mistake." Her eyes glittered with hate. "And leadin' on my George, what gall—"

"*True Detective* magazine should've taught me about killing, that women are tougher than men," I said. I wouldn't give her the satisfaction of denying that I led on her darling boy. Led on, ha!, he did his own leading when mama wasn't on the scene.

"It's the price we women have to pay sometime," Beatrice declared, "to protect our children. And no price is too high to protect my George. He's the one who matters. Herlihy and Revak were loose ends that needed tyin' up. And you're a loose end, too, Mrs. Applesnoop, with your endless sniffin' around—"

"Wait a minute, Bea," Harry said. "You can't mean that! After all, I know about Herlihy, too!"

"Yes, Harry, and I wish you didn't." Beatrice eyed him. "Because that makes you a loose end, also." She pointed the gun at him. "Too bad, you were very entertainin'—"

"Bea, you said you were crazy about me! I'm wild about you, you know that!" He started toward her, arms raised as if to embrace her.

"Get back, now! I'm sorry, Harry, really, you were very amusing. But George comes before any man."

And before I could even open my mouth to scream, the gun went off BANG.

thirty-three

Harry slumped back against the prescription counter. Then he fell down.

George's mouth opened and his face turned ashy. He gave a strangled gasp.

"My God, George," I yelled at him, "your mother just killed Harry, she's really crazy! Do something! Take away her gun! You're bigger than she is!"

"Oh, my George knows that what I'm doing is for his own good, don't you, darlin'?"

He glanced down at me, tied up in the chair like a mummy from Egypt I saw in the Art Museum. Then he looked at Beatrice. "Mother, I never left you, did I? Didn't you believe me when I promised you that I wouldn't?"

"Of course, dear, but you are a man, and lately you've had your mind on a woman, so anything can happen—especially with a connivin' type like her—"

"Listen, Beatrice—" I talked fast, listening to me would give George a chance to grab the gun away. "What you're doing will never work! Too many people know the story already. Look, I myself told Jim the detective all about you and Herlihy, it's no secret no more—"

"*Any* more, your English is a disgrace. And who do you think you are, Sherlock Holmes?" she said. "The police know very little, actually. You see, I called the station and talked to a young fellow with a lovely Irish brogue—what was his name,

Rafferty?—and he told me that they were looking for a John Hicks. That's their chief suspect in the Revak case. Do you know who this Hicks is?"

"He's Marcia's brother. You know, the girl behind the fountain in the drugstore—"

"Oh, the blonde. How was her brother involved with Revak?"

Good, a chance to keep her talking. "Well, it seems Revak made a big play for her. She thought he was going to marry her, she believed his lies. Then, when he dropped her, she thought she was pregnant. So John got furious at the way Revak treated her. And he has a whole collection of guns. So he—"

"That's enough. It's plenty to keep the police busy," she said, swinging the gun. "They'll never suspect me."

"George, listen," I said, trying to get his eye, "you can't go along with cold-blooded murder! She's making a bigger mess every minute! You still got a chance, you didn't kill yet—"

"George, dear," said Beatrice, "there's an ampoule of five-percent cocaine solution and a syringe in the bag. You know what you have to do. Just get it over with, that's the only way."

"But, Mother," he began, "this is different, don't you see?" He moistened his lips. "It's not Belle's fault, let her alone. I promise—we'll go away together, mother—Rio, Buenos Aires, anyplace you say. We can leave tonight!" His forehead knotted. "How do you know about cocaine? Did Harry—"

"Darlin', my head is splittin', don't try to sidetrack me. Can't you see, this way we'll be in the clear from now on? And how could you fall for such a woman, she doesn't even speak proper English!"

"I do, too!" I yelled. "Miss Wallace gave me an A in Evening English!" Who cared about grammar rules right now, anyhow. "What solution? What are you pushing George to do?"

"Very simple and foolproof," she said with her ritzy air.

"George will inject a solution of cocaine into your vein. Won't hurt a bit, he'll tell you that. In fact, you'll positively enjoy it! When the police find you they'll know you were a drug addict.

"Drug addict? What're you talking about?" I shouted.

"Ah, we'll put this gun in your hand. You came in, asked Harry for cocaine, he refused, so you shot him. Then you opened the narcotics cabinet and injected yourself. With an overdose, unfortunately. You see, all the loose ends will be tied up." She smiled at George.

An addict, yet! How could she figure out such a plan? But then, she killed Revak and made it look like someone else did, and fooled everybody. Only George was more of a surprise to me than Beatrice. After all, I thought I knew him. Where was the baseball player, the pitcher? A tall athlete with powerful arms, why didn't he grab Beatrice from behind and make her drop the gun? He stood there like a *shlemiel*.

"Hurry, darlin', we've got to get this over with." Beatrice glanced at her watch.

In the silence I could hear a train puffing into the North Station yards, I wished I was on it. Appleman, I told myself, you got to THINK! There must be a way out of this if I just put my mind on it. When would the cop on the beat come by, he might hear a lot of yelling? Who knew what time it would be?

Appleman, never mind the detective stuff, you're a woman, can't you reach George? Imagine, just a short time ago he was holding you close and raining kisses down your throat. Why not whisper something in his ear—?

But he wouldn't look at me, he was reaching into that miserable canvas bag and taking out a hypodermic syringe and a tiny bottle with a rubber top. He took a deep breath, then stuck the needle through the top and drew out the stuff inside. It looked like plain water.

"George, what're you doing?" I screamed. "When you became a doctor you swore to help people, not kill them! If she's a nut, that's her funeral, not yours!" What was it they said in baseball? "Don't strike out, George! She takes the stuff all the time, just look at her eyes!"

"Never mind her," scolded Beatrice. "What does she know, she's only an immigrant. You have a real mission in life, that's what matters."

"Immigrant, what do you mean?" I yelled. "I'm an American citizen, I've got the papers to prove it!"

"Mother, don't you see?" George was begging her. "This'll never work—I just can't do this—"

"What? Of course it'll work! And you can do it, it'll all be over in a few minutes, this is no time for silly sentimentality! You'll have lots of girls—"

He wriggled his head around as if he was in pain. Then he took a deep breath, reached in the bag, and yanked out a piece of rubber tubing.

"George—" My throat was so dry, it didn't sound like me. "Don't you remember how we danced under the stars—and what about Colorado—the ranch—and the mountains—"

"Colorado? What are you up to!" Beatrice shoved the gun right under my nose. "You shut up, I know your kind! Leadin' a man on, usin' every trick in the book, I saw how you behaved in my own house! One more word and I'll gag you!"

George pushed up my sleeve and tied the rubber tubing around the top part of my arm. He rubbed the inside of my elbow for a minute. Then he tipped up the syringe, pressed the plunger, and shot a little stream into the air.

"George, look at me—please don't do this—" My throat was parched and my stomach was jumping up and down.

He turned to Beatrice. "Mother, I can't do it—" It sounded as if he was crying.

"Oh? Then I'll just shoot myself, is that what you want?" She put the gun to her forehead. "It'll be your hand pullin' the trigger, darlin'—"

"No, no, don't!" he yelled. "All right, you win, you always do!" He picked up my arm and stuck the needle into a blue vein that was getting fat in the middle of my elbow. Then he pulled the tubing away and let it drop on the floor. His thumb began pushing on the plunger.

"George," I moaned. "I'll go away with you—"

But then things started to happen. I noticed the back-room light was getting brighter. I looked at the bottles on the prescription shelves. Funny, the labels were so clear. TINCT. OPII, SYR. CERASI, ELIX. SIMPLEX. I looked at Beatrice's face, every line stood out like rivers on a map of Massachusetts. Nothing Harriet Hubbard Ayer made would ever make her look young again.

I couldn't move, but my heart started to beat faster and faster. My brain tried to sort out stuff. I knew where I was, I knew what was happening.

But it all felt so good, who cared. That was some stuff he was putting in my arm, all right!

My eyes followed George's thumb, it stopped moving, it left the plunger. My ears heard him saying something. Was he actually talking back to his mother? She was screaming at him.

Then the thumb came back to the plunger and moved it a little bit forward. I wasn't interested, I didn't care about a thing. Things around me were happening on a big movie screen. This was better than the Wilbur Theater.

The back-room light got even brighter. The bottles and cans of medicine started to move on the shelves. My heart was banging like the drum in Jimmy Dorsey's band. I wanted to stop it but I didn't know how. Noises started to come into my ears, first from far away and then nearer. I heard a sharp bang, like a firecracker, was this the Fourth of July?

Then I thought I heard my name, Belle, Belle, being called way up somewhere. Daniel, helping me, telling me to come join him in heaven. I tried hard to get up out of the chair to go to him.

But first the top of my head with all my hair was going to blow right through the ceiling.

thirty-four

I opened my eyes, where was I? Everything was a fuzzy white and my head ached. But it couldn't be heaven, the white figure bending over me wasn't my Daniel, no such luck. Not even an angel. Anyway, heaven would've had whiffs of Chanel No. 5, or something like it. This place made my nose wrinkle up. "Something smells awful . . ."

"I'm Dr. Bancroft," said the figure in white, "and this is the Mass. General Hospital. How do you feel? That's just the smell of ether."

I wriggled my feet under the bedclothes. "Okay, I guess. Everything looks fuzzy—"

"That'll pass, you're going to be all right," he said. "You had a narrow escape, now just rest. You have some visitors, but they can't stay long."

The white figure melted into Sarah, wearing a halo. Or was it a straw hat? "Belle! You're breathing! *Gottenyu*, you're really alive!"

A face with glasses showed up next to Sarah's. "Belle? You're okay? We got you just in time!"

"Nate? Sarah?" My mind was working like a clogged sink. "What happened? How did I get here?"

The halo bobbed up and down. "We took you in the car. You weren't awake, you looked something terrible, we were scared to death—"

The deeper voice spoke. "The doctor said you had anaphy-
lactic shock, we were worried plenty—"

A movie screen with pictures in it lit up in my head. Beatrice
Parkland pointing the gun. Harry falling down, blood spilling
from his head. George's hands tying the rubber tubing on my
arm—getting the needle ready—sticking it in my vein—his
thumb pushing the plunger.

Those pictures who wanted to watch? "How did you know
where I was?" I asked.

"Because—" Sarah and Nate started to talk at the same time.
But he was a gentleman and waved his hand at her.

"When you didn't call by eleven-thirty, after that date, I
started to get worried," she said. "By midnight I was plenty
scared. So I called Nate. And he right away called up—oh, here
he is—"

"Top of the mornin', and how's our lovely patient this fine
day?" A new voice in the room. Things were getting clearer, it
was Jim, at last. He bent over the bed. "Belle, m'darlin', does my
heart good to see you alive and kicking. Doc says you'll be good
as new."

When Jim uses all that blarney, he's usually good and mad.
"So you finally got to the store, Jim. Oh, how I prayed for you
to show up! What happened? Harry's dead, no?"

"Harry? He's got a tough hide, don't you worry about him.
In a room just across the hall."

"Harry? But she killed him with that gun! I saw the blood!"

"Oh, the bullet hit him, all right, but it just creased his skull."
Jim grinned. "Luck of the Irish!"

"But the blood—you're just kidding me—"

"Pretty common in head wounds, Belle. Plenty of bleeding,
but it's mostly from those little capillary blood vessels. I remember one night when I got called to an accident at a carni-

val. Had a new ride called the loop-the-loop. Dumb guy standing right under it got whacked plunk on the head. Everyone
thought he was a goner from all that blood. Turned out all he
had was a big scratch and a headache."

I let out a giant sigh. "Thank God! And thanks, Jim, for
saving my life. I tried to call you—"

"Don't thank me, thank Nate. Why, he's been keeping watch
over you from that first night when that crazy woman tried to
run you down on Allen Street."

"It was nothing, just out getting some fresh air," said Nate.

"Nothing?" Jim asked. "After you staying up night after night
to make sure she got home safe?"

So now I knew why I had that feeling someone was watching me. No wonder Nate was right there to help me when John
Hicks pushed his way into my place.

"And last night, when Parkland picked you up, Nate made a
note of the make of his car and the license number. As soon as
Nate called me to say Sarah hadn't heard from you, I picked
them up. We drove all over the West End trying to spot the car.
Until Nate had a hunch to check the drugstore."

I reached my hand out to Nate. "Thanks a million, thanks
for everything."

He took it and squeezed it for a second. "My pleasure."

"Nate's worth a hundred doctors, see, I was right," Sarah said.

"What got me," Jim went on, "was that when we got there,
the lock on the front door was open. So we just ran in! There
you were, tied in the chair, knocked out, Harry on the floor.
And George Parkland—" He stopped.

The picture of Beatrice holding the gun to her own head
came into my mind. What happened after I passed out? How
come I wasn't dead like she planned? That last camera shot I
had of George's thumb on the plunger—that was the way to
finish me off.

"What about George?" I asked at last.

Nobody spoke for a minute.

Finally Jim said, "I'm sorry, Belle. He's dead."

"Dead?" I couldn't believe it. "What do you mean dead?"

"We finally got the story out of Mrs. Parkland, but it wasn't easy, she was in pretty bad shape. It seems George refused to finish injecting the cocaine into you, so she decided to shoot you. He argued with her and tried to get the gun away from her. While they were struggling, it went off. And killed him. When we came in she was holding him in her arms like a baby, hysterical and raving."

A shiver went through me. Imagine, Beatrice killed George herself. I couldn't help saying out loud a line from a poem that Daniel used to read to me, it always made me feel sad: "'Yet each man kills the thing he loves—'"

"'By all let this be heard,'" Jim continued it. "'The brave man does it with a knife, The coward with a word.'"

Sarah and Nate stared at him.

"Jim knows lots of poetry by heart," I told them. "Listen, Jim, I'll bet that bullet in the wall in Revak's house'll be a good match with Beatrice's gun." He nodded. "And she's the one pushed Herlihy in front of the train." I told them what I found out about George's license. "Beatrice was convinced she knew what was best for her son. Poor George, he never got away from her." Colorado I wouldn't mention.

"Mother love gone haywire, it seems. Well, now," Jim said, putting on the brogue again, "I won't say what I'd like to till you're recovered. It was foolish you were to take such a chance."

"I know, I know. But we caught the murderer, no?"

"That we did."

"Wait, Jim, what about John Hicks?"

"He's off the hook for the Revak murder, of course. But that club of his, the Boston Patriots—well, the Commissioner let them know he wasn't exactly happy about what they were plan-ning to do. So we won't be hearing much about them in the future." His smile disappeared. "Nate told me what Hicks was doing in your apartment. I'd be happy to pick him up on an assault charge, if you want."

I shook my head. "No, Marcia's had enough trouble, and her family, too."

"Ah, you're blessed with a heart. But one thing does puzzle me. How come the front door of the store was open? Doesn't it lock automatically again when it closes?"

I began to laugh.

"What's so funny?"

"It's funny because the door lock used to be that kind. But Harry told me he got sick and tired of putting the key back in the lock from the inside every day, the door should stay open. So he put in the kind, I forget the name, where you open it once with the key and it stays. You got no place to put the key in from the inside, just a little handle."

"Oh, a dead-bolt lock," Jim said, nodding, "and she didn't notice."

"What life is," said Sarah, shaking her head. "Living and dy-ing, sometimes it depends on such teeny things—"

"In any case," Jim said, "the Department is mighty grateful to you for solving the Revak murder. You'll have to be our chief witness for the prosecution—"

"That I wouldn't miss," I told him.

The door flew open and a frizzy-haired nurse marched in. "Mrs. Appleman has had quite enough company for now!"

"I'll be in touch, Belle. And if you ever want to hang out your shingle as a private eye—" Jim winked, then he bent down and gave me a kiss on the cheek.

"I'll come by in the morning," said Sarah, and kissed me. "See, I brought you a plant." She pointed to a geranium on the sill.

"And that fellow brought flowers," said the nurse, nodding toward Nate. On the bedside table was a vase filled with gorgeous red roses. "Oh, thanks, Sarah, Nate, I owe so much to you both—"

Nate kissed my cheek also. "Belle—"

But the nurse shooed him and the others out the door, saying, "Try to get some sleep, Mrs. Appleman."

Everything they told me was spinning around in my head. George dead, was it possible? Dead because he tried to keep me alive, in spite of his mother. So I was wrong, he was no *shlemiel* at all, he died defending me. A real hero. I worried so much if he was serious about me, I hardly thought whether I was serious about him. So I was guilty, too.

If I had agreed to run away to Colorado with him, he'd still be alive.

thirty-five

The door of my room opened again and a bandaged head stuck through.

"Belle!" It was Harry, in a striped bathrobe. He was holding a blue china automobile with a plant in it. "Rosalie left this with me to give you."

"Harry—I'm so glad to see you alive! Tell Rosalie thanks, it can go on the windowsill."

He set down the plant and turned around. "Belle—I—I don't know what to say—except thank God you're here—"

"Harry, there's nothing left to say, it's all over but the shouting."

"But it was all my fault, I'm the guilty one!" he burst out. "If I'd told you sooner about Herlihy and—and Beatrice, you would've guessed that she—she—" His voice got chokey and he slumped down in the chair near my bed.

"Harry, stop blaming yourself for the whole thing." I put out my hand and touched his. "You're not the only guilty party. Life isn't a map you can follow, we all get a little *tsemish*, sometimes. But you got to forgive yourself, nobody's perfect, nobody on this earth, anyway."

"But I had everything, and I made such a mess of it—" He couldn't look at me.

"Look, the important thing is you should make up with Rosalie. You've got a wonderful wife, make sure you hold on to her, don't let this business break you up."

"Easy for you to say." He rubbed his eyes with his fist. "I didn't get up the nerve to tell Rosalie the whole story yet . . ."

"So don't tell her the whole story." My own words surprised me.

He gaped. "What do you mean?"

"Look, Harry, a squealer I'm not. So maybe it's better the business with Beatrice gets buried along with Herlihy and Revak. Tell her about the gambling, how it was all driving you crazy. Tell her about the blackmail with George's license. It's enough, she'll believe you. More nightmares she doesn't need." She sure didn't need to hear where Beatrice got her cocaine.

"But is that fair to her?"

"Fair-shmair! Sure, you'd feel better to get the whole thing off your chest. But she'd maybe never get over it, and neither would your marriage. So go better and have a session with Arnie Silverstein, he's a terrific psychiatrist. And don't make more aggravation for Rosalie, she's had enough. You got to make a whole new start together."

Harry finally looked right at me. "Gee, I'm glad you feel that way, Belle, you've got a real head on you. Besides, I already began on a new start. A few weeks ago I got an offer for the store. Truth is, I'm sick and tired of the whole pharmacy racket. Owning my own place, look what happened."

"No kidding, you're going to sell the store?"

"On the level. This guy, Nathan Miller, comes from Newton, he's buying the store with his wife."

"With his wife?"

"Yeah." He looked down at the floor again. "This part I hate to tell you, Belle. She knows cosmetics. So he's keeping Marcia and Jerry for the fountain. But your job, I'm afraid—"

"I got the picture, Harry." I leaned back. "*Nu*, maybe Nate can get me back in the factory. Don't worry, I'll make out. How about you, what'll you do?"

"For years Rosalie's brother's been asking me to come in with him in the auto parts business. Let him be the big boss with the headaches, this way I'll sleep nights."

"*Mazel tov*," I said. "I'm glad the bullet only gave you a part in your hair!"

"Thank God George finally stopped taking his mother's advice with that injection," Harry said. He came over and gave me a kiss on the cheek. "See you later, Belle. And don't worry about the cost of all this." He waved a hand. "The private room is on the Charles Street Pharmacy."

"Thanks a million, Harry," I told him, "you're a sport."

He waved another kiss to me before he closed the door. A minute later, before I could even shut my eyes, the door swung open again and in came Arnie Silverstein.

"Belle!" He bent over, gave me a big smack on the cheek, and put a box at the foot of the bed. Five pounds of Schrafft's chocolates. "I came soon as I heard! Are you all right?"

"You know me, Arnie, I always bounce back."

He sat down in the chair. "Good for you. But listen, Belle, I don't know quite how to say this—"

"What? What is it, Arnie?"

His round face was serious. "I have to take back that offer of marriage I made—things've changed—"

I almost asked him what offer. The whole thing had almost slipped my mind. So I gave him my Bette Davis big-eyed look and said, "Oh? What happened?"

"My wife changed her mind. So we're going to try it together again."

"Your first wife or your second?"

"Second. Maybe we can work it out this time." He took off the cover of the box of chocolates. "Five pounds is their biggest size, I asked. Go ahead, have one, Belle. No? I will, I'm starving." He picked one out and chewed it. "Mm, a caramel."

He eyed me. "I hope I haven't hurt your feelings too much, Belle?"

I shook my head no. "It's all right, Arnie, we'll always be friends. Tell me, what do you think of the whole business? You knew Beatrice Parkland. Could you believe that about a woman like her—intelligent, educated, rich—she had everything!"

Arnie's eyebrows twitched. "Everything? Most of my patients are people like that. By your standards they have everything—me, too—" He picked out an oblong chocolate and chewed it.

"So what made her do such things, Arnie? All right, mothers worry. But George was so good to her! And what did she need that cocaine stuff for?"

"Hey, Belle, I didn't know George that well, and I hardly knew his mother." Arnie studied the chocolates like they were a painting. "Anyway, you don't need a whole lecture on obsessive maternal love, you were there. So you know her whole case history, right?" He glanced at his watch. "Hey, got to run, Muriel's waiting. Get better fast, so we can see you in the store, Belle." He grabbed a couple chocolates, threw me a kiss, and hurried out.

"No, you won't," I muttered to his back going out. Goodbye, Arnie. Goodbye, townhouse on Mount Vernon Street. I shlepped the box of chocolates over and put it on the table for the nurses to nibble. At last, time to lean back and close my eyes.

Imagine how much started with a girl coming in the drugstore and collapsing. Still, by now the whole puzzle got practically solved—except for the most important part. The heart of the whole affair.

What was the answer to why Clara Borofsky did what she did?

You've never been in a private room in the Mass. General, you haven't lived. Some difference from the City Hospital— even a telephone next to the bed!

A phone. That made a thought at the back of my head come back. I called Information, got Fay Winkler's number, and dialed.

"Sure I remember. How are you, Belle?" she said.

"Listen, I was wondering if you ever remembered anything else about what I asked you. You know, the day you told me Marcus Plaut carried Jenny Borofsky's kid upstairs?"

"Funny you should call. Just the other night I couldn't sleep, it was so hot, so I was thinking about it. And I did remember something else."

"What?" I straightened up. "What did you remember?"

"I remembered it happened the time Hilda's sister in Worcester was having a birthday party for her son, so Hilda took the boys and went there for a couple days. Why I remember is my own boy, Erwin, complained to me there was nobody around to play with, Hilda's kids were away. So that's it. Does that help at all?"

Goosebumps popped out on my arms. "Absolutely! Thanks a million, Fay, you really made my day!" My head began to swim, so I sank back on the pillow.

Puzzles are a cinch when you got all the pieces. I began putting together what Fay told me with what she remembered when I saw her. So I didn't even hear the door opening. When I looked up Eddie Plaut was standing there with a pile of magazines in his arms. *True Detective* was on top.

"Hi, how do you feel?" he asked, coming closer.

"Who's taking care of the store?"

He laughed. "I knew you'd ask. Relax, we got that other fellow back, Milt."

"Only this time you're not in jail." I smiled at him.

His mouth twitched as he put the magazines down next to Arnie's chocolates. "Thanks to you."

"Sit down, Eddie, I got to talk to you . . . I think got it figured out at last. Why your Clara had to—do what she did."

His eyes opened wide. He leaned forward.

It wasn't easy to tell him. "See, Sol Borofsky was a salesman then, away on the road a lot. And Clara's mother was left alone with her young children. One day when the youngest girl— was that Zelda?" He nodded. "—was small, she took a tumble on the sidewalk. Your mother was away visiting your aunt in Worcester, but your father was home—"

Eddie interrupted. "Oh, we used to visit my aunt's in Worcester, sure, but I don't see—"

"Zelda was moaning, and your father ran out and picked her up and carried her upstairs to her mother. On the way he told a neighbor, 'She had a nasty fall.' I found that neighbor and she still remembers the whole thing."

"What're you getting at?"

He was no baby, he had to know. "You got to remember, this was a long time ago. We're talking now about two very young people, younger than you are now probably, one of them's maybe very upset. Maybe Clara's mother was worried sick if her little one hurt herself real bad with that fall, had a concussion or even worse. And your father was trying hard to help her out, he got pretty upset, too. And he was trying to calm her down. So you know how it is when you're young and alone together—"

His brow wrinkled. "I'm not sure I'm getting your drift—"

"You're young yourself, no? Two young people thrown together, one thing leads to another—"

He sat bolt upright. "You mean my father and Jennie's mother—I don't believe it!"

"Eddie, stop and think. What went so wrong between the two families, yours and Clara's? Maybe there were bad feelings from the old country mixed in, one German family, one Eastern European. But would Clara's father and mother have been so strong against you two—and your folks—stop and think—"

He gave a groan. "That's what I could never get—my father's never had any kind of prejudice, never—it didn't make sense that he was so set on breaking us up—he wouldn't even listen—"

"But, Eddie, don't you see why? Maybe Clara could've been—well—"

He jumped up. "My God! Clara might have been my sister!"

Poor Eddie, it was a lot to dump on him. I put on my Fay Bainter wise-owl face. "Maybe they weren't sure. But Clara's mother and your father must've know it was a possibility. So you can imagine how they felt when you and Clara wanted to get married. They had to join in and try to break it up between you, what else could they do? On top of the whole mishmash, such a secret—what a burden!"

Eddie's jaw was tight, he sat down slowly. "And my mother, did she find out? And Mr. Borofsky?"

I gave a shrug. "Who knows?"

"But why didn't Clara—"

"Don't you see? When Clara told her mother she was really going to marry you, Jennie must've panicked. So she told Clara the truth. But Clara couldn't tell her mother she was already pregnant. You can imagine how she felt—her own brother, even her half-brother, the father of her baby? She couldn't even tell you. So what could she do, poor thing? She broke off with you and went to Revak to have the abortion."

"My God!" Eddie closed his eyes like he couldn't stand the light, he rubbed his forehead with his knuckles. "Poor Clara—all by herself—" His shoulders twisted around. "Oh, God—"

I put my hand on his. "Eddie, you got to stop feeling guilty. Revak's mistake wasn't your fault, you had nothing to do with that. And the whole business goes way back before your time. Tell yourself it's not your fault!"

He gave a giant sigh. "Our own parents—it's so hard to believe! Why didn't they tell us right away?"

"Oh, yeah, why! Have a heart, Eddie. One little mistake, sometimes—" Wasn't that what George said? "But you shouldn't be mad at them, neither. Don't go pinning guilty labels on them, or on yourself. Just try and understand."

Eddie sat quiet for a while. Finally he spoke. "One of the things I came to tell you was that my father and mother have agreed to send me to medical school. I have enough credits from the College of Pharmacy to get into B.U. Med."

"*Mazel tov*! Congratulations!"

"It'll be hard for them to swing it," he said. "But it's what I always wanted to do." He bit his lip. "I suppose it's Dad's way of making things up to me."

"Never mind, go and make good! That's what counts. And when you start an office, I'll send everyone in the drugstore to be your patients!"

What drugstore? *Nu*, forget that.

Eddie nodded. "You're a real friend, Belle." Then he stood up, gave me a hug and a kiss on the cheek, and went out.

My eyes could shut now for a little rest. The movie in my head started playing again. Fenway Park on a bright, sunny day. George winking as he bought me the Red Sox pennant that still hung over my bureau. His blue eyes shiny as he pointed out Babe Ruth to me. His first love, baseball.

And after all that dancing, when he asked me to marry him. And to leave with him that night for Colorado. Why weren't you smart enough to see it was his last chance, Appleman? What if you had said yes?

The door creaked and I had to look. Nate stood there, frowning. He came over to the bed and bent over me. "Belle, there's something I got to ask you. Right now! Before that buttinsky nurse—" He took off his glasses and stuck them in his breast pocket.

His brown eyes, usually hidden, were dark and velvety. "Nate, listen. A million people have been pecking me on the cheek, you too. What's wrong with a regular Clark Gable kiss?"

He grinned and got a little pink. "Anything to oblige a lady—" He bent his lanky frame down some more and gave me a long delicious smack right on my lips.

"Well! I thought all visitors were gone!" The plump nurse stood there, arms folded, staring.

Nate straightened up with a sigh. "I'm going, I'm going." Then he turned to me. "But I'll be back tomorrow soon as I'm off from work. Listen, Belle, you get better fast." He marched out with his head high. The nurse followed.

What was it Nate was going to ask me?

Suddenly I felt terribly sleepy. Too much happening all at once. Anyway, Appleman, I told myself, you finished what you started out to do. My eyes began closing. Before I fell asleep, I remembered what Harry told me. *Nu*, tomorrow was another day.

"Oh well, Appleman," I yawned, "catch a murderer, lose a job!"